# MAP

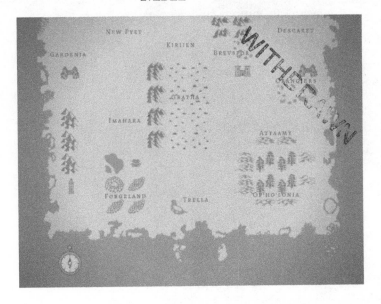

THE EX-PRINCESS

**First edition. October 1, 2018.**

ISBN: 978-1-7328774-0-5

Written by Fiona West.

Dedicated to Mr. West: I think writing books will be the crazy scheme that sticks, but even if it doesn't, I know you'll stand by me because that's the kind of man you are. Thank you for being the Parker to my Abbie. I love you.

FW

# CHAPTER ONE

AS ABELIA STOOD ON the platform, anticipating the vibration of the public light rail train's arrival, she never imagined it would be the last time.

It was a Wednesday, so those without train allowances were walking to work, streaming swiftly by like the waters of a brook, most babbling into their phones. She gripped her travel mug of coffee with one hand and stuffed the other deep into her uniform overalls to avoid human contact as people jostled around her. It made no sense to change at work, especially when one might sit in something sticky on the train.

Abbie loved riding the train. She loved watching the spaces between suburbs fly by. She loved the retro look of the seats and the conductors in their little hats, scanning people's phones for tickets. She didn't have a smartphone, so she dug around for her paper pass in her oversized bag.

She loved riding in the opposite direction from most people. It took no time at all leaving the city in the morning compared to all those suckers riding into downtown, standing up like cattle. She rode from Tanner's Point through Binderville past Cottage Grove and Blakewood. The woods were lovely this time of year; spring was just arriving and the trees were all buds and possibilities. It made her want to sit by a creek and watch the fish jump. The window she peered out of seemed to stand still as the trees and buildings scrambled by. The recorded voice announced Beaver Landing, the last stop, and she hopped off.

Work was another story. It was hot underground—less like being in the sun and more like being in a sauna. A smelly sauna. The overalls were stifling but mandatory, their color indicating rank and their fabric soaking up unwanted chemicals from the air. They'd been specially designed, but they didn't work as well as their manufacturers claimed. And worst of all, being inside all day made her white, freckled skin even paler than it would naturally be. Then again, a waste reclamation plant was never going to be an attractive job.

"Start down on the end and work toward me," Abbie called to her team over the hissing air coming out of the vents. "We should be able to finish this load before lunch. Watch out for the aluminum, you missed some yesterday." As they dispersed, she went back to her clipboard and began looking over the day's quotas.

"Abbie?"

"Yo," she answered without looking up. Someone cleared his throat.

"Abelia Olivia Jayne Venenza Ribaldi Porchenzii?"

At this, she looked up slowly, her pencil still poised over the paper. Two people who looked to be related were smiling excitedly at her, then at each other. Their pale skin looked almost green under the fluorescent lights.

"Your Highness, thank the Woznick we found you! We need to speak with you."

Abbie set her mouth in a hard line. "I'm busy." She turned and walked back toward her office without another word.

They followed.

"Your Highness," the woman began, but Abbie spun around, holding up a quelling hand.

"I left that title behind a long time ago. Please don't use it."

"What should we call you, then? Light of our hearts? Gracious one? Your worship?" The woman sounded completely serious. Abbie tried not to roll her eyes.

"Just Abbie is fine," she said, her gaze returning to her clipboard.

"That won't do," whispered the woman to the man. She snapped her fingers. "We'll call you sister, then?"

"Are you in a cult? Because I have no interest in cults. Coffee is my religion."

The man removed his hat. "Perhaps Your Highness would like to discuss this somewhere more private?"

Abbie forced herself to smile politely. Hanging up her clipboard on the wall, she badged them into the corridor of offices where things smelled a bit better and led them to hers, closing the door behind them.

"Please allow me to introduce ourselves," said the man. "I am Rubald Jerrinson, and this is my favorite wife, Rutha." He pronounced it "*Root*-ah," a name Abbie hadn't heard before in her 23 years. He cleared his throat nervously as she paged through the stack of papers in her inbox. "We're on a diplomatic mission from Orangiers," he continued, "a mission of the gravest importance."

At this, Abbie's eyebrows flew up. "You've come a long way, then."

"Yes, Highness."

"I thought we'd agreed on *sister*, Mr. Jerrinson," Abbie said, though they'd agreed on no such thing. She heaved a sigh. "I don't want these people knowing who I...was."

In truth, Gardenia's capital city was a popular spot for erstwhile princes and princesses of all sorts, and she knew several, though none from countries as large and powerful as Brevspor. Most were perpetual philosophy majors at the university, living off trust funds. By working at the plant, she had been able to keep her identity under wraps. Until now.

"Yes, apologies, erm, *sister*," Rubald said with a nervous little cough. "We've been sent to bring you to fulfill your contractual obligation to marry His Royal Highness, Second Son of Orangiers, Prince Edward Kenneth Keith Francis Benson Broward. We must leave as soon as possible."

Abbie stood up and walked to the corner of her office where a mini-fridge and a coffeepot lived. She pulled out a pink toaster pastry, her go-to when-I'm-stressed-out food, and poured herself another cup of coffee. She sat back down at her desk without offering the two emissaries anything.

"That contract became void when I renounced my title and position in line to the throne," she said through her first enormous bite of pastry. Despite her best efforts, her heartrate was starting to climb.

The couple smiled at each other knowingly, and Rutha pulled a thin stack of papers out of a satchel Abbie hadn't noticed she was carrying. "This copy of the contract says otherwise," the woman said. "You can read it yourself if you'd like, Your Ma—ah, sister. We've just highlighted the salient conditions there, under 'bridal conditions'...your royal status isn't one of them. Please remember that international marriage contracts are enforceable in any country on the continent or across the Sparkling Sea, so your presence in a foreign country is no obstacle. We have spoken to the leaders of Gardenia privately, and they've agreed to extradite you to Orangiers if necessary."

A vise tightened in Abbie's chest, her fear rising fast in a hot, panicky wave. "I need some time to look over this contract," she said, her voice surprisingly even to her own ears. She stood up and walked to the door. "Would you both please come back tomorrow, say around ten, when we can discuss this further?" Her thoughts were already racing ahead of her to her best friend Lauren with her law degree, to a large glass of wine, and to the "go bag" with a stack of new identities in a train station locker she'd been renting for five years. Anything but the terrifying specter of a thousand-person church wedding and a gold circlet back on her head.

"There's something else, sister." Rubald paused. His pale face was grave. "It's your father." At this, Abbie crossed to the desk and sat back down. Rutha rose and quietly shut the door she'd left open.

"He's written you a letter. I have it here." She reached out and took the large manila envelope Rubald offered. Her father's wax seal straddled the flap. She broke it quickly and removed the fine linen sheet. It was shorter than she'd expected.

*Dearest Abbie,*

*You are missed more than you can imagine. Things are not going well here, and your help is needed. I am ill. The people do not wish your brother to ascend to the throne. Brevspor has been a matriarchy for sixteen generations, and the people do not accept the way things are now. They tolerated my leadership after your mother passed away, knowing that you were too young to shoulder such responsibility, but no more.*

*They have petitioned me to enforce your marriage contract. Under your joint leadership with Edward, they believe Brevspor would flourish, and of course, I agree. Brevspor would come under control of Orangiers as a territory with you as its steward, and they would have a Porchenzii queen they trust once more.*

*There is more. Other ruling powers know what a powerful alliance this would be, and are working swiftly to prevent it. You are in danger where you are. I'm sorry for this, but thought it better that you know.*

*Come say goodbye to me, my darling daughter, and take your rightful place...for all our sakes.*

*Love,*

*Paul Daniel Trevor Washington Frakes Porchenzii...aka Dad*

All the royal training in the world wasn't enough to keep her emotions under control. Five years of silence, broken with such news. She couldn't stop the tears that blurred her vision, and she wiped at them with angry swipes. She reread the first line over and over: *You are missed more than you can imagine.*

"What kind of illness is it?" she asked quietly.

Mr. Jerrinson shrugged, his expression helpless. "I'm sorry, Highness, I don't know." She didn't bother correcting him. Suddenly, another line caught her eye. She wiped the snot escaping her nose on her sleeve and asked, "What does this mean, 'your joint leadership'? Is Edward now first in line for the throne as Second Son?"

Rubald nodded. "The First Son, Lincoln Atticus Jonathan Norris Bryant Broward, tried to seize power before his father announced his intention to step down. He's been deemed unfit to rule and currently sits in exile in Op'ho'lonia. He mounts an army there even now to attempt another coup—that is, until his brother marries you and gains the advantage of your territory's forces, at which point he'll be..."

"Irrelevant," she finished.

There was a knock at her door, and without thinking, she called, "Come in!"

Two low-level employees stood in the doorway, eyes wide. "Um, we had a question about the sewage temperature as regards to the feasibility of reclaiming mercury..." one started, but trailed off when he took in Abbie's tear-stained cheeks.

"We'll come back," the other said, and the door shut once more.

Abbie wiped her face again, the tears still refusing to stop. Rutha offered her a handkerchief, which she gratefully took.

"Damn it," she whispered. "Damn it all to Jersey."

"Majesty," Rutha said quietly, "regarding the danger your father spoke of, we believe you should plan to leave here as soon as possible."

"No," she replied, blowing her nose. She stared them down through reddened eyes that matched her hair. "You may leave now."

Twin expressions of shock appeared on the couple's faces, but Rubald found his voice first. "Majesty, we both feel—"

Abbie rose to her feet and slammed her palms down on the desk, scattering papers and the pastry wrapper to the floor. "I do not care what you feel, what you think, or what you want," she enunciated slowly and clearly. "I have left that life behind permanently. I will *never* return to a royal life. You are welcome to try to extradite me if you dare."

"Oh my," Rutha muttered, and Rubald just shook his head. They stared at her, Rubald's face turning a mottled red, but didn't move until she cleared her throat.

"Let me be more clear. Get. out."

# CHAPTER TWO

ABBIE TOLD HER SUPERVISOR she was ill and fled. She was sure she looked as sick as she felt, so it wasn't a lie—not that lying bothered her one iota right now. She headed for the train station, checking over her shoulder to see if Rubald and Rutha had hung around; they hadn't.

Her fingers itched for something to do, and she clung to the straps of her bag with both hands. The other pedestrians largely ignored her, their eyes trained on their phones—a piece of Veil Technology allowed by the magic curtain that encased this part of the country. What it didn't allow was motorized vehicles; the pollution collected inside the Veil and made its inhabitants sick. She'd thought about going into Veil Tech instead of waste management, but ultimately her love of nature had won out over VT's better pay.

She passed Damsey Park, tall oak trees towering over her with butterfly milkweed, asters, and wild bergamot planted neatly around their bases. Gardenia was known for its natural splendor—it was what she'd enjoyed most about the last five years she'd spent in the country. As she walked, she found herself tumbling into the memory of when she'd first arrived, desperate and alone.

Hungry. She'd never been so hungry; it had felt like she was turning inside out. It kept her awake at night, curled inward on herself on rough concrete in that very park until a policeman told her to move along. A young man in a heavy plaid jacket had been watching her since what should've been dinnertime. He leaned against a tree and bobbed his head at the policeman, who bobbed back and said nothing to him. Abbie'd scowled. *What made that guy special?* She still wasn't used to being treated like a second-class citizen because of her gender; in Brevspor, women were more important in the social hierarchy than men. There was no other way to say it. That clearly wasn't the case here, and she'd already encountered that fact in numerous ways: being shoved aside at customs and immigration, called "girlie" by police officers, getting her backside pinched on the train...it galled.

The young man had approached slowly, and she'd wondered in passing if he worked for her mother, if he'd been sent here to look for her. Her hands had curled into fists as she got to her feet. *No way*. She'd fight him with her bare fists before she allowed herself to be hauled back home. Seeing her posture, he'd slowed and put his hands up.

"Just wanted to talk." His clothes were ratty, dirty, but his face and hands were clean, and he kept his eyes on her face. She kept her spine straight, her feet braced to fight or run.

"So talk."

"I'm Ward. What's your name?"

"None of your business."

He chuckled. "Right. Not from around here, eh?"

"What makes you say that?"

He'd taken in her auburn hair and light skin. "Your coloring. Your accent."

"So?"

"Could use someone who looks like they're not from around here. Got food to trade."

"I don't spread my legs for food."

The man had taken a step closer, smirking, and cold sweat broke out along her spine. "Not what I wanted, but good to know." He'd looked around then, like he was sharing a secret. "Find a nice guy to protect you, or you may not get that choice." Backing away, the man gave her a meaningful look, then turned to leave. Abbie trembled.

"Wait..."

Stirred from her reminiscing by the crackle and buzz of the electronic announcer calling out arrival times, Abbie looked around in a daze. She'd arrived at the train station. She sat on a wooden bench, watching the doors to see if anyone had followed her in. She recognized no one, either by their face or their body language. After a few steadying moments, Abbie rose and went to her locker, the one that had been her fallback all this time. She rifled through it until she found the cash, the pepper spray, and the jerky and trail mix that were probably still at least borderline edible, then tucked it all into her bag. But when she got to the passports, the tears came back.

*I'm choosing to lose all contact with Lauren, with Melinda, with Davis, with Ward, Patty, Jenny. I'm choosing to live paycheck to paycheck again...find a new job, and ugh, Jersey—new doctors, too. Change my name. I'm choosing to let my father die without saying goodbye. That's what I'm choosing right now.*

She felt for the same steel resolve she'd grasped when Ward had first approached her in the park that night, the same inner voice that promised she could control her own life, that she could fight for what she wanted—and came up empty. This wasn't right. She put the passport back and slammed the locker. There would have to be another way.

# CHAPTER THREE

BEFORE SHE LEFT THE train station, Abbie used a public phone to call Lauren.

"Hey. I'm in big, big trouble. I need your help. Can you leave work now and meet me at my place?"

"Um, okay?" Lauren replied slowly, voice full of concern.

"Great, see you soon," Abbie said, hanging up before Lauren could start cross-examining her.

Walking was too slow; she took a carriage rather than risk public transit. Lauren was already waiting outside her building when she got there. Abbie unlocked the outside door to her dingy building, glancing over her shoulder for what felt like the hundredth time. Any one of the five stationary men hanging out on the street could be watching her. She pushed Lauren inside. "Jeez, watch the suit, Abs, I've gotta go back to work without people thinking this was a booty call."

"Stop joking around for once. I'm in real trouble here," Abbie hissed, then softened her tone, her shoulders slumping. "My old life caught up with me."

Lauren's eyebrows shot up. "What? Then why aren't you on your way to the train station? I thought you had a plan."

"There are...complications." Abbie unlocked her apartment. She brought Lauren up to speed as she warmed coffee in the microwave, Lauren reading over the contract silently. Eventually, she put down the thin stack of papers and sighed.

"This thing's a piece of work, Abbie. It's entirely based on something called the Hapsburg Test, which traces your lineage and compares it to your proposed husband's. The lines can't run too close together or the test fails. Finding royalty who aren't already related is getting tougher and tougher."

"So, what does that mean for me?"

"It means—or at least I think it means—that the only way to get out of this contract is to get new parents. Can't be done. It's predicated entirely on your genetics; your role as potential queen of Brevspor was incidental, really."

"There's no purity clause?"

Lauren's mouth dropped open, and she shot Abbie a lascivious look. "Girl, did you finally get laid?"

Abbie shook her head. "That's fixable, though."

Lauren took off her glasses and stared at her. She leaned forward across the table. "Are you serious?" Abbie looked out the window and said nothing. "We've never really talked about this part of your life before. What was so bad? Why'd you leave?"

Abbie was quiet for a long time. When she spoke again, the words felt like they were being pulled out of her by some unseen force. "When I was thirteen, things changed suddenly. I wasn't supposed to succeed my mother, but my sisters..." Abbie took a sip of her coffee. She cleared her throat. "My sister Allegra was supposed to ascend."

"Allegra? Have you told me about her?"

Abbie circled the rim of her mug absently with one finger and shook her head.

"Why not?"

Abbie shrugged, staring into her cup. Good thing she was all cried out from earlier. "She's gone, Laur. There was an accident, and they...they died."

Abbie didn't look up at her friend, not wanting to see the expression of shock and pity that would surely greet her if she did. A moment later, she felt the weight of another hand on her own.

"I'm sorry, hon," Lauren said softly. "I shouldn't have pried. But it makes the contract's conditions make more sense. Even if you ascended in your kingdom, Edward wasn't being considered for ascension in his kingdom, so there'd be no conflict."

"Queendom," Abbie corrected. "In a matriarchy, it's called a queendom, beginning with Patrice Evelyn Georgina Deering Fletcher Compagnia in 37 A.B." She couldn't believe how easily that ridiculous information, which had been dutifully drilled into her head since childhood, came back to her after all this time.

Lauren squeezed her hand. "Girl, are you okay? What can I do? Wine? Toaster popper? Chocolate?" Abbie shook her head. They sat in silence as the elevated train went by, rocking a lamp atop a bookshelf and setting the curtains swinging.

A thought zinged into Abbie's head as the train's rumbling faded. "Wait, you said something about...you said my only way out was new genetics."

Lauren put her glasses back on. "Right. This contract is predicated on your genes. But I don't think that's scientifically possible just yet—"

"Who needs that when I can do it the old-fashioned way?"

Lauren furrowed her brows. "I'm not following you, hon."

"If I got my father to deny his parentage, would that work?"

Lauren made a skeptical face. "Well, I think so, but isn't that going to really hurt your father? I mean, you're basically asking him to lie for you."

Abbie shook her head. "It's very possible that my mother was unfaithful to him. I may not be his daughter at all. He could say they lied, which means they'd have to figure out who my real father is in order to run the test again. That delay buys me time to convince Edward Kenneth Keith Francis Benson Broward that he doesn't want this marriage anyway and to find someone else to take my place."

Lauren scrunched up her face again. "I know your freedom is important to you, but this isn't going to get you there. It's flimsy at best, and there's very little legal precedent for it. Can't you just, I don't know, tell them the truth?"

"The truth about why I can't do this?"

"Yes. Is that so unreasonable?"

"Do you know the shitstorm that would bring down on my head? On my family's heads?"

Lauren tipped her head to one side, casting her gaze over the second-hand living room furniture. "I get that, but this is...this is just..."

"Callous? Coldhearted? Unethical? Abso-freakin-lutely. And that's exactly what I'm going to do." She stood up, shoulders square and a grimace on her face. "I'm going to Brevspor to break my dying father's heart."

There was a forceful knock at her door, and the two women looked at each other with wide eyes. "Did you lock the door?" Lauren whispered, scrambling for her phone. Abbie shook her head.

"Your Highness, we know you're in there!"

Abbie's shoulders relaxed, and she let out a breath she didn't know she'd been holding in. "It's just those envoys from Orangiers, it's all right," she whispered.

"No highnesses here," she called across the room, feigning confidence, "just a mid-level sanitation worker and her lawyer. Go away."

There was muffled conferring outside the door. "Majesty, please. We were given a mission and we intend to fulfill it. It's a matter of honor. Don't make us bring the authorities into this. That'd be a rocky way to start off your reign."

Abbie stormed to the door and threw it open, startling the couple, who stepped quickly away from the door. "I do not intend to reign. And you can tell the Second Son that—"

"Actually, His Highness wishes to speak to you himself," Rubald said, holding up a smartphone, and Abbie saw that it was already connected.

"Call declined. You can tell him that—"

"He can hear you. You can tell him yourself."

Her voice hardened. "Do not interrupt me. You can tell him that I will be flying to Brevspor tonight to sort this mess out once and for all."

"*No!*" Abbie startled as three voices, including the one through the phone, all shouted at her at once, especially when she'd expected them to be delighted by this news.

"Your Grace, you cannot fly. Shooters on the border of Gratha are gunning down all dirigibles that attempt to cross their borders, and the Trellavik government is already combing the countryside for you. They are determined to prevent this union at any cost. Don't you see?" Rubald's voice had taken on a pleading tone. "It is not safe for you here, nor any place between Brevspor and Orangiers."

"But it would take weeks to go overland!"

"We have horses," Rutha piped up, as if this made the situation any more appealing.

"Yes, thank you, Rutha," said Rubald, nodding. "We have horses, and can most likely cover at least thirty miles a day. We estimate that it would only be three weeks at most."

Abbie massaged her temples. "I'm going to lose my job," she muttered.

"Be realistic, dear! You don't need a job when you're a queen," Rutha said cheerfully, then sobered after seeing Abbie's answering glare. Abbie half-closed the door and said quietly to Lauren, "So, about that purity clause..."

Lauren paged through the document quickly, eyes flicking back and forth, then shook her head.

Abbie opened the door and grimaced. "I'd like to leave as soon as possible."

"Wonderful. Did you hear that, Your Highness?" he asked, putting the phone to his ear and turning away from the doorway. Rutha stood there, her hands clasped in front of her chest, grinning. "May I come in and assist you in packing?"

Abbie half-closed the door again and gave Lauren a pleading look.

"Don't look at me," she said, her eyes still on the contract. "I don't believe in lawyer-assisted suicide."

"Please come in," Abbie replied to Rutha as she opened the door.

# CHAPTER FOUR

ABBIE LAY IN BED THAT night, wide awake. The moonlight poured in through her window onto the quilt on her bed, one of the few vestiges of her old life. Her grandmother had made it for her—not her royal grandmother, but her father's mother. She'd made it from dresses and t-shirts Abbie had worn as a child. Camp Soggyboggy t-shirts...she'd given her palatial guard more than they'd bargained for the year she disappeared from her bunk to watch shooting stars with Penelope Cunningham. Brevspor Nationwide Music Festival Best Bassoon Solo. Highlands Junior Equestrian Competition participant t-shirt. Porchenzii Family Rendezvous '07. The pastel pink satin dress she'd worn when she was first presented at court. A little magenta corduroy jumper with monkeys on it. The prom dress she was wearing when she'd gotten her first kiss (*not* from Edward Kenneth Keith Francis Benson Broward)...she smiled ruefully at the memory of her father punching her date in the nose. Arthur should've known better; she'd already signed her marriage contract, and he was just supposed to be standing in as a friend. Her dad had always come to her defense.

She wiped a tear away and sighed deeply. He would understand what she needed him to do. He had to. She pulled the quilt up under her chin and rolled onto her side. She'd miss sleeping under its calming weight, her fingers entwined in the simple satin ribbon ties her grandmother had used to finish it. She'd leave the quilt here tomorrow, along with the rest of her belongings, with the exception of a few essentials for the road. She'd be back soon enough.

From the next room, Abbie heard Mr. and Mrs. Jerrinson talking in low voices. They'd refused to leave once they'd finished helping her pack. Rutha had even made them lasagna for dinner, the leftovers of which Lauren had quickly claimed as she exited. Abbie peeked through her cracked bedroom door. Rubald sat dozing in an overstuffed chair he'd moved against the front door. His phone chimed, and he adjusted to read the message. Abbie could just barely see Rutha's graying head resting on the arm of the couch. If she held her breath, she could just barely hear them.

"He says Lincoln prepares to invade Orangiers at the southern border, near the Tupelo Crossing," said Rubald.

"He intends to go out to meet him?"

"Yes."

"It's the right thing to do, but not the easy thing, especially for him. He deserves to succeed his father," Rutha said.

"Yes. But all we can do is get her there. The rest is up to him."

Rutha shook her head slowly, sadly. "Woz help him."

"Yes, he'll need that kind of help, I think." Rubald was quiet after that, and Abbie thought he had drifted off. Then, his voice thick with sleep, she heard him murmur, "You're my favorite wife, Rutha."

"I love you, too."

Abbie crept back to her bed to stare at the moon and force sleep to come.

ABBIE DRIFTED OFF JUST before dawn and woke to the smell of bacon, eggs, and her best friend, coffee. She stumbled out of her room in a white camisole and boy shorts and Rutha quickly averted her eyes. Abbie saw Rutha pass the spatula to Rubald, who didn't seem to know why until he looked around and saw Abbie. He quickly averted his eyes, as well.

"Sister, why don't I help you dress?" Rutha offered, attempting to lead her back into the bedroom. Abbie shook her head and shuffled to the coffee pot. There was a stale silence in the room, broken only by the train rumbling by...the one Abbie should've been on going to work.

Rutha coughed. "Highness, it isn't proper for us to see you like this. Let's get you presentable."

Abbie took her first swallow of coffee with closed eyes. "Propriety is not a priority for me. I am not majestic, and you're gonna see me in worse shape than this before we arrive in Brevspor, I promise you. This is my house. This is how I dress in my house." Then she smiled sleepily at Rubald, who was staring very intently at the kitchen table.

"What about a robe? A good compromise? Hmm?" Rutha asked.

"Sure. But I don't own one. I don't have many guests sleep over. Also, your eggs are burning."

Rutha snatched the spatula back from Rubald, who was still frozen in place like some embarrassed statue, and hurried into the kitchen. Abbie hadn't noticed how round she was until she saw how she jiggled when she ran. It was endearing, she thought as she watched Rutha take bacon out of the oven.

"Where'd you get this food?"

"Rubald purchased it at a local supermarket last night." Rutha smiled at her, making real eye contact for the first time that morning. She handed Abbie a plate, then a second one for Rubald. "Your stores were insufficient for the journey," she continued. "As it was, we could only pack enough for a week."

Abbie set the plate down. "Did you pack coffee?"

"No. Essentials only," Rubald said between bites of bacon. "Simple food that's easy to cook. Coffee requires special equipment."

"Mr. Jerrinson, look at me."

Rubald forced his gaze from his plate and to her face, turning an even deeper shade of red than his previous tomato hue.

"Coffee *is* essential equipment. I will carry the press. I'll forego the cream."

"It'll break."

"No, it won't."

Rubald gave a resigned shake of his head. "I also bought Your Highness a cell phone," he said, "at the Second Son's request."

"That doesn't sound like an essential. Better leave it here. It might break."

"He desires to speak with you. I have not given out the number to anyone else."

"A cell phone's magical properties make you easy to track. We're trying to be untraceable, right? Leave it here. I haven't needed one for five years, so I don't think I need one now."

Rubald shook his head again, looking back at his plate, then his expression turned thoughtful. "Wife, how long has it been since we were outside the Veil?" Rutha pursed her lips and touched the spatula to her mouth, making Abbie glad she'd already been served.

"At least two years, I'd say. It'll be interesting to see how things have changed. Or rather, haven't." Rutha turned to Abbie. "And you, sister? When did you last pass through?"

"Never."

Both her guests dropped what they were holding, and Rubald began to choke on his food. Rutha whacked him on the back with the spatula.

"Never, sister?" she asked, growing pale. "How can that be?"

Abbie shrugged, bringing her mug to her lips again. "Never bothered. I've always lived in Veiled countries. But I've camped before in the Thundercreek Highlands, so I think I know what I'm in for."

Rubald muttered something to Rutha in Orangiersian, and Rutha replied softly. Abbie's temper began to rise. "Don't talk about me like I'm not here. Translation?"

Rubald turned to look at her. "You have no idea what you're in for. With all due respect, Majesty, Unveiled countries aren't like *camping*. I thought you'd been through before, I thought...I didn't realize this was your first time across. We should've prepared differently." He wiped his mouth and rose from the table, crossing to the door.

"Where are you going?" Abbie asked his back.

"To buy coffee and a robe," he replied. The door slammed behind him. Abbie smiled and picked up her plate.

BOTH WOMEN WERE FED, dressed, and packed by the time Rubald got back from the store.

"We have some decisions to make," he said, cracking open a new map and flattening it on the kitchen table. "I just received a call. His Highness the Second Son says that there's a military transport going to Orangiers from Gardenia leaving in two days."

"Where in Gardenia?"

"Fairisle."

Abbie ran her fingers through her hair. "But that's southwest of here. That's in the wrong direction."

"Correct."

"Will they wait for us if we're delayed?" Rutha asked.

Rubald shook his head. "The Second Son fears that will arouse suspicion and make the vessel a target. Its forces are also needed for the coming armed conflict against the Exiled Son. It cannot delay."

"How fast could it get us there?"

"Three days." Abbie sighed and sat back, arms crossed. She stared at Rubald, who stared at the map.

"You know the terrain better than I do. Six days is a lot better than three weeks. What do you think we should do?"

Rubald seemed taken aback. "I—I don't know, Majesty. The Second Son wanted to make you aware of the opportunity, but gave no recommendation himself. He's still asking to speak with you, by the way."

Abbie ignored this and turned to address Mrs. Jerrinson. "Rutha, what do you think?" The older woman had left the table and was washing the breakfast dishes, humming quietly to herself. She wiped her sudsy hands on her dress and shrugged.

"It seems worth trying to me, Majesty. Especially with your father's health being fragile."

Abbie hadn't thought about that. It was no use getting to Brevspor and finding him dead. She'd never get out of her contract that way. She hated the way her own voice sounded in her head, cold and calculating. She had missed him all these years, and losing him without getting to say goodbye would be...the voice in her head trailed off. She couldn't say it, even when she wasn't saying it.

Abbie shook her head to clear it of that line of thinking. "We'll go to Fairisle. It's bound to be more secure, both on the road and on the ship, and it'll save time. The sooner we get this mess cleared up, the better." She pushed away from the table and began to lace up her boots.

"Majesty..." Rutha began gently.

"This is the last time you get to call me that," Abbie growled, her knee to her chest. "Once we're outside this apartment, you'll endanger my life if you do. So knock it off."

Rutha sighed. "Majesty, no one has ever gotten out of an international marriage contract. Perhaps you should consider—"

"No thanks. Ready to go?" They both nodded, and with a brief, final glance around her home, Abbie swept through the door and locked it behind them.

# CHAPTER FIVE

IT SHOULD'VE BEEN EASY: Fairisle was at the southern border of the continent, on the coast. Go west until you hit the ocean, then go south. But here they were, idling between two corn fields, trying to figure out which way the sun was moving like a bunch of bumbling bumpkins.

Abbie wore a wide-brimmed cowboy hat and a long-sleeved plaid shirt with jeans. Boiling didn't begin to describe it. She tugged at her sleeves and tried to shift in the saddle to relieve the pressure on her tailbone. "Doesn't your phone have GPS?"

Rubald squinted against the sun, trying to shade the screen of his phone. "There's no internet here, and apparently, this part of the map didn't download before we left the house...I'm sorry, sister." They were all sweating profusely. The horses were happy, munching the scrub grass at the edge of the gravel road. Abbie stared up into the cerulean sky, soothing herself by murmuring "cerulean" over and over as a mantra against yelling. Her caffeine headache was growing. She scratched a persistent itch on her arm absentmindedly.

"How about some lunch?" Rutha asked, dismounting clumsily. Abbie followed suit, but with more panache, and sat down in the meager shade of the corn by the razorwire fence, taking off her hat. Rutha began to rifle through her saddlebag, pulling out cola in glass bottles, peanut butter sandwiches, and apples. She walked bowlegged over to Abbie, holding the drink out first, which Abbie politely declined. Mr. Jerrinson was still looking around, scratching his head, muttering to himself as he reached for the map in his saddlebag.

"Chafing?" Abbie asked.

Rutha shook her head. "Arthritis. This is a bit more physical than my normal work." She smiled brightly at Abbie. "You looked right at home up there, though."

Abbie nodded, smiling a little at the memories that surfaced. "I had riding lessons for years as a kid. I had a horse named Elvis that I used to ride all through the lake country."

"Yes, I've seen pictures."

Abbie lifted an eyebrow. "You have?"

"Of course, dear! You're going to be part of his family!" she said, setting Rubald's lunch in the grass next to his hunched body. "You were such a cute little girl."

"I know. What happened, right?"

Rutha's eyes widened in embarrassment. "Oh no, sister, that's not at all what I meant! His Royal Highness delights in you. You mustn't think otherwise. Your beauty befits your station."

"You have to say that," Abbie said, snorting in a decidedly un-queenly manner.

"We wanted to know all we could about you, we were all so thrilled. And the internet is such an invention, isn't it? Such a marvel—"

"Based on this map," Rubald interrupted, ignoring Rutha's good-natured eye roll, "our plan to head south first was ill-advised. At the southern end, this mountain range is going to be impossible to cross on horseback. I think if we head west now, we can cross the coastal range before it gets too high."

"Great—however, this road seems to run north-south. Do you want to turn back or press on?"

Rubald sighed and squinted at the sun. "I think we have to turn back." Dejected silence followed.

"Food, Rube. Eat." Rutha pointed at his lunch, which he promptly dug into, still looking at the map. Rubald rummaged around in his front pocket and pulled something out, tossing it to Abbie. She caught it on reflex, then groaned.

"What's this?"

"Your phone. I believe you may have mistakenly left it behind."

"You know that's not true. Diplomats are the worst."

"Well, no one will accuse you of holding that honor, then."

Rutha snickered, seeing Abbie's mouth drop open in shock.

"Mr. Jerrinson, I believe my respect for you just went up," she muttered when she'd recovered.

"Call him," he barked.

"No, thank you."

Rubald's expression darkened. "Sister, when the future leader of the fourth-most powerful country in the world asks you to call him, it's not really a request."

Abbie sighed and shook her head. "Well, I see no way around it, then. Let's get this over with." She solemnly held her wrists out to him, pressed together. "Charge me with treason."

"I'd certainly like to. Not to mention the disrespect you're showing your future husband."

"Says the guy who keeps interrupting his wife. Don't lecture me about spousal respect, mister. And now, I need a nap." Abbie stretched out in the grass, her hands behind her head, and stared up at that sapphire sky.

"Sister, if you've got something to say about my—"

"Rube, someone's coming." Rutha nodded toward the road where a horse-drawn cart was quickly approaching. Abbie could just make out a figure, black hair flying out behind her, a young woman snapping the reins to urge her team on. It was hard to see who was chasing her, if anyone.

Much to their surprise, the woman yanked back on the reins as soon as she saw them. In one smooth motion, she leaped to her feet and nocked an arrow on a large bow she'd slung down from her back. She aimed it at Abbie, who was now on her feet, and Rube immediately stepped between them.

"You don't want to do that, sister," he said, his voice dropping an octave lower than usual. The woman did not lower her weapon. She shifted to look into Abbie's eyes.

"Are you her?"

"May I ask who you're looking for, sister?" Rutha asked. "We're passing through; perhaps we've seen—"

"Shut up!" the girl shouted and repositioned her weapon. "Are you her?" she repeated, and Abbie held up her hands, something she realized she should've done immediately. Damn, kidnapping training was a long time ago. "Don't know until you tell me who she is, hon."

"Stop with the honeys and the sisters. Are you Abelia?"

Abbie tried to see Rutha's face over Rube's shoulder, but her horse, Stargazer, was in the way. Was there any chance this black-haired woman was actually trying to help her, and she should tell the truth? But the woman's face was all intensity and no concern.

She was on a hunt.

"Look, my name's Sarafeen. I don't know anyone named Abelia," Abbie said smoothly. "This is my father, Gerald, and my mother, Brica. We're heading to Fairisle to see my brother, who's just gotten out of the Navy."

The woman eyed them a moment longer, then lowered her bow and slid her hat off in a huff.

"Woz, I'm never going to find this chick. You're the fourth set of travelers I've held up today. Sorry about that, folks."

"That's all right," Rutha said evenly, "it was an honest mistake. Has this Abelia done your family some wrong? Or is she wanted by the law?"

The woman nodded. "The last one, in a way. There's a million-dollar reward for her capture alive. The warlord-in-chief of Gratha issued the warrant this morning."

"No prize if she's dead?" Abbie asked.

The woman sneered. "Nope. Wish I'd known that before I confronted the first group. Anyway, sorry to keep you. Please thank your son for his service. I dated a serviceman once. Love those uniforms."

"Will do," said Rube, tipping his hat and moving toward his horse. The woman snapped the reins and took off down the road, already scanning the fields for other travelers and the roads for clouds of dust. They waited until she was out of sight to confer.

"A price on my head? Are you kidding me? What the Jersey would make him do that?"

Rube stroked his beard. "He's trying to ingratiate himself to His Royal Highness the Second Son. If he brings you safely home, he's guaranteed a lucrative alliance with the new joint kingdom. Very shrewd, actually."

"*Shrewd?*" Abbie hissed. "That woman shot some poor lady this morning because she looked like me!"

"You have to agree, Rube, this isn't what we thought it would be," Rutha added.

"We need to get beyond the Veil as soon as possible," Abbie said. "The sooner we get away from Gardenia City, the better."

"You're right. Let's put some distance between us and here; we can figure out how to get over the mountains later. The story you created will work fine, Abbie; we'll stick to that. Does the brother have a name?"

"Uh, Sajek?" Abbie spluttered.

The couple nodded. They turned toward their horses, but Abbie laid a hand on Rube's arm.

"Thank you for...thank you for defending me."

He shrugged. "If I fail in this, I may as well be dead. Everything depends on this."

"I know how you feel," Abbie said, putting her hat back on.

# CHAPTER SIX

ABBIE WOKE UP DISORIENTED. She rolled toward the zipped door of her tent and her body immediately protested. Right—she'd ridden a horse all day yesterday, because she was traveling across Gardenia. Her back was particularly angry. She'd been sleeping with a rock under her right hip after she'd basically collapsed when they'd made camp after sundown.

They were at the foothills of a rather impressive mountain. Being springtime, the rather impressive mountain didn't have snow, but it was still a mountain. A mountain she had a maximum of forty-eight hours to cross if they were going to meet that military transport. She'd tell them later that she suffered from debilitating seasickness.

She could hear Rutha and Rubald talking softly, chuckling over something she couldn't hear. Finding her boots, she tucked the laces inside and slid her bare feet in, then stood up. That's when her body began to protest in earnest. In fact, it was more of a coup; she fell down.

Rutha and Rube turned to look at her from the stumps they were sitting on. They'd made a fire, where they were toasting pastries sans toaster.

"Morning," she croaked as she attempted to pop back up to her feet. She managed a lurch rather than a pop. "Anything else for breakfast?"

Rutha's eyes went wide. "I saw you eating these the day we came to your office. I assumed it was a preferred food."

33

Abbie shook her head. "I'd prefer something else."

"Let me cook you up some oatmeal," Rutha said, rising quickly and going to her pack.

"Is it instant?"

"Yes..."

"Don't bother, then."

She saw Rutha and Rube exchange a look out of the corner of her eye as she went over to check on Stargazer, who was standing placidly near a group of birch trees. She had some trail mix in her saddle bag that would do for today, but she hadn't brought enough for three weeks. She knew the Jerrinsons must be wondering at her rudeness about the food, but she didn't have the energy—or, frankly, the desire—to explain.

ABBIE HAD TAKEN TO referring to Edward as "he" or "him," partly for security's sake, but mostly because her hostility toward the man himself was actually growing. She'd been gone for five years; couldn't he have found someone else to marry? Wasn't it obvious she wasn't interested anymore? What was the point of enforcing their contract? Surely it wasn't saving him more than a few weeks at most, and they were already using that to travel clandestinely across the continent.

"Rubald, has he said anything about my father's condition?" The envoy seemed to have given up on her calling Edward on the phone he'd bought her for the moment, but his reply was terse.

"No. He's a bit busy fighting a war right now."

"Well, doesn't he have any ministers who could look into it? Who's looking after his kingdom while he's gone? This is just the kind of sloppy, backwater—"

Rubald rose to his feet and pointed his pastry at her. "Watch it, sister. Royalty or no, that's my kingdom you're talking about." Rutha patted his hand.

"Oh, keep your hat on," Abbie muttered, "it was just an observation." She sat down and held out her mug. Rutha poured her some coffee.

"Sister, I'm sure you're concerned about how your father's illness is progressing, that's understandable." Rube sat down, muttering under his breath, throwing pine needles into the fire, and Rutha continued. "Isn't there anyone in Brevspor you could call? Your brother, maybe?"

"Kurt and I were never close. He's still pretty pissed that I stuck him with the throne, I'd guess. He's not likely to take my calls. I don't have his number, anyway."

"You've not stayed in touch with anyone, then?" Rutha shook her head sadly. "Family's so important in Orangiers. I just can't imagine."

Abbie cleared her throat. "It's important in Brevspor, too. We have a saying: 'Grandchildren are the crown of the aged, and the glory of children is their fathers.'"

"Finally!" Rube grunted. "I thought you'd forgotten all your sayings."

"Meaning?"

Rutha smiled. "It just means you Brevsporans are famous for your 'sayings,' for having a pithy quote for every situation."

Abbie smirked. "I'd never thought about it, but I guess we kind of do."

"My favorite," Rutha continued, "is 'better a small serving of vegetables with love than a fattened calf with hatred.' Sums up my life very well, I'd say." She glanced at Rubald, who appeared not to notice, being more interested in staring into the fire.

"What about you, Mr. Jerrinson? Do you have a favorite saying?"

"Yes."

"And what is that?"

"Eat up. We're crossing the Veil this morning." With that, the Jerrinsons stood up and walked over to begin dismantling their tent.

"Funny," Abbie said as she picked the chocolate chips out of her trail mix, "I don't remember that one." Rubald's backpack was sitting next to her. Abbie couldn't resist. She slipped the phone out of her pocket and began to unzip the front pocket of his pack.

"We leave in ten minutes," he called from inside the tent, startling her. Abbie stuffed the hated thing back into her pocket and called over her shoulder, "I don't even have my shoes tied!" Exasperated, she tossed the nuts and raisins still in her palm into her mouth and hurried to get packed as quickly as her stiff muscles would allow.

THE TRAIL, IF YOU COULD call it that, was steep. Abbie couldn't decide what was more annoying: the switchbacks that made your progress feel immeasurably small, or the straight-up, hold-onto-your-hat, feels-like-I'm-falling as-cent that made her abs hurt. Abbie assumed she had abs, though she'd never seen evidence of them. Still, they were probably in there, somewhere.

The forest was all dry pine needles and scrub. A few Ponderosa pines towered over them. The innumerable juniper trees looked stubby and stunted, not lanky and windswept like in Brevspor, probably because the mountains blocked the wind. The junipers obscured the top of the mountain, which added to the feeling of walking endlessly on a tread-mill. Abbie tried to focus on the trail, watching for rabbits and weasels. Maybe Rube could catch one and cook it for them. The sun was high in the sky when Abbie finally spoke up from the middle of the caravan.

"When do we cross the Veil?"

Rube turned his head to call over his shoulder. "Already did, about two miles back."

"What? No, we didn't."

"There was a sign. It was green."

"What did it say? 'Now crossing the Veil...exit at your own risk'?"

Rubald cleared his throat. "No, it just says, 'Good luck and goodbye.'"

Abbie pursed her lips. "Rutha, did you see the sign?"

"Truthfully, no, I missed it, sister."

"Well, I'm disappointed. The Unveiled seems perfectly safe to me. People can be so melodramatic. And shouldn't it say, 'Goodbye and good luck'? Doesn't saying goodbye after good luck kind of seem like jinxing it?"

No one responded.

"There is another saying that applies here. 'Let a man meet a she-bear robbed of her cubs rather than a fool in his folly.'"

Rube circled his horse around to see her face. "And how does that apply?"

Abbie pointed east. "There's a bear over there."

It was the biggest bear Abbie had ever seen. She had no cubs with her, but it was hard to tell if she'd noticed them or not. And then it wasn't. The she-bear started toward them, first at a walk, then picking up speed into a lope.

"Go!" Rube yelled to Abbie and Rutha, and he gave her horse's rump a sharp slap. Stargazer didn't need to be told twice. He took off crashing through the brush, trying to go straight up the slope instead of following the trail. Abbie jerked at the reins, desperately trying to regain control, but holding the reins meant she couldn't hang onto the horse. Abandoning the reins, she latched onto Stargazer's soaked neck, his powerful muscles flexing under her arms, her face pressed against his maple coat. She closed her eyes, the smell of his sweat and the dirt that clung to his coat strong in her nostrils. His frenzied breathing was strangely comforting; at least one of them was still drawing air.

By the time Stargazer slowed, Abbie was afraid to open her eyes. She'd held onto her horse, but with her eyes closed, she had no idea which way he'd charged. There was a breeze on her face, which meant she'd crested the hill...but which hill? And did Rube and Rutha see which way she'd gone? As much as she didn't want to be with them, she didn't want to be without them, either. She opened her eyes to a spectacular view of the ocean in the distance and choked back a sob.

"The worst part is," she said to Stargazer, "they have all the food."

"That *is* a shame," he replied as his breathing slowed.

# CHAPTER SEVEN

EDWARD KENNETH KEITH Francis Benson Broward sat on the edge of his army cot, his head in his hands, his ebony skin blending into the darkness as night took hold. He stared at the abused, sun-starved grass under his boots. He listened to the sounds of men outside by the fire, laughing at each other's embellished stories. He considered the tension in his shoulders, the tightness in his back, the throbbing in his temples. He pressed his fingers into the tight dreadlocks on his head. He read Rubald's text again.

*Separated from A in a bear attack; none wounded. At-tempting to track her phone. Will update soonest.*

The prince sighed deeply. He never should've sent Rubald. The man had amazing protection instincts and he was loyal to a fault...but he should've just sent a strike team to drag her back to Orangiers kicking and screaming, so they could talk face-to-face. He'd intended to try to start their re-lationship off on the right foot; give her the benefit of the doubt that she'd do the right thing by sending a diplomat in-stead of a military man...the right thing being to come quick-ly and quietly. Clearly, that was expecting too much.

Now Edward was torn between concern for her wellbe-ing and despair at his own situation—assuming, of course, that it hadn't been her intention all along to slip into the Un-veiled and disappear. According to Rubald, she knew hardly anything about the area, so she may have overestimated her opportunity to shake them. Edward's head spun sickeningly. He heard someone pause just outside his tent.

"Yes?"

Colonel Gasper, his right-hand man, poked his head into the darkness, his eyes searching. "Sorry to bother you, sir. They're waiting for you."

"I'll be right there." Edward picked up his phone and quickly texted Rubald back.

*If A not found within 8 hours, additional measures will be necessary. Keep me informed.*

He knew Rubald would never admit if he couldn't do the job; if Edward needed to send backup, it would damage the man's pride significantly. He'd been on his father's council since before Edward was born. He called him Uncle Rubald, for Woz's sake. While he didn't wish to insult him, it might be necessary. Edward chafed at the long-term implications of the decision already. He ducked out of the tent and the colonel fell into step with him as they crossed the camp.

"Sir?"

"Yes, Colonel."

"Is the light fixture in your tent working? If not, I can send someone to replace it."

"No, Colonel, it's functional. But there is something..." He paused at the door to the mess tent. "Could you have dinner delivered to my quarters after the meeting? I neglected the opportunity to go by the mess hall earlier."

The older man smiled. "You never have to ask, sir, or explain yourself. Just give the order."

He shrugged, smiling. "Right." Giving orders. That's what military men did...and kings. Clearly, it was going to take more getting used to. Edward walked toward the mess tent, which was doing double duty as a meeting place for his council and strategists at the moment. Edward started into the tent, but Gasper cleared his throat.

"Excuse me, sir, but you must be announced, even for informal settings."

"Very well, Colonel."

Gasper cleared his throat and barked out, "On your feet for the heir to the throne, Edward Kenneth Keith Francis Benson Broward, the Second Son." He hated that title. A constant reminder that he wasn't the original heir, that he was the spare. The people standing around the table had a variety of skin tones, and he thought fleetingly that they represented the diversity of Orangiers well. Edward motioned for them to sit down, and he sat as well.

They stared at him in silence, waiting for his cue. Edward looked at Gasper, who cleared his throat.

"Start with the status of the regents, Paris."

"Yes, sir," said Lieutenant Paris, rising from her chair. "Ambassador Brighton in Brevspor reports that officially, King Paul's condition is unchanged. However, he hears rumors that his condition has improved somewhat."

"Wait—improved? Then he's not dying?"

"We can't come to that conclusion yet. However, if it's true, it buys us time before Brevspor plunges into chaos. They may be more likely to send troops to support our efforts if the king is making a recovery, even a temporary one. But the political situation there remains fragile, especially with Abelia's intentions still in question."

"Have you been able to make contact with her, sir?"

Edward shook his head. "Jerrinson delivered the phone to her, but she hasn't used it yet, to my knowledge."

"That doesn't bode well."

*No,* thought Edward, *that's what I expected from her. Being lost in the Unveiled, however...that doesn't bode well.* Outwardly, he simply nodded. "What about my father?"

"The court report said he's doing well, given the situation. He's somewhat fatigued, but other than that, he's in good health. Concerned for both of you, of course."

Edward blinked. He actually hadn't stopped to think about whether his father worried about Lincoln. He pushed down the shame that was oozing up inside and turned his attention back to Gasper.

"What numbers is Lincoln showing?"

The colonel paged through a stack of papers on a clipboard, shaking his head. "Well, it's better than we'd hoped. He's got 5,000 troops right now, mostly from Op'ho'lonia. He's also gained some Grathan mercenaries."

"Do we know how he's compensating them? Or what he's promising them, I should say?"

General Tybald chuckled at the end of the table. "Grathan mercenaries don't fight on promises, sir. They only take cash, in advance. Someone's investing heavily in this venture, and if I had to guess, it would be the Kiriiens. Brevspor imports a lot of their goods, and if Orangiers and Brevspor unite, they'll lose a lot of that commerce. Not to mention Lincoln's contract with Heather."

"I think Descaret's in the mix, too," Gasper added. "They're racist as Jersey; they want their monarchy to continue as it always has, with black royals: period. No mixed race suitors for Princess Crescena. They've always had designs on getting her into Abelia's seat after she took off. That would really expand their territory, too, give them the whole northern coast."

Edward shook his head. "Not possible. Even if Malieka had the funds, which she doesn't, they need our alliance. It goes deeper than political ties for us."

"Sir, we're still unclear on what is Lincoln hoping for, ultimately. He's dividing the continent, and not along neat lines."

Edward sighed. "It's always been about control with him, manipulating things. He'll want the penultimate control and benefit, whatever that looks like. I'm sure he's spinning all sorts of tales and promising all manner of things he won't deliver. There's no second place with him. Something to keep in mind as we go forward."

"Your Highness, the Jerrinsons also report that someone held them up at arrow-point looking for Abelia. They were able to fool their assailant, but she claimed the Warlord-in-Chief of Gratha had set up a large reward for Abelia's capture alive. So it looks like he's planning to cash in from both sides."

"Sounds like Gratha," Colonel Gasper and General Tybald said together, and everyone laughed, except Edward.

"This is a serious threat to her security. I'm concerned that some will misunderstand his offer and try to harm her; put ears to the ground and see if we can get confirmation of this offer before we start getting ambassadors involved."

"Yes, sir," they chorused as they quickly sobered, and Edward grimaced inwardly. *Fascinating; giving orders is easier when my future wife's life is at risk.*

"General, your plans are in place for all six scenarios we discussed regarding Lincoln's advancement at Tupelo Crossing?"

"Almost, sir. Once we have the troops from Fairisle, we'll be ready."

"Good. Dismissed."

EDWARD DIDN'T LINGER at the table. He dialed her number as he crossed the camp. It began ringing as he ducked into his tent...that was new. His heartrate went double-time. Two rings. *Come on, Abelia, just pick up the phone.* Three rings. *Pick up, damn it, I can help you.* Four rings. He took a deep breath, preparing to leave another voicemail.

"Hello?" The voice was businesslike, and for a moment, he wasn't sure if it was her.

"H-Hello, is this..." *Should he use her real name?* "...Abelia?"

"Yes, how are you, Uncle Ed?" Her voice was steady, but he could sense the edge in it; he heard other voices in the background, some of which sounded like children. *Okay, so she's with people, but she doesn't know if she can trust them. Smart.*

"Right now, I'm just glad to hear your voice. Rubald told me what happened. Are you okay? Are you hurt?"

"I'm fine, but I need to get a message to Mom and Dad..." *Mom and Dad; her mother's dead, so she must mean Rubald and Rutha.*

"Yes, I can do that." He felt around the pitch-black tent for a pen and paper.

"Tell them I'll meet them in Fairisle, at the docks."

He froze.

"No, Abelia, do not advance without them. That is a *terrible* idea. Just tell me where you are and I'll have them come to you."

"Love you, too, Uncle Ed."

"Activate Locate My Phone so we can get a lock on your—"

"Okay, talk to you soon!"

"Abelia! Do not go on without them! Do you hear me? That's an *order!*"

The connection broke. Edward slumped down onto the bed again, this time landing in the dinner tray they'd prepared for him.

# CHAPTER EIGHT

ABBIE SLID OFF STARGAZER and walked around to look him in the eyes. This was surprisingly hard to do with a horse, since his eyes were on the sides of his head. She settled for one eye.

"Did you just say, 'That's a shame'?" she asked.

"Yes, I suppose I did," he replied.

"When did you learn how to talk? And more importantly, *how* did you learn how to talk?"

He flicked his long, black tail. "I believe it was when we passed through that electrified curtain. I already had all the words in my head, but suddenly found that I could use them. Quite unusual."

"Gotta agree with you there," Abbie said, shaking her head. *Talking horses. Of course there would be talking horses.* "Curtain...you must mean the Veil."

"If you say so, dumpling."

Abbie lifted one eyebrow. "I'd prefer you call me Abbie."

"Oh? My previous owner always called me dumpling. I assumed it was a generic word for acquaintances in polite conversation. My apologies, Abbie."

"Actually, it's a type of food and a term of endearment."

"I see. Tasty food?"

"Yes, but you'll be hungry again an hour later."

Abbie walked to the edge of the ridge the way they'd come as Stargazer seemed to consider this new information. Perhaps she could spot signs of Rubald and Rutha. Seeing

47

the Veil from this angle, it looked like the valley was encased in a watery cube that extended to the upper edge of the troposphere. Its barriers were sharper than she'd imagined. Its integrity appeared unaffected by the birds flying through it. There was a marbled shimmer moving across its surface that wasn't as translucent as the rest of it.

"Abbie?" Stargazer said behind her. "I'm thirsty."

She sighed. "Yeah, me too." She stared down the hill, looking for signs of movement. They both listened. "I can't hear anything. Protocol dictates that you stay in one place if you're lost...but I don't have time for protocol. At the same time, I'm never going to make it to Fairisle in time to meet the ship without the Jerrinsons. I clearly have no idea what's going on here...given that I'm talking to my horse."

Stargazer nodded his huge head, tossing his mane. "It's a conundrum."

"Right." Abbie stalked over to Stargazer and swung up into the saddle. "Let's go back down and see what's happening. Which way did we come?"

"I'm not sure..." Stargazer swung his head from side to side. "That way, maybe?"

"That way it is." Stargazer didn't move, and Abbie looked down at him. She cleared her throat. "Sorry, I feel uncomfortable kicking you now...can I just ask you to go?"

"Oh, that. I hardly feel it. You're pretty weak compared to me, you know. I think of it like a tap on the shoulder."

Abbie smiled, then clicked her tongue to urge him on. They followed the ridge for half a mile before they found a path, not knowing if it was the one Rutha and Rubald would be using or not. Following it down, they could hear running water. She gave Stargazer his head and he led them to its source, a trickling stream surrounded by scrubby grass and low bushes. Looking around, she realized this probably wasn't the smartest place to be, on the off-chance Rubald hadn't actually killed the bear. It was all so peaceful, it was hard to believe they'd just nearly been attacked by a wild animal. Abbie got down to get a drink as well and noticed a narrow, well-traveled path going up the rise, a cabin sitting near the top.

"Stay here," she said to Stargazer, "I'm going to see if they went that way. If either of them are injured, they might have gone there for help."

He flattened his ears against his head. "Actually, I'll come," said Stargazer, "it's creepy here by myself."

"Suit yourself, but it's pretty narrow."

"I've been up worse. Did I ever tell you about the trek I did with Susan through the Bluebrook mountain range?"

"No," said Abbie, starting up the hill. She decided not to bring up the fact that he couldn't talk until just a few hours ago.

"Oh, well, it was quite the experience, let me tell you—"

"I'd like to hear about it...later."

"Oh. Not now?"

Abbie tried to hide a smirk. "No, not now, Star. In fact, let's go ahead and hide your ability to speak for the moment."

"Oh, I see."

Abbie looked at him over her shoulder, and he smiled, showing all his big, yellow teeth. She laughed, unable to help herself.

"Who's there?"

Abbie turned at the child's voice. A thin girl wearing a too-small T-shirt and cutoff denim shorts peeked out from behind a ponderosa pine. Two thin, red braids trailing limply from the sides of her head framed her freckled face.

"I'm Abbie. I'm looking for some—for my parents." Damn, she'd given her real name. *That was stupid,* she thought, smiling at the child.

The girl stepped out from behind the tree. "Ain't seen nobody's parents. Who you talking to?"

"Just me. Don't you ever talk to yourself?"

The girl offered a small smile, but shook her head. "You're welcome to come sit on the porch and rest a while. You can meet my sister."

"Certainly. Thank you." *It's the middle of the week,* thought Abbie. *Why isn't she in school?*

The girl turned and scampered up the slippery pine-needled hillside. The sun was beginning to slant sideways through the tree trunks, illuminating the dust that rose behind her like steam off a lake at dawn. The house was wood with a corrugated metal roof; the structure leaned heavily to the left, and she couldn't help but wonder how on earth they got the front door open when it wasn't at a right angle. When the second girl climbed out of a ground-level window onto the porch, her question was answered.

"Hello, I'm Abbie," she said. The two girls sat down on either end of the swing, picking rocks out of the beans, stealing cautious glances at her, so she sat down between them. "Your parents own this place?"

The girls shook their heads. "Parents died awhile back. We're staying with our Auntie Marie now."

"Working for her, you mean," the second girl muttered.

"Quiet, Fadline. You'll get us kicked out." The redhead turned to Abbie. "Auntie ain't here right now; she'll be back soon. I'm Theresas." Abbie offered a hand and the girl gave her a firm, dusty handshake. As Abbie drew back, the girl gripped her harder, staring at her face more closely. "You're...a Sparkler?"

"What's that?" Abbie asked, gently trying to withdraw her hand from Theresas' unyielding hold.

"Pokerbelly, you're right, sister," said Fadline, coming closer to Abbie. She failed to dodge the finger Fadline jabbed into her cheekbone. "Look, it's even in her hair!" Both girls began combing their fingers through her ponytail, beans forgotten.

"Sorry, but can you tell me what you're talking about? Please? And give me a little personal space?" Both girls stopped petting her, but it was obvious they were put out by it.

"We've heard that people inside the Box have the stars in their skin...I knew it was true!"

Abbie shook her head. "My skin's the same as yours."

Theresas yanked her arm over, pushed up her long sleeve, and held it next to her own arm for comparison, and Abbie gasped. Her skin was iridescent, glowing with a shimmer like the one that moved across the surface of the Veil. She rubbed at her skin, but the shimmer only glowed brighter.

Abbie tried to keep the panic out of her voice. "Excuse me, girls, I have to wash this off."

The girls laughed. "It doesn't come off, silly, it's part of you. You just can't see it in the Box."

Abbie glanced at Stargazer, who was munching grass at the edge of the yard. He bobbed his head at her, but she couldn't tell if he meant anything by it. Her mind was spinning.

"I'm sorry, girls. I should keep looking for my...my parents."

"Auntie Marie's been out and about; maybe she's seen them. Would you like us to call her?"

Abbie suddenly remembered that, for once, she also had a phone. Scrambling to get into her pocket, she pulled it out and turned it on. Thirty missed calls. Boy, that Edward certainly was persistent—there was no way she was involving him unless she was desperate. Rubald had been true to his word: he didn't have her number. Integrity wasn't really paying off so far.

Without warning, the sun went out.

"Oh, pokerbelly," Theresas muttered in the blackness.

"Well, that's it, then. Nothing more we can do tonight." Abbie felt the swing tip back as they leaned over to drop their bean-sorting baskets with sighs just as heavy.

Abbie shook her head, heart thundering. "What's happening?"

"Oh, the sun went out. We're done working," said Fadline, as if this were a completely normal thing to say.

"But I have to find my parents tonight!"

Theresas and Fadline giggled, their faces suddenly illuminated in the light of their phone screens. Abbie crossed her arms and tried not to huff audibly.

"When does the sun...come on again?"

Fadline smiled and nodded. "How many stars are in the sky?"

Theresas elbowed her and said, "Oh, I've got one—when will the mountains fall into the sea?"

Fadline clapped her hands. "Oh! What about this: How many licks does it take to get to the center of a—"

"What are you doing?" Abbie asked, unable to keep the exasperation from her tone.

Theresas didn't look up from her phone. "We're doing what you're doing. Playing The Unanswerable Question game."

Abbie's face reddened, and she was momentarily thankful for the darkness. "My question was in earnest. I was serious."

Theresas and Fadline giggled again, then sobered. Theresas cleared her throat. "Sorry, sister. My mama used to say that the king has archers who are constantly firing flaming arrows toward the sun, in hopes of lighting it up real quick."

"That's not true," said Abbie. "That's impossible."

"I heard," put in Fadline, unfazed by Abbie's bewildered skepticism, "that the sun itself is shielding us from falling stars that would otherwise kill us all, and that's what reignites it. Is that it, then?"

"Of course not!" Abbie shouted, losing her temper, and the girls jumped, looking down at the ground and hunching their shoulders in almost perfect unison. There was something uneasy about these sisters, something...wary, despite their giggles and juvenile jabs at Abbie's ignorance. "I'm sorry, girls, I didn't mean to frighten you. But the sun never went out like that when I lived—"

"Inside the Box?" Theresas asked softly. "Yes, I know. But sister...you're under the open sky now."

"Isn't it the same sun?" Shoulder to shoulder, she felt them shrug. It occurred to Abbie that there might be an obvious reason for their alarming ignorance. "Shouldn't you be in school? It's Friday, right?"

"Auntie and Uncle say we don't do our work quick enough."

Fadline added softly, "Auntie said maybe next year, if we're good."

Abbie slid down, letting her weary head rest against the back of the swing, staring up at the stars, which had suddenly appeared as well. The realization came over her that there were all kinds of prisons in the world that required no bars or chains, just a master manipulator and a victim without the means to leave.

"Shouldn't do that," said Fadline as she stared at her phone.

"Do what?" asked Abbie despondently.

"Look up."

"Why not?"

"When the sun reignites, it'll blind you. And you never—"

"Right. You never know when that'll be."

# CHAPTER NINE

SITTING IN THE DARK, Fadline dialed the girls' aunt, and Abbie nervously cleared her throat as it rang.

"Fadline, what the Jersey are you doing on the phone? I swear, if that garden's not weeded by the time we get back, sun or no sun, you're not going to—"

"Yes, hello, my name is Abbie, and I lost my way in the woods. Your nieces were kind enough to let me use a phone." Embarrassed silence followed, so Abbie took a deep breath and filled it. "Anyway, I was separated from my parents in a bear attack, and I know you're on your way back here...I thought perhaps you've seen them."

"Oh my, you poor dear, that's quite the tale," the woman cooed, shifting away from the harsh tones of her introduction into something ingratiating. "I'm afraid we haven't seen them, but I can leave word with our neighbors to keep an eye out. Have the girls been polite to you, dear? We'll be headed up to the Poutine wedding when we get back, but you'd be welcome to join us."

Abbie stiffened. The more people who saw her, the longer she had to hang around, the more likely she'd be recognized.

"Oh, that's so kind of you, but I couldn't impose."

"No trouble—we insist on it. Besides, it's good luck. I'll lend you a dress if you need one. Gonna be lots of good food."

Abbie swallowed her objections, unwilling to offend probably the only person standing between her and sleeping in the woods alone tonight. "Thank you so much, Mrs....?"

"Rogier. Marie Rogier."

"Mrs. Rogier, I so appreciate this, and please extend your thanks to your husband as well."

The girls giggled, and Abbie wondered what she'd gotten wrong this time.

"I'll certainly pass your thanks on to my man. We'll see you soon." She hung up.

Fadline nudged Abbie. "Auntie and Uncle aren't married, silly. They're too poor for that." She took her phone back and carried her lit lamp to the back of the house, where Abbie could just make out a large vegetable garden. With a sigh, Fadline sank to her knees beside Theresas, peering between the leafy green plants to spy out the offending seedlings.

ABBIE DIDN'T INTEND to doze on the swing, but it had been quite a long day, and the previous night's sleep had been a little, well, rocky. The gentle swaying motion, the closeness of the girls, the chorus of cicadas who'd decided to sing despite the fact that it was only three in the afternoon, the lack of lunch...

She awoke to giggles and selfies she didn't know were being taken. This skin phenomenon must have been quite the attraction if they wanted to take pictures of her in her sleep. She blinked, squinting. The sun was back on...er, reignited. The girls had resumed their previous work, wicker baskets back on their laps. Stargazer nickered a soft warning, and she looked up. A couple was approaching on horseback, and Abbie tried to see if it was Rubald and Rutha without looking too desperate, but it wasn't them. Where the Jersey were they? Her concern for them was rapidly growing, and they must be worried sick about her...should she go out looking for them? As focused as she was on meeting that carrier, it wasn't worth sacrificing someone else. Including herself.

The couple approaching the crooked cabin appeared to be the aunt and uncle whose porch she was occupying. Their arrival sent their nieces into a flurry of activity, opening the gate, leading the horses to the back, drawing water hand over hand with an old margarine bucket from the well embedded in the hard dirt near the garden. *Like cold water to a thirsty soul, so is good news from a far country.* Ever since Rubald had brought up those old proverbs, they'd come floating back to her, like deflating balloons riding a breeze that could carry them no longer. Woz knows she'd tried to keep them aloft, batting them away, trying to end that chapter of her life for good. But she needed good news now. She'd rarely needed it more.

"Abbie? Welcome! Let's get you changed," Mrs. Rogier said, smiling. Although she was as white as the girls, the similarities ended there: she had a curvy hourglass figure, her long, thick hair dyed an unnatural shade of blonde, and her clothes fit nicely. She held out her arm through the open window Abbie was meant to climb through. "You ever been to a wedding outside of the Box?"

Abbie smiled and shook her head, ducking into the house. She expected rough-cut furniture, scrapped together from remnants, as crooked on the inside as the outside. Instead, she stepped onto waxed wood floors, gleaming in the low fire's light. High-backed benches sat around a long table, and as her eyes adjusted, she realized the backs weren't just embellished with patterns, but whole pictures. Bears with open jaws over a cowering farmer, pitchfork falling from his hand. Mountain lions swiping at soldiers astride their steeds from low branches. Wild horses galloping across a shallow river...Abbie reached out to touch the intricate detail of the water droplets splashing up from the horses' hooves, and Mrs. Rogier cleared her throat.

Abbie quickly withdrew her hand and stood up. "I'm sorry," she began, but the woman waved her hand dismissively.

"It's nice to see a Sparkler admire his work. Marc's got a talent for craftsmanship, but few notice it." Abbie wanted to ask why he hadn't put that skill to work on the frame of his house, but held her tongue. She followed Marie into the bedroom, which boasted a headboard marked with the same impressive detail, only this time, the subject was Marc and Marie, barely clothed, horizontal and embracing. Years of art appreciation classes meant that she wasn't easily embarrassed by nakedness, but she fought the urge to look away all the same, and the woman snickered and turned to a small closet.

She pulled out a stretchy polyester dress with a turquoise-and-white chevron print and held it up to Abbie. It was a halter top, short, and very fitted. Abbie couldn't imagine anything worse.

"You've got a nice, sexy figure, honey, this ought to work," Marie said frankly.

"Um...I'm sorry to be picky, but I really look better in sleeves."

The woman shook her head. "No, you won't. This dress will be wonderful on you. Try it on and let me see."

*Temper, temper, temper,* her heart cautioned her with each beat. *This isn't worth a fight. Wear the dress. Get their help. Find your escorts. Move on.* Abbie put on a fake smile and took the dress, then turned to find a bathroom or even a space behind a door...only to find Marie, arms folded across her middle, looking annoyed.

"We're late already."

"I'm sorry," she muttered, turning away so she at least didn't have to watch Marie staring at her. She unbuttoned her shirt and tried to kick off her hiking boots.

"Oh, you'll need shoes, too, won't you?"

"Yes, I guess so. Thank you again for including me."

Marie waved her hand again. "No trouble. What about these?"

Abbie turned and Marie handed her a pair of shiny, three-inch pumps in silver. Abbie stared at her, dumbfounded. "How do I ride a horse in these?"

Marie threw back her head and laughed so loud it rang in the confined space. "Girl, you don't ride a horse in these! We'll take the wagon so we don't get mussed. You can leave your horse here." She continued before Abbie could protest. "You're lucky you came to us before some of the others around here spotted you. Their Common Tongue isn't as good as ours." She puffed up as she finished speaking, eyes proud.

Abbie's eyebrows lifted. "Really? Even so close to the...Box?"

Marie nodded. "Many speak just enough to say, 'Give me one dollar,'" she laughed. "Not many travelers cross the borders this way...except those that don't want to be noticed." She glanced at Abbie out of the corner of her eye as Abbie turned to pull the dress down over her chest. Abbie ran her fingers through her hair and tried to smile reassuringly, ignoring the implication in the woman's tone.

"That's interesting. My parents and I are on our way to receive my brother at Fairisle; he's just getting out of the Navy. We just wanted a more enjoyable trip through the lovely, cool woods instead of a dusty highway."

"I see," she said. "Marc!" she called through the doorway, "aren't you going to Fairisle tomorrow?"

"Sure, I was planning on it," came the reply.

Marie shrugged a shoulder. "See? Problem solved. Marc can take you tomorrow, and we'll leave word with everyone at the wedding that your parents know they should meet you there. They'll get the message."

"Oh, I appreciate the offer, but I can't go on without my parents."

"Sure you can. It's no problem, Marc's going anyway."

"*No*, I can't." Her true feelings had bubbled to the surface for a moment, and she kicked herself for how sharply she'd spoken. Marie looked up quizzically from strapping on her own unreasonably tall shoes.

"Why not?"

"They're...they're elderly, you see. I'm afraid something's happened to them. I can't go on until I know they're safe. I'm afraid the bear got them."

"Who, Betsy? She's harmless, they'll be fine. They've lived this long, haven't they? Don't think them so stupid, girl." With that, Marie turned and left the bedroom, calling out to Fadline and Theresas to get in the wagon. Abbie followed, grimacing. *Betsy?*

She eased herself through the window head first, then slipped her knees through together in order not to tear the hideous garment she wore. She stuffed her clothes into Stargazer's saddlebag and detached it, dragging it with her.

"Girl! Let's go!" called Marc from around back. Abbie tried not to bristle at the man's choice of address.

"Be right there!" she called back, then more quietly to Stargazer, she said, "Follow us. Don't let them see you." He bobbed his head, and she smiled and patted his strong neck. Then she hurried, as much as one can down a narrow dirt path in three-inch heels, to catch up with her strange hosts.

# CHAPTER TEN

ABBIE SAT IN THE BACK of the open wagon, rocking and swaying between the sisters, who were passing makeup back and forth across her lap. She was pretty sure someone was going to put an eye out; she just hoped it wouldn't be her.

"Let's do yours, Abbie!" Fadline said, a twinkle in her eye.

Abbie shook her head, laughing. "I don't think so."

"Dontcha want to find a beau?" Fadline passed the mascara, and Abbie noticed light bruising just above her elbow, as if her arm had been grabbed, twisted. She was too distracted to hear the question accurately.

"A what?"

"A boyfriend!" Theresas squawked, applying iridescent eyeshadow heavily and unevenly.

"Oh, I've got one, actually." *Not technically a lie,* she thought.

Abbie's phone rang, and the girls squealed.

"Is that him?"

She looked at the screen, which displayed an Orangiersian cell phone number. Abbie hesitated.

"Answer it!" the girls prompted in unison, and she could feel Marie's attention turn toward her from the front seat. Abbie took a deep breath and slid her thumb across the screen.

"Hello?"

"H-Hello, is this...Abelia?" His voice was much deeper now than it had been the last summer they'd spent together, but she knew it immediately.

How could she forget her best friend's voice?

"Yes, how are you, Uncle Ed?" The sisters sat back, disappointed, and went back to fixing their faces. To his credit, Edward didn't comment on being dubbed Uncle Ed.

"Right now, I'm just glad to hear your voice. Rubald told me what happened. Are you okay? Are you hurt?"

"I'm fine, but I need to get a message to Mom and Dad." *Would he know what she meant? He used to be pretty sharp...*

"Yes, I can do that," he replied without pause.

She heard Marie clear her throat, and she hoped her racing heart wasn't as obvious as it felt. "Tell them I'll meet them in Fairisle, at the docks."

"No, Abelia, do not advance without them," he said, his voice suddenly full of tension. "That is a *terrible* idea. Just tell me where you are and I'll have them come to you."

*Not possible, buddy.* "Okay, give my love to Aunt Viv."

"Abelia, activate Locate my Phone so we can get your loca—"

"Yep, talk to you soon."

"Abelia! Do not go on without them! Do you hear me? That's an *order!*"

That seemed like the perfect opportunity to hang up. The last order Abbie had been given was when she'd been told to show up "properly dressed" to the Christmas Eve Ball six years ago. Her plaid flannel pajamas hadn't gone over too well, even if she had curled her hair. She tucked the phone back into her satchel.

"Well," Marie said from the front seat, "now you can go on to Fairisle tomorrow with Marc. No problems."

As Abbie nodded, her phone made a sound like a stone being dropped into a pool. *Blunk.* There was a text message.

*E gave me your number. Felt you might be in a compromising situation. Call soonest.*

She locked it and turned to Theresas, who was still staring at her skin. Her bony shoulders stuck out from her dress's sleeves in a way that would be comical if it weren't so disturbing. Fadline's were no better. Didn't they get fed? Marie and Marc looked like they ate well enough.

As the wagon bumped along and the girls continued to split their time between layering on more cheap makeup and ogling Abbie's iridescent skin, Abbie made a decision.

"Would you girls like to come along with us? Do you get there often?"

There was a long silence; Theresas opened her mouth but glanced at Marie before speaking. She shut it again, looking down.

"Surely you know the way?"

Theresas nodded.

"I'd gladly pay you for your time; I realize I'd be taking them away from their work. I just so enjoyed getting to know them this afternoon, they'd make wonderful traveling companions."

"And I don't?" Marc huffed, and at that, all the ladies laughed.

"I suppose they could go, as long as they came straight back, and as long as we're compensated..." Marie said, ignoring the girls' excited faces.

They'd crested that same hill and were descending toward the coast when Abbie noticed a small general store.

"Can we stop here and ask after my parents? Please? I'm so sorry to be a bother."

"Make it quick," Marc said, and the girls helped her jump down from the wagon. Out of the corner of her eye, she could see Stargazer keeping his distance, moving off the trail into the thicker part of the underbrush.

Abbie hurried inside and walked through the aisles away from the windows. She muddled her way through the settings to activate the location feature, then called Rubald.

"Oh, praise the Maker; she does know how to operate the device."

"No time for jokes. I'm at the general store near the top of the hill on the main road. You know it?"

"Yes. We passed it about five miles back."

"Get here quick. I'm going to try to stay here, but they may not like that."

"Understood."

"Also, how much money do we have?"

"Plenty. Why?"

"You'll see. Just get here." She felt a hand on her shoulder and turned around slowly.

Fadline and Theresas were grinning at her. "Who you talking to?" they chorused.

"My parents, I was able to get in touch with them after all."

"Oh, that's nice," said Theresas, still clearly disappointed she hadn't been talking to the love of her life.

"You girls want a cookie?"

Both nodded eagerly, and she glanced out the window at Marc, who'd jumped down from the wagon and was trying to peer into the windows of the store.

"Are you happy with your aunt and uncle?"

Both girls froze. They stared at her open-mouthed, all traces of their bubbly joy over applying makeup and talking about boys gone in an instant.

"I don't have much time here. Happy or not?"

"Not," Fadline whispered, and Theresas elbowed her, but said nothing, her eyes wide. Terrorized. *I knew it,* Abbie thought with a sick twist to her gut.

"Stick with me. Agreed?"

Marc appeared in the doorway and the girls jumped. "What's takin' so long?"

"Sorry, the girls wanted a cookie."

"They don't need that, there's plenty of free food at the party. Let's go."

"Actually, I've made contact with my people, and they'll be meeting me here. I'd still like the girls to go with us if you agree. My parents aren't very familiar with—"

"No." Marc moved aside as the girls hurried out to the wagon. "I don't know who you are or who you think you are, but these girls is ours. Stay here if you want to. Good luck to you." He started to walk away, then turned back. "Oh, and leave Marie's dress and shoes with the shopkeeper. He'll get them back to her."

Abbie's mind was racing. She couldn't give up that easily. Those children were enslaved, property. Just the thought of them weeding in the dark had red-hot anger clouding her vision, and Marc was clearly just as controlling as Marie. Possibly worse.

*Voice, don't shake. Don't shake. Steadily, confidently...* Abbie strode out to the porch and said, "I'll buy them from you."

Marc tossed her satchel over the side of the wagon and it landed in the dust with a *poof*.

"No. You go your way. We'll go ours." He snapped the reins, and the horses took off at a trot up the lane into the forest. Theresas and Fadline were holding hands in the back of the wagon, tears in their eyes, their lips clamped shut. Marie didn't even turn around. As Abbie watched them disappear into the woods, shaking with rage, she knew she'd made a huge mistake. And even worse, that she wouldn't be the one to pay the price.

THE SHOPKEEPER HAD already left for the wedding by the time Rubald and Rutha arrived. Abbie didn't think the older lady could dismount that swiftly, and she suddenly found herself on the receiving end of a very ardent embrace. Abbie patted Rutha's back stiffly, still tense and drawn from her encounter.

"Thought we'd lost you," Rutha whispered as she withdrew and grabbed Abbie by the shoulders to see her better.

"No such luck." Abbie gave her a tight smile. "I'm glad to see you, as well."

"You all right?" Rubald asked, looking her over as he brushed the dust of travel from his hat. Abbie nodded. "What's with the dress?"

"They loaned it to me to take me to a wedding."

Rubald and Rutha looked at each other and laughed. "Because you're good luck?"

"Yes, how'd you know?"

"Oh, it would've increased their stature in the community considerably if they'd been successful. Sparklers are good luck, everyone knows that."

"I didn't," said Stargazer, and they all turned to look at him.

"Oh, pardon me. Rubald, Rutha, this is Stargazer."

They stared, and Stargazer smiled with his big yellow teeth. Abbie felt some of the heaviness lift from her heart. *You did what you could,* a small voice inside her said. *You tried.* She heaved a sigh and scrubbed at her face with both hands.

"Well, that's a surprise," Rubald muttered, walking back to his horse. He and Rutha didn't seem to have noticed her state of mind, but that was probably for the best. Rubald had one foot in the stirrup when he suddenly stopped, quirking an eyebrow at his mount. "Horse, do you...can you also...?"

"Oh, no, sir, your horse doesn't appear to have the same abilities," Stargazer put in. "I tried to strike up a conversation earlier on the good quality of the clover here and was ignored. Perhaps I'm just boring, but I don't think so. He seemed genuinely confused."

Rutha covered her smile with the back of her hand, and Rubald shook his head.

"Good. Let's get out of here while we can still see where we're going."

# CHAPTER ELEVEN

THE THREE TRAVELERS descended into the valley as the sun began to set. In all her time in Gardenia, Abbie had never been to the ocean, and watching the sun appear to sink into its depths had her transfixed. It burned and throbbed on the horizon, painting the ships trying to get home before dark in vibrant pinks and oranges. *I wonder if it'll go out again tomorrow.* The whole experience had left her shaken. The sun felt like one of those things you should be able to count on, like gravity. *What if gravity stops working? Is there an emergency procedure for that? What if I'm alone again?*

Her mind kept drifting back to Fadline and Theresas. *I should've fought harder. I should've done more. Maybe if I'd just jumped on Stargazer and taken off with them...he probably couldn't have caught us with the wagon slowing him down. Yeah, it was stealing—but weren't Marc and Marie stealing their whole childhood from them?*

With a clicking of her tongue, she urged Stargazer to catch up to her guardians as the road widened. "Rubald," she said softly, as she pulled up alongside him. "I have a few questions."

"Fire away, sister."

"When the sun went out..."

"Oh, yes."

"Does that happen frequently here?"

He shrugged. "It depends on where you are. It doesn't happen in all the Unveiled."

"They don't call it that. They said we were...under..." She tried, unsuccessfully, to shake the tired from her brain.

"Under the open sky?"

"Yes. What does that mean?"

"Not certain. But most people in the Unveiled do not envy life 'in the Box,' as they call it."

"What? That strikes me as...well, bizarre. And why do we sparkle? And is slavery legal here? Why haven't they killed that bear? And—"

Rubald's sigh seemed to come all the way from his heels. "Perhaps the guest house will have a copy of *Traveling the Undignified Road.* I think it would help answer some of your questions. It's just another mile or two. It's not safe to travel at night, so I made a reservation earlier today when it appeared we wouldn't be arriving at the port."

"Those people I was with—one of them is traveling this road tomorrow. It would probably be best if we didn't meet him again. We didn't part on the best terms."

Rubald lifted an eyebrow. "It's best if we don't involve ourselves in local politics, sister."

Abbie looked straight ahead and said nothing, sighing in frustration.

"Don't you agree, sis—"

"Absolutely. Makes sense to me."

She heard a soft whinny from Stargazer. "Abbie?"

"Yes, Stargazer?"

"Are we almost there?" He sounded exhausted. She'd forgotten that he'd hardly eaten anything today, either.

"Soon, I think. I'm sorry, I haven't traveled this way before, either."

"I'm so hungry I could eat a human."

Rubald and Rutha both tried to cover their snickers.

"I can hear you, you know. Horses have *excellent* hearing."

A fluorescent light appeared through the trees. A poorly maintained cement-block building that was only half-painted sported a sign reading best time guess house in green. A swimming pool full of leaves sat to the right of the entrance. Abbie peered into it as they passed by, and the water rippled.

"*What was that?*" Stargazer shot forward at a trot, until Abbie pulled back on the reins.

"Take it easy, new guy. Let's play it at least a little cool, okay?"

"I apologize, I don't hide my emotions well. I have literally no practice at it."

"Well, you're spooking the nonverbals, so cut it out."

Abbie dismounted and handed the reins to Rubald, who led the horses back to the barn. Her legs were shaky, her head hurt, and her pack felt like it weighed five hundred pounds. She stumbled into the reception area and was greeted by no one.

"Hello?"

An apathetic employee shuffled out of a back room, rubbing his face as though he'd been asleep.

"Reservation?" he mumbled.

"Yes, we made a reservation."

"Jerrinson," said Rutha, appearing at her side. The man rifled through some papers as Abbie watched the gadflies throwing themselves at the single overhead lamp. Sighing deeply, he found what he was looking for and launched into a well-rehearsed speech.

"This is Best Time Guest House. Welcome. Don't drink water in the sink. Don't open windows. Don't run fan. Breakfast at seven. Your room, top of the stairs to the right."

"Sir?" The man didn't realize Abbie was talking to him until she cleared her throat.

"Yes?"

"Where do I get drinkable water?"

He pointed to an empty five-gallon jug upside down in a dusty, unplugged water cooler.

"That's empty."

He nodded. "Water guy comes morningtime."

"I need water now."

He gestured over his shoulder, still shuffling paperwork in a way that couldn't possibly be productive. "The man doesn't come now. Creek that way."

"Is it safe to drink from the creek?"

He cocked his head at her.

"Creek water clean?" She didn't mean to mimic his accent, but it did seem to help him understand her.

"No."

Rutha put a hand on her arm. "We have tablets to help with that. They taste...effective. I'll give you some of my water, dear."

Abbie nodded gratefully. Rutha unclipped her canteen and passed it to Abbie, who accepted it. They stood there silently.

Rutha blinked at her wearily. "Aren't you going to drink it?"

"I will in a minute." There was no way she was pulling out everything here in the lobby.

Rubald came in, still dusting off his hands. "What are we waiting for?" he barked.

Abbie had many times been accused by Lauren of being "hangry," a combination of hungry and angry. Her limited experience with Rubald made her want to call Lauren and ask what the word would be for tired and out of calm..."tim-patient," maybe? Or maybe just impatient was enough.

"Keys, dear. It's all under control."

"Keys, son?" Rubald had raised his voice at least ten decibels.

The man dug around in a drawer without finding them. After trying two more drawers, he turned around with a bright smile and handed one to the couple and one to her.

"Two keys, just one room." Abbie grimaced. Great. Nothing between her and Rube's snoring again tonight, though she was reaching new levels of exhaustion that would probably negate that as a factor regarding sleep anyway.

"Let's go, ladies. Upstairs. If I don't get out of these boots soon, they're going to become a permanent part of me." He led the charge up the uneven cement stairs, and Rutha and Abbie fell in dutifully behind him.

"You? Miss?"

Abbie turned back at the foot of the stairs.

"You are...from the Box?" Abbie waited a beat, but that seemed safe enough to disclose.

"Yes."

"You are very beautiful."

Abbie swallowed hard, and she felt her face redden. Maybe sharing a bedroom with Rubald playing the role of Overprotective Dad wasn't such a bad thing, after all.

"Thank you."

"You have a phone number?"

"Uh..."

"I would like to speak better Common Tongue. Maybe I call you, show you my place, you can help me talk better."

"I'm sorry, I can't. I won't be here long."

"I need money. My wife, she needs an operation. Woman problems." The man's expression went from flirtatious to sorrowful in an instant.

*Oh, that's just too much.* Abbie dropped her bags and crossed her arms, walking slowly back to the desk.

"Why are you calling me beautiful and inviting me over if you're married?"

The man shrugged. "Maybe not married for long—woman problems, I said. Not a lot, just $500."

"Oh, is that all?"

He misinterpreted her sarcasm as interest, and his eagerness intensified. "Yes, that is all, very inexpensive, right?" His eagerness to get her money repulsed her, and she had zero emotional reserves at the moment. She was about to give him a piece of her hungry, sleep-deprived mind when she heard Rube's heavy footfalls at the top of the cement stairs.

"Daughter?" he bellowed, leaving her hoping he hadn't just woken up the other guests.

"That's my father. Good luck with your problem. Coming, Dad!"

Put out, the man shuffled back to the office. Abbie hoped she wouldn't have to talk to him again. She tried to drag her pack up the stairs without lifting it to her shoulders, and she heard Rubald come thundering down.

"I've got it," she said without making eye contact. Without a word, he lifted the pack and motioned her ahead of him. Rutha was already in her modest nightgown, rubbing a white cream on her face, her graying hair loose in waves down her back. She sat on a pulled-out couch, the mattress practically folding down the middle.

"You're in the queen-size bed, sister."

"No, I'm on the couch."

Rubald lowered his voice. "Majesty..."

"Nope. I don't give a burnt brownie about your customs. There are two of you and one of me. Plus, it ruins the illusion of a happy family if I have the big bed. Do not even consider arguing with me, because I will lose it, you hear me? I. will. lose. it."

The couple exchanged a look before both nodded.

"Good. Where's the bathroom?"

"Downstairs next to the front desk."

Abbie sighed. "Don't take your shoes off just yet, Rubald; I need an escort, and Rutha can't go down like that."

"Oh, come now—surely not. You need an escort? To pop a squat?"

"Rubald, language," Rutha chided as she stifled a yawn.

"Look, there was some...unpleasantness with the man at the front desk. He'll leave me alone if you're with me."

"Just because he looked at your skin..."

"It was more than that."

He folded his arms across his chest, an unpleasant hardness to his gaze. "More, eh?"

"Yes. Just trust me. We're saving time in the long run; you don't want to have to bail me out of jail for assault."

Rubald muttered something under his breath before striding out into the hallway, and Abbie hurried to grab her meds bag, pajamas, robe, toothbrush, and Rutha's water. The older woman was already under the covers, her breathing steady and deep.

They descended the stairs as quietly as Rube's boots would let them, but there was no sign of the desk clerk, much to Abbie's relief. When she flipped on the light, five cockroaches the size of her thumb went scrambling for a crack under the tub, and she shuddered. The walls in the bathroom were tiled. Abbie stared at the work, the identical pieces lining the walls nearly to the ceiling. *They can't paint the outside of the building, the water isn't drinkable, but the bathroom walls are tiled.* She shook her head. The priorities of these people were incomprehensible.

Abbie lined up her meds on the edge of the tub. At home, she had a dispenser that she could refill once a week, but being gone for three weeks she'd had to bring the bottles. She'd also been concerned about border crossings with unlabeled pills. There was nothing too radical in her current lineup, but they might not believe her.

Prescriptions first...did she take her steroid yesterday? She could probably take it again. Her entire body was raging, angry, her knees and shoulders swollen and stiff. Forgetting about the cockroaches, she slipped to the cold floor and sat down. It felt good to be alone. It felt good to sit without

Stargazer's jarring gait rocking her. She sighed and shook her head, refocusing on the drugs. Methotrexate, yes. Aspirin, yes. She wanted an NSAID, too, but she couldn't afford that...Belimumab, yes. Fish oil, yes; that one was like a bowling ball going down, and she coughed, trying to get it to turn.

"Daughter? You all right?"

"Yes, I'm okay, thanks, uh, Dad."

Vitamin E, yes. D3, skip; she'd had plenty of sun. Too much, probably. Double turmeric for the joint pain, spirulina, magnesium, MSM, DHEA...that was it for tonight. As if that wasn't enough. Abbie tossed back the last one, leaving a tiny bit of water in the canteen. She swept the bottles back into her bathroom bag, quickly changed her clothes and brushed her teeth, not stopping to check her reflection. She didn't want to see the rash; she could feel it well enough and if she ignored it, maybe it would fade by morning. Abbie sighed longingly at the shower, then left the bathroom.

Upstairs, they entered the room quietly. The overhead light was off, but Rutha rolled over.

"Someone texted you, dear."

"Me?" Rubald asked, rummaging through his pack.

"No, not you-dear, Abbie-dear," Rutha clarified, as if knowing the ex-princess for two days gave her every right to call her "dear." Abbie mumbled an apology and fumbled around in the sheets until she found it. She knew who it would be from.

*Dear Abbie, I'm so relieved to know you're safe. Please call me in the morning; we have much to discuss. —Uncle Ed*

*Wow, semicolons in a text message. Lighten up, Uncle Ed.*
She smiled tightly before silencing the phone, setting it to
charge, and collapsing onto the failing mattress for the night,
only to stare at the ceiling.

# CHAPTER TWELVE

FIVE MORE SIT-UPS. Five more sit-ups, and then Edward could check his phone. He was almost done with set five of his PT pyramid routine, and he'd already decided that he wasn't going to interrupt his workout again to check it. He would check it between sets, and he would check it at the end, but there was no need to be pathetic about it. *Unless it rings*, he told himself, getting to his feet. *If it rings, that's another story.*

"You're behind, sir." Lieutenant James was grinning at him, red-faced. He was two sets behind everyone else already, though everyone else was too polite to mention it. Exercise, though one of his least favorite things, felt easier with his old company, and since he was about to be in charge of, well, *everything*, his advisors hadn't complained.

"He's waiting for a girrrl to call," Simonson panted in a singsong voice in between sit-ups, his walnut skin glistening. "Guess the grass isn't always greener on the other side..."

Edward was used to their ribbing and just shook his head, grinning, as he started his push-ups. Company D had been home until his abrupt promotion following Lincoln's attempted coup. His sit-ups got faster as he thought about it. He checked his phone while he caught his breath. No calls, no texts, still. It was 6:30 in the morning; he was certain Rubald would have them on the road by now. If not, they'd have no chance of making the carrier. She'd call soon...he hoped.

Edward was about to set his phone back on the tree stump when it began to ring. The men around him erupted into spontaneous applause, and he backed away from the group in order to hear better.

"Hello?"

"Good morning, Edward...how are you?" Edward winced and shook his head, and the mannerism spread quickly to the men around him.

"I'm fine, Crescena, how are you?"

"I'm very well, thank you. I'm worried about you, though."

"That's very thoughtful of you, but I'm fine. Really."

"I don't see how you could be," her gentle voice pressed. "If one of my siblings betrayed us like that...I don't know how I'd cope."

"It was a shock, certainly." Edward didn't want to tell her that his anger was keeping him going just fine. He only started to fall apart when he thought about what might happen if he failed and Lincoln won. Scary words like "exile" and "execution" came to mind.

Crescena sighed on the other end. "Well, I'm sorry all this has happened. My people and I are thinking of you in this difficult time. Please let me know what I can do to help. Our nations have always had a friendly and...intimate relationship, and we certainly want to do all we can going forward to assist and support you."

Edward gave her a tight smile she couldn't see. "Thank you, Princess. That's very kind of you. I'll pass your good wishes and offer on to my parents."

"Take care, Edward."

"You too, Crescena." It took a good deal of self-discipline to set his phone down on the tree stump instead of throwing it, but Edward managed it.

"What did she want, then? Came right out and said it, did she?" called James.

Edward chuckled bitterly. "Oh, no, they seldom do. Just offered all her help and support in any way she could or some nonsense like that. But yes, implicitly, she offered to marry me in a heartbeat."

"Boy, these princesses and their dirty talk."

Edward rolled his eyes. "She did use the word *intimate*." That drew groans from the men.

"Doesn't she know you've got a contract?"

"Of course she does, he and Abelia signed it at twelve, didn't they? It's common knowledge, isn't it?"

Saint took a swig of water, then wiped his forehead with his shoulder, leaving a streak of dirt across his white skin. "I've dated Brevsporan women before, and I have to tell you, sir—they're not easy to tame. You're in for more of the same, your whole life."

"Whereas Crescena seems a bit more...eager." That got the rest of them laughing, except Edward. He frowned at his phone again. *Call, Abs.*

"Are you gaming with us tonight, sir?"

He nodded. "It'll be a welcome distraction." Edward stalked off toward the showers, trying to hide his bewildered irritation with Abbie. What had he done to warrant this kind of disrespect, this obvious disdain she had for him personally? Yes, she'd run away. But did she really think everything was off, just like that? A breeze kicked up and it rattled the tree above his head, releasing the smell of the orange blossoms. The scent transported him back to the summer they were ten.

"Aren't you coming up?" Abbie was a cute redhead, freckle-nosed, long-legged. She almost always won their foot races, even when she wasn't wearing shoes. He crossed his arms, staring up at her in the tree.

"That kind has thorns."

"Don't be a wimp, just come up!" she chided. "Ouch!" She leaned back on a branch, bracing her feet against the trunk, trying to get a better look at her wound. Edward found himself charging up the tree.

"Are you bleeding?"

She nodded, but smiled. "See? I knew you could do it."

"Is it bad, though?" He grabbed her hand to see it better, but in the dappled light, it was hard to tell how deep the puncture went.

"Look, we can see the ocean! I love the ocean."

He shrugged. "I can always see the ocean. You'll see it all the time when you live here, and then you won't even care."

"Who says we'll live here? We're totally living in Brevspor."

"So far from the ocean? I thought you just said you loved it."

"Let's build a tree house up here, so we can climb up without thorns and watch for pirates."

"My father's navy does an excellent job of preventing pirates, so that's unnecessary."

Abbie groaned and slapped her forehead. "Why do I bother? You're hopeless."

"Not as hopeless as you swimming across Frillicum Lake."

"Hey, you had a head start, it was totally unfair!"

"Rematch?"

"Race you there."

She'd beat him to the shore, of course, diving in fully clothed, much to the dismay of the nannies.

He started to chuckle, then realized that laughing by yourself probably wasn't the most credible sign of good leadership. Best of all, Lincoln had been away that summer visiting his own betrothed, so they'd had the run of the property: the orchards, the vineyards, the beach, the lake, everything.

Lincoln. He'd ruined everything.

If Edward could have gone to Abbie, seen her in person, talked things out, surely it would've gotten everything off to a better start. Still, she was on her way now, and that was something. But Rubald didn't seem to think she was too keen on fulfilling the contract.

He had a headache again. Shoot, his phone—oh well, he'd double back for it. More than likely, he'd only miss more calls from clamoring princesses in neighboring countries. If only the only princess he wanted would pick up the phone.

# CHAPTER THIRTEEN

BETWEEN BITES OF HER third hard-boiled egg, Abbie dialed Edward's number. He *had* been helpful during the bear debacle. She felt the slightest twinge of guilt about how she'd treated him—not just since the Jerrinsons had shown up at work, but since she'd left her country at age sixteen. Maybe if she'd been honest with him from that awful time forward, he'd have already moved on by now.

One ring. They'd boiled the heck out of the egg, a gray layer around the yolk, but at least it was healthy protein, and she could take a few with her for lunch. Two rings. Abbie reached for a banana as Rubald came into the dining room.

"Time to go, sister."

She motioned toward the phone and tried to ignore the glimmer of delight in his eyes as he backed slowly out of the room. Three rings. Geez, maybe he wasn't as anxious to talk to her as she'd thought he was.

"Hello?"

"Hello?" She echoed, confused. The accent was Orang-iersian, but it wasn't his voice. "Is this Edward's phone?"

"Yes, this is Lieutenant James. Please hold one moment, we're trying to locate him for you, Your Highness."

"That's fine," Abbie said around her mouthful of banana, enjoying the uncomfortable silence on the other end of the line. Then she decided she could do better. "How's your day going, Lieutenant?"

"Excellent, Your Highness." He had his speaking-with-a-superior-officer voice on, and it made her smile.

"Really? What's been the best part so far? It's only 7:30, after all."

"Speaking with Your Highness, of course. It's a pleasure to hear your voice."

"Are you flirting with me, Lieutenant? I'd hate for that to get back to the Second Son..."

"Um, no, no of course not, Your Highness, uh..."

Abbie grinned, stifling a laugh. Poor guy. She shouldn't torture him, but it was just too easy.

"Here's His Highness now. Thank you for holding, Your Highness, and I hope you have a wonderful day."

"Hello?" An out-of-breath Edward. That was more like it.

"Morning, Uncle Ed."

"Good morning. I trust you slept well?"

"I slept fine, thanks. Just not long enough. Your emissary has a perverse sense of timing."

"Thank you for calling me back. I've been anxious to speak with you." Abbie could hear water running in the background and joking voices.

"Where are you?"

"I've just finished a shower following our physical training this morning. Where are you?"

*Still so formal,* Abbie thought with a creeping fondness. "Eating breakfast, if you can call it that."

"You find the offerings for breakfast inadequate?"

"Quite," she said, mimicking his accent playfully.

"Hmm. I'll speak with Rubald about improving your accommodations."

"No, that's okay," she said quickly, "I don't think there's a lot of options around here."

They were both quiet for a time, until Edward cleared his throat.

"By the way, what did you say to my lieutenant?"

"Oh, that."

"Yes, that." If she didn't know him so well, she'd think he was genuinely unhappy; thankfully, she was very experienced with his dry sense of humor when it chose to show itself.

"I called him out for flirting with me. He was totally brazen about it."

"Was he now?" She could hear his eyebrows going up through the phone.

"He said my voice was as melodious as birdsong and that he wanted me to bear his children."

"Well, I've always enjoyed your voice personally, so I can understand that. Still, it's wholly inappropriate; shall I have him court martialed or drawn and quartered?"

"Maybe just a slap on the wrist this time. You don't want them to think you're a tyrant before your reign even begins."

"Perhaps you're right. Very well. Your mercy is boundless." She could hear him grinning, and she bit her lip. Guilt, guilt, guilt. Why was she flirting with him? Stupid, stupid, stupid.

"You said we had much to discuss in your text message; is that what you had in mind?"

"Not precisely, no, I..." He paused. Having suddenly forgotten how to breathe normally, Abbie simply held the air in. *What if he asks if I'm going to fulfill the contract? What should I say?* Panic shot through her like an electric shock.

"Rubald's calling me, I've gotta go."

"Wait—would you please call me when you stop for the night?"

Abbie squirmed. "If it's not too late."

"Even if."

"Um, sure. I'll try."

"All right. Goodbye, Abbie."

She hung up without replying and let out an exasperated sigh that startled the chicken that had snuck into the dining room looking for crumbs. Rutha appeared in the doorway, arms crossed.

"Strange, I didn't hear Rubald calling you, sister."

"Eavesdropping is rude, you know."

The older woman smiled knowingly, but it was tinged with sadness, and Abbie rubbed her eyes.

"Please don't look at me like that. I wasn't ready to talk to him about it yet." She couldn't put her finger on why, but Rutha could draw the truth out of her like she'd drugged her. It was disturbing.

"Very well. Before you ask, we've had no official update on the other situation yet, but we will keep asking. Shall I braid your hair for you this morning, daughter?" She said the last bit louder as an employee walked by with a mop and bucket of dirty water.

"Sure." Abbie sat up straighter as she finished her banana. Rutha was already hacking away at her mass of dark ginger waves, which she'd done nothing with since the previous morning. Hair was such a nuisance; why not let Rutha deal with it, if it made her happy?

Abbie lowered her voice. "What's the unofficial update?"

Rutha's expression clouded. "Oh, dear, I don't know if I should say."

"Hello!" It was the man who'd been staffing the desk the previous night. "How come you don't talk the same? Same family, right?"

Abbie cleared her throat, annoyed at his nosiness. "Yes, same family, but I'm adopted."

"Adopted? What's adopted?"

"Adopted? Oh, well, um, when I was small, my parents died, so my new mom and dad took me into their house and took care of me. Adopted."

"Ohh, oh, okay. That's okay." The way he smiled at her made her want to shower again. She thought he might walk away, but instead he sat down at the table with her as Rutha continued to work through the snarls. "You are going where today?"

"Fairisle," Abbie said, sticking with the standard lie partly because she wasn't sure he was completely buying their story.

"Why Fairisle?" *Mind your own business,* Abbie thought, but she smiled.

"My brother is getting out of the Navy. We're picking him up."

"No, you can't go Fairisle today. Big protests, people say port taxes are too high. They block the road, no shipments, no transportation in, no transportation out."

Abbie did not look at Rutha, but felt her stiffen. *Rubald will not be pleased...*

"No horse for him?"

"I'm sure we can find one there for him," Rutha put in, threading her fingers through the hair high on her scalp. Based on the man's face, she was giving him a stern expression that told him he was overstepping. He was undeterred.

"What is brother called?"

"His name is Sajek," Abbie said. "What's your name?"

"Daisy."

Abbie snorted before she could stop herself. "Daisy, like the flower?"

"Yes," he smiled, "like the flower and the milk."

"Milk?"

"Big yellow can of milk, milk like sand. Discount for the name."

Abbie tried to pivot to see Rutha, forgetting that the woman's fingers were firmly fixed between the bundles of hair. "Any idea what he's talking about?"

"Let me see...Daisy Dry Milk, you said? Why yes, I do remember something about that many years ago. They ran a promotion where they gave a discount to children named Daisy, about twenty years ago. His mother must have heard about it."

Abbie tried not to let her jaw drop open. "And she named him that *for the discount?*"

He shrugged. "Children need milk."

"How many children does she have?"

"She is pregnant ten times, but only four live. I am the lowest one."

"You mean the youngest," Abbie corrected gently, trying to imagine losing six babies. Rutha's practiced hands were nearly finished now. "How did they die?"

"Diarrhea. Cholera. Dengue fever. Tooth infection." The man ticked the causes of his siblings' deaths off on his fingers as he named them.

"That's terrible."

"My wife, she has six children."

Abbie scowled at him. "Aren't they your children, too?"

"They might be. I cannot know." He shrugged. "Without surgery, she won't live. If she goes, those six will die also. You cannot help me?"

"Ladies!" Rubald was clearly over the waiting around. Abbie jammed the last of her breakfast into her mouth as Rutha tied off her hair. She ran a hand down the length of it; it felt good. Very secure. She shrugged apologetically to Daisy, who nodded as if he understood. He stared after them as they cleared their dishes away.

"Goodbye, Daisy," Abbie called. He waved. Conflicting emotions roiled in her chest as she watched his face disappear around a corner. This trip outside the Box had brought nothing but since she'd set off, and she didn't think it was going to get any simpler.

# CHAPTER FOURTEEN

AS ABBIE ANTICIPATED, Rubald was about as happy about the protest news as a hive of hornets hit with a baseball bat. He shook his head, fuming, scrolling through social media on his phone.

"The potential violence aside, we can't risk exposing your face to that many people. We'll have go around. We can't make the transport." He stomped off, dialing Edward and muttering curses under his breath.

*Could this have been intentional? A protest that just happens to block our way to the ship? To force us to cross the Unveiled and make me vulnerable to those who would claim the price on my head?* Abbie wiped the sweat off her brow with an ice-cold hand as Rubald came back to the two women.

"So, sister, we've decided to cross through to the south through Trella rather than try to go north."

"Through Gratha? Considering that they're trying to kill me, I approve."

"Good," Rubald grunted. "And thank you." These last words seemed to pain him.

Abbie glanced at him sideways. "For what?"

"For calling him."

"He did help me out when I was lost. I figured I owed him at least one call."

"One? You're only going to call him *once*? Of all the blasted, contrary—" Rubald stopped when he caught sight of the grin sliding across her pale face. "Don't toy with me, woman."

"It's my nature. Also, you deserve it."

They were on the road, talking softly so as not to be over-heard, not that anyone was paying them much attention. At most, they were met with long stares as heads turned to fol-low them, mostly from children. She so wished her dumb skin would stop standing out; Rubald assured her that the sparkle would fade the longer she was outside the effect of the Veil's harnessed magic. Under the hat and long sleeves, the shimmer was less noticeable. At least her skin color was common here; Edward would've felt even more strange, most likely; his skin stood out more on this side of the con-tinent.

*No,* she chided herself, *there's no need to empathize with him. He's the enemy, even if we have history together. He's the enemy of all that I've built and worked for and created with my own two hands. It's over. He just doesn't know it yet.*

"So, sister, what do you like to do with your free time?"

Rutha had been trying to get to know her better, and Ab-bie found herself surprisingly amenable to it. They'd started into the deep woods, the rock walls on either side of the road closing in as they entered the narrow channel through the mountain instead of over it.

"I like to read novels. Watch movies. Knit."

"Oh really? No sport, then?"

"Only when chased."

Rutha laughed. "We're cut from the same cloth, you and I."

"You like horror movies?"

"What?" Rutha looked aghast. "Oh, no. I like happy endings."

"It's a happy ending for the ones who survive."

"But how can you enjoy something that's so full of fear and misery and pain?"

Abbie shrugged. "I find it actually helps me face my fears. Whenever I'm in a situation that's uncertain, I just think, 'Well, at least I'm not locked with a madman in a basement full of crossbows.'"

"You remind me of Jack a bit; don't you think, Rubald?"

He grunted his agreement.

"Who's Jack?"

Rutha's smile lit up her face. "He's my second son, my third-born."

"How many kids do you have?"

"Ten."

Abbie's eyebrows shot skyward. "Wow, you look great for having had ten babies!"

It wasn't a lie. Abbie did think she looked pretty good—her salt-and-pepper hair was straight and much less unruly than her own, and her breasts were still pretty perky for having fed ten hungry little mouths. Rutha smiled and waved her off, chuckling.

"Rubald, don't you think Rutha's beautiful?"

He grunted again. Abbie gave him a meaningful stare, and he cleared his throat.

"I find her very lovely."

"See? I'm not the only one."

The older woman was blushing, but her suppressed smile told Abbie she appreciated the kind words.

"So, what's Jack like?"

"Oh, he was a quiet boy. He loved stories, he was always tugging at my skirt to read with him. He had a bit of a dark side to him, but he was a good boy, nothing sinister. He just liked to be frightened a bit, like you. He was always pulling practical jokes on the others."

"The peanut butter," Rubald muttered.

"Oh, I'd forgotten about the peanut butter!" Rutha bent forward, laughing. "And when he sewed all our socks shut halfway down!"

"I thought it would take you a week to undo that one. We all had to wear our shoes without socks to Katie's graduation."

Abbie laughed along with them. "Well, I can't wait to meet him. I can't believe I never met you all during my summers at Bluffton Castle."

"Oh, we always took summers with my sister Jurie out in the countryside. I couldn't be expected to keep the royal children and mine happy all summer, now could I? Plus, they wanted to give you two time together without too many mother hens pecking around."

"I know you were close to Ed—uh, to him. He talked about you. He said you told better bedtime stories than his mom."

"Oh, nonsense. I just knew he liked pirate stories. Her Majesty was exhausted from a full day's work." She took a sip from her canteen. "He talked about you, too, dear. He was utterly enamored with you. We were just sure that one of those summers, he was going to stow away in your suitcase and go back to Brevspor with you. Did you two have a nice chat this morning?"

It had been, actually. He was still a pompous know-it-all, but he was funny. She'd always liked his sense of humor. *But that changes nothing.* Abbie felt her silence going on too long, but she didn't want to talk about Edward.

"Tell me about his brother."

Rutha paused, shifting uncomfortably in her saddle. "How do you mean?"

"I mean, what happened there? How do you go from First Son to their first political exile in 200 years?" Rubald and Rutha exchanged a glance, and Rubald nodded slightly, looking around.

"He's always been...temperamental."

Rubald snorted. "You call it temperamental, I call it volatile."

"And what? He just snapped?"

"He was pressuring His Majesty behind closed doors to step down. King Ignatius is getting older, he was forming a transition team, but Lincoln was tired of waiting. He didn't want to respect tradition, didn't want his father's advisers telling him what to do."

Rubald lowered his voice. "It isn't public knowledge, but we're trusting you here." He gave Abbie a hard look, and she swallowed, nodding.

"He tried to kill him."

"Who?"

"Lincoln. He tried to kill his father."

Abbie shook her head, hardly able to believe it, but Rube looked deadly serious. "Who stopped him?"

"Edward. He walked into the room just as Lincoln pulled out the knife. The coward turned and fled before Edward or His Majesty could find their voices to call for the guards."

Rutha sniffled, and Abbie looked over to find tears on her face.

"I'm sorry, Rutha, I didn't mean to upset you."

"No, no, I'm fine. Truly. I just feel so sorry for his mother and father, his brothers and sisters. They've always been such a close family, until now."

"The others are still close."

"Yes, of course they are. Yes, of course." Rutha sniffed.

"Let's see if I can remember," Abbie said, trying to shift the conversation to a lighter place. "There was Lincoln, then Edward..."

"No, Rhododendron is older, she's First Daughter."

"Okay. Lincoln, Rhodie, Edward, Ginger, Dahlia...oh shoot, I can do this. Forsythia?"

The couple chuckled.

"Wait, wait! Oh, come on, brain. Lincoln, Rhodie, Edward, Ginger, Dahlia, Andrew, Forsythia, Simon!" They clapped patronizingly, but Abbie didn't mind.

"So you *were* listening during your matrimony preparation lessons?"

"Only to the good stuff."

"Such as?"

"What ancestral properties we would likely have access to and whether they were suitable for horses."

Rutha laughed, wiping the tears from her face with the back of a dusty hand.

THAT NIGHT, THEY DIDN'T set up camp until after dark, so Abbie texted Edward to say that she wouldn't be calling. He responded right away to thank her for letting him know. The next three days, Abbie survived mostly on her snacks. They camped just off the main road on public lands at night. The terrain was largely forested in tall cedars, towering for what seemed like miles overhead, and she was thankful for their ample shade. Sword ferns, thimbleberry, and sugar maples competed for the weak light at the lower level of the canopy, weaving their way between the warp of the taller trees. At times, the trail became so narrow they went single-file through steep ravines, coated in moss and lichens, slippery with the mist of waterfalls that seemed to have no respect for the trail, crossing it at will. They were mostly stopping before dark, but she was still pushing it too hard, she knew that. The fifth night after crossing the Veil, the food situation came to a head.

"What's wrong with it this time?" Rubald had been in a foul mood since Rodeo Drive got too close to Stargazer and they almost got kicked. He was glaring at her over the freeze-dried sweet-and-sour pork he'd just rehydrated.

"Nothing. I just don't want it."

"It's just pork. Rice. Fruit. That's healthy."

"Yes, pork, rice and fruit...drowned in refined sugar and preservatives."

"What do you want me to do, catch a pig and slaughter it in front of you?"

She squinted at him across the fire. "Could you?"

"That's it." Rubald got to his feet. "Woman, we won't be catering to your peculiarities regarding food any longer."

Abbie swallowed a bite of her jerky. "That's going to extend our journey considerably."

He glared at her. "Is that a threat?"

Abbie glared back. "No, it's a fact."

"All right, you two, enough," Rutha said wearily. "It's been a long day, let's talk about it in the morning."

He turned on Rutha. "She's wasting away! I can't deliver the Second Son an emaciated bride!" Abbie paled. She thought she'd been losing weight based on how her jeans fit, but she hadn't known it was obvious to others.

"Okay, fine—I should've told you before I left that I have...unique dietary preferences."

"You don't have the luxury of preferences out here, sister!"

Abbie stood up. "Unique *needs*, then. Call it whatever you want; I can't eat food that's full of gluten and sugar and weird chemicals."

Rubald crossed his arms. "So, you'd rather eat rice and beans."

"Gladly."

"What about plain oats?"

"Love it. Even better with peanut butter and honey."

He pointed at her. "That's sugar."

"No, that's naturally occurring sugar, not refined sugar."

He crossed his arms again.

"Will you eat fruit?"

"As long as it has no sugar added."

"How can fruit have added sugar?"

"Most dried fruit does."

"Eggs?"

"Yes."

"Does it matter how they're cooked?" Rutha asked softly.

Abbie shook her head. "I can eat dairy in small amounts, and any natural oil."

Rubald stared at her for a moment, then pointed at her. "Get Rutha a list of what you can eat tomorrow. I can't have you fainting and falling off your horse." He turned sharply and strode toward his tent.

"As someone who's known Rubald for 43 years, I can tell you that he's just acting like that because he's worried about you, dear. It comes out as harshness, but it's concern."

Abbie nodded. "I should've told you earlier. I just...I didn't want..." She covered her face with her hands. "Sorry, I don't know what I'm trying to say. I should just go to bed."

"Yes, good thought. Let's all be off to bed."

"Goodnight, Rutha."

The older woman put her hands on Abbie's shoulders and gave her a light squeeze.

"Goodnight, dear. Thank you for filling us in on your...situation. We want to make this journey as comfortable for you as we can."

Abbie felt a lump rising in her throat, so she just nodded and headed quickly for her tent.

# CHAPTER FIFTEEN

SAINT AND SIMONSON were thumbing their controllers frantically and were just about to blow the troll's north gate when Colonel Gasper came through the door, breathing hard. Edward stood up, dropping his gaming controller, and the others scrambled to follow.

"What's happened? Is it Abbie?"

"No, sir. Good evening, sir." The man gasped for breath. Edward had never even seen him move quickly, let alone unable to speak for lack of breath.

"Here, sit down." He offered the colonel his own chair while his friends scrambled to offer theirs instead.

"Thank you, sir." Gasper seemed to have recovered somewhat. "I'm sorry to alarm you, sir. We just received word from our spotters that there are ships...ships coming up the river."

Edward's stomach rolled. "What flags are they flying?"

He shook his head. "It's hard to tell in the dark. But we need to contact your father to send reinforcements no matter what."

Edward turned to his friends. "Gentlemen, keep this to yourselves, please."

"Yes, sir," they chorused in unison.

"Sorry to leave you shorthanded. Take down that troll." When they didn't respond, he put his hands on his hips. "That's an order, gentlemen." They managed weak smiles as they saluted his departure.

"Is the council assembled?"

"Not yet, sir," replied Gasper.

"Do you think we should wake them?" He checked his watch: it blinked one in the morning at him.

"Yes, sir. In fact, we should call artillery to battle stations."

"How far away are they?"

"About twenty-five kilometers."

"Is it possible they're reinforcements? For us?"

"It's possible." The older man was struggling to keep up with Edward's long strides. "But unlikely. We would've been notified by diplomatic communications first."

"How deep is the river?"

"I...don't know, sir."

Edward let out a sigh. "Then find out, please." He turned to enter the mess hall, then stopped.

"Wait—why weren't we guarding the mouth of the river?"

Gasper's expression was pained. "We weren't anticipating the battle moving to the river because all the nations with naval forces are our allies."

Edward was silent for a time. "So, someone may have turned on us."

"It's likely, sir."

*Damn it all.*

The prince nodded curtly to Gasper, who saluted and turned to leave without another word. Edward ducked into the mostly empty dining hall. A young soldier was still wiping down the tables.

"Why aren't you in bed, private?"

"Sorry, sir. Just finishing up."

"I need the room. You're dismissed."

He dialed his father as the young man collected his bucket and left out the back toward the kitchens. His father's aide answered.

"Good morning, Crown Prince Edward. Your father is still asleep."

"You'll have to wake him."

"Very well, sir. Would you like to hold or shall I have him call you back?"

"I'll hold."

"Very good, sir."

Edward kicked at the ground under his feet. This was his land. No one was going to steal his country's future. Not Abelia, not Lincoln, no one. And whatever nation had sent this fleet, they weren't going to get close enough to do any damage if he had anything to say about it. He just had no idea how he was going to stop them.

"Do we need your mother for this conversation?" his father's deep voice rumbled on the other end of the line.

"Hi, Dad. No, you can let her sleep." Edward heard his father murmur something and his mother sigh.

"What's up, son?"

"Business call, I'm afraid. There are ships coming up the river, and we need reinforcements."

His father didn't miss a beat. "How deep is the river?"

"I'm finding out."

"What are they flying?"

"Too dark to tell."

"Don't fire yet, they could be allies."

"I told them that." Edward kicked at the ground. He pushed down memories of his brother, standing next to his father's desk with a gleaming knife in his hand and a look of reluctant determination on his face. *What if I hadn't come to get him for dinner? What if we'd just called him? Thank Woz Lincoln's such a coward.* He was counting on that personality flaw now.

"Okay." His father was still waking up, but he was still the king. "What do you need?"

"I was hoping you could tell me that."

His father chuckled. "I'm not in charge down there. Pretty soon, your mum and I will be sleeping in late, taking our breakfast on the patio...maybe staying in bed all day..."

"Dad, focus, please."

His father chuckled huskily. "Lighten up, son. You've got this. But you have to tell me what you need. You're there, I'm not. Can't do this for you."

Edward's temper flared, but he quickly doused it in guilt. "I know, I know. Just...tell me what kind of light steam frigates you've got available."

"I've got six here. Do you want them all?"

"What does it leave undefended if I take them all?"

He could hear his father scratching at his chin as he thought. "Good question. That would leave the northern border unguarded with Descaret."

"Crescena called me the other day. She didn't mention anything about sending troops, but it sounds like they're not exactly openly hostile, either."

His father sighed. "They still think they have a shot at marrying her off to you."

"They don't."

"Maybe..." His father paused. "Maybe they should."

"We've talked about this. I have a contract."

"She's not going to sign, son."

"We don't know that yet. Let's just wait and see."

"You don't have time to wait and see, Parker." Though his dad meant it affectionately, Edward winced at his childhood nickname.

"Dad, I—I can't just..."

Out of the corner of his eye, Edward saw his advisors gathered at the doorway, talking softly. He motioned them inside.

"I am needed. Send the six."

"Very well. Take care, son."

"Say hi to everybody for me in the morning."

"Will do. Love you."

"Love you, too."

THE NEXT FEW HOURS were a blur of maps and phone calls and tea and troop mobilizations, but the start of the Brothers' War didn't feel real to Edward until the first shot was fired. He was just about to take a sip of his Duke of Darlington when he heard the cannon go.

"Whose was it?"

"Ours, sir," one of his men said. "We've identified the ships: they're Trellavik."

General Tybald shook his head. "That's the last country I'd expect to get themselves involved in this mess. Kiriien or one of the northern countries must be putting pressure on them somehow." Trella was a tourist destination, ruthless only when it came to keeping their beaches clean. *What in the world do they hope to get out of this? They do share a border with Attaamy, which circumscribes* Op'ho'lonia, *Lincoln's main ally.*

*Borders...Abbie.*

He whipped out his phone.

"Sir, I need your—"

"Just a moment."

"But sir—"

"I said I need a moment!" Edward shouted, and the crowded tent went silent. *Pick up, pick up, pick up. You cannot cross that border. Don't cross that border, Abs.*

"I apologize," he said to the room as the phone rang. "Abelia's supposed to be crossing into Trella today, we've got to stop her."

One ring. Two rings. Three rings. Four. Voicemail.

"Hi, you've reached the voicemail of someone who isn't allowed to use her real name. Mysterious, I know. If leaving a message for a mystery person appeals to you, you can do so after the tone."

"Gasper, call Rubald. Tybald, call Rutha. Everyone, get on the damn phone!"

# CHAPTER SIXTEEN

AT THE GATE TO THE city, the trio dismounted their horses. Large signs declaring the entrance to a secure area advised them to turn off their phones or have them confiscated, and one look at the mounted police told Abbie they were serious about this. She brushed the dirt off her clothes and looked around. There was a winding line of people waiting in the hot sun, fanning themselves with passports and immigration paperwork.

"Looks like we'll just have to—" She stopped and looked around. Where were those two? Scanning the crowd, she saw them over by a small awning that read find out your wait time here in unfriendly lettering. She waved, and they hurried back toward her. "Don't worry, I got you one. It's all fruit, I checked," Rutha called as they got closer as she held out a strawberry popsicle. Abbie took it, confused.

"Did you find out our wait time?"

"Our what?" Rutha asked, sucking on a grape popsicle.

"Our wait time, the awning, it says..."

Rube and Rutha laughed. "Oh, that's not a thing anymore. Now they just give you free popsicles. I suppose it's cheaper than building somewhere out of the sun for you to wait," said Rube. Her dripping dessert threatened to stain her sleeve, so Abbie quickly licked the liquid up. It tasted amazing. She quickly began to suck on it...the strawberry flavor was bright and intense, and she began to dream about her last Centennial celebration, sneaking strawberry shortcake with her brother and sisters in the woods while her mother wasn't looking.

Abbie shook her head. Her vision had gone all soft and fuzzy. Rube and Rutha were sitting in the grass, their eyes glazed over...then her eyes drifted toward the line. No one in line had a popsicle. *Why would no one in line have a popsicle to help keep them cool? What could that have to do with—*

"Wait!" she shouted at Rube and Rutha.

Rube scowled. "You startled me. I almost dropped my pop!"

"You said you've never been inside this gate. Why?"

Rutha shrugged. "Usually, we come from the other side."

"The Attaamy side? The Veiled side?"

"Yes, I suppose so..."

Abbie threw her popsicle into the road, spooking Stargazer.

"Put those down and let's get in line. They're drugged."

"What?" Rutha and Rube stared at her and their jaws dropped in unison, exposing their purple tongues.

"They're poisoned. They make you forget why you came. It weeds out the dumdums, the unmotivated, the ignorant. Or at least I'm sure that's what they'd say. I'd just call it discrimination. Let's go get in line *now*."

Rube picked up his pack and got a slip from the valet for Rodeo Drive, but did not put down his popsicle. "So you're saying," he said, hurrying to catch up with her, "that the *pops* make us forget."

"Yes."

"Ridiculous," muttered Rutha. "There's nothing wrong with a good popsicle, she's just uppity."

Abbie pivoted slowly. "Excuse me?"

"You're uppity, I said. You don't like things that drip or stain or turn your tongue a funny color. You're frigid and stiff and a real—"

"What's my name?" Abbie asked, folding her arms.

Rutha stopped. "What?"

"What's. My. Name."

"Well, it's, um...it's Rutha!"

"That's your name."

"It's...Rube!"

"That's your husband's name." The people around them started to snicker. Rube took her popsicle and threw it into the field. Several already stoned individuals waded out into the long grass to get it, giggling.

Rutha scowled at him. "My pop! You've ruined it now."

"What's her name?"

Rutha crossed her arms and said nothing, still pouting.

"Sister," said Rube, pointing at her, "you've got a good head on your shoulders. I should've figured that out immediately."

"Can't believe I gave *her* the strawberry pop..." muttered Rutha, still clearly not herself, and they shuffled forward in line. Forty-five minutes later, they were so sweaty that Abbie was starting to sorely miss that popsicle, even knowing what mischief it contained. The immigration officer rattled off his speech while stamping them through the first carrel.

"Papers-please-photos-showing-ladies-take-off-yer-jewelry-men-take-off-yer-belts-and-shoes-and-be-prepared-to-remove-yer-phones-from-their-cases-NEXT!"

"Well, that wasn't so hard," said Abbie, taking off her post earrings.

A short, stocky woman looked at her papers next. "Sorry, no admittance. NEXT!"

"Wait!" Abbie cried, her stomach flipping over. "Why not?"

"Well, it's not because you ate the popsicles, though I can see the pink around your mouth...*dumdums,*" the woman muttered as she cleared her throat. "You're Brevsporan?"

*Didn't it say so on her passport?* "Yes, I am."

"And your friends are...?"

"They're from Orangiers."

"Well, non-Trellavik visitors such as yourselves must be certified free of Squealing Nose Malady, and the forms are in Mr. Percy's drawer."

Abbie leveled her best steely glare at the woman. "And that's a problem because...?"

"Percy's out."

"Can't you just...get one out of his drawer?"

The customs agent stood up. "Don't make me call security, lady."

Abbie stepped back. "I'm sorry, I'm sorry, I'm just really—I just really need to get inside the gate today. Is there any other way?"

The lady sat back down. "Well, you could wait for the doc to examine you."

Rutha and Rube began to protest, but Abbie took her papers back from the customs agent, nodding. "Great. Where do we do that?"

They were led to a windowless room furnished with nothing but two unpadded folding metal chairs. The once-white walls had been touched by a lot of very dirty hands. Ironically, they sported several posters about personal hygiene. The tile floor was chipped and cracked in a few places, but more or less clean.

Rube stood while the ladies sat.

For the first hour.

Eventually, even he slumped to the floor, staring at the ceiling.

"Rube."

"Yeah?"

"What are you looking at?"

"Ceiling."

"Mmm."

"We could play a game," Abbie said.

They both looked at her.

"It's called Twenty Questions. You pick something in your head—anything—and then the others ask questions to try to guess it. Okay?" They nodded. "Okay, Rube, you go first. Got something in your mind?"

The older man screwed up his face in concentration. "Yep."

"Rutha, ask him a question that tries to narrow down what it might be."

Rutha paused. "Is it the ceiling?"

"Yep."

At that moment, the door opened and a woman stuck her head in. "Miss...Anderson?"

Abbie and Rube jumped to their feet, and even Rutha slowly stood. "Yes?" said Abbie.

"The doctor will just be a few more minutes."

They all sunk back down.

"Look at it this way," said Rutha. "We're out of the heat, in a nice, air-conditioned room. We're sitting in chairs..." Rube shot her a look. "Well, some of us are sitting in chairs, and...well, it could be worse."

"I'm hungry," said Rube.

"Me too," said Abbie. "Anyone have any food?" They both shook their heads.

"I was planning a resupply inside the city," Rube grumbled.

They sat in silence for a few more minutes, until Rutha suddenly took a deep breath and turned to Abbie.

"Sister, I'm real sorry for what I said to you earlier, about the popsicles. You're none of that, sister. You're wise and friendly and real as the sky, and I'm glad to be with you, even here, where we will probably wait until we die."

Abbie squeezed her hand and looked into her eyes. "Don't worry about it, Rutha. That was the pop talking." Rutha nodded.

"It was, utterly."

They sat some more.

"You don't think this is another test, do you?" said Abbie, musing aloud. No one said anything. Abbie stood up and walked to the door. They watched her with such pitiable desperation that she had to open it. Abbie cracked the door open and stuck her head out. A woman in a lab coat with her hair in a tight bun was walking by.

"Excuse me," Abbie said, and the woman stopped and turned to her, pinching her nose. Ignoring this, Abbie went on. "Are you the doctor?" The woman shook her head and pointed to the badge on a nylon lanyard around her neck: chief cabbage examiner. Abbie tried not to let the hysterical laughter bubbling up in her throat out, schooling her features into what she hoped was a serious expression. "I see. Do you know where I could find the doctor? My friend isn't used to being in confined spaces, and we've been here for hours. I'm afraid he's losing his marbles a bit..." Abbie winked surreptitiously at Rube, then cracked the door open so the examiner could see in, then held her breath. To her surprise, Rube played right along.

*"Deep into that darkness peering, long I stood there wondering, fearing,"* he intoned in a booming baritone.

*"Doubting, dreaming dreams no mortal ever dared to dream before;*

*But the silence was unbroken, and the stillness gave no token,*

*And the only word there spoken was the whispered word, 'Lenore?'*

*This I whispered, and an echo murmured back the word, 'Lenore!'—*

*Merely this and nothing more."*

The examiner made a face of thinly veiled distaste, and through her precautionary nose pinching, she asked, "Is that his wife's name? Lenore?" Abbie shook her head sadly. "No, his wife's name is Rutha. He's quoting a poem about a talking bird. You see what I mean." The woman nodded, backing away slowly, and held up a finger to indicate that Abbie should wait here and she'd be right back. Abbie closed the door and smiled at them. They smiled weakly back. A few minutes later, the door opened.

It was the customs officer Abbie had argued with earlier, Officer Svoboda.

"Who opened the door?" The woman snarled. They stared at her, then at each other, unsure what to say.

"I did," Abbie said, smiling brightly. "Is there a problem, Officer?"

"Yes, sister, there is a problem. If you have Squealing Nose Malady, you could infect the whole staff! Have you no consideration? Trella is a decent place and we don't allow unseemly diseases to run rampant!"

"That's a wonderful ideal...but we don't have Squealing Nose Malady."

"It can lay dormant for *years*, Ms. Anderson! You don't know if you're a carrier until you've been *examined.*"

*All right*, Abbie thought, patience fraying to its last thread, *that's enough*. She stood up calmly and spread her hands out wide. "Here's the thing: trapping us in this room, keep us from continuing on our journey, refusing to even provide us with enough chairs, not offering us food or water...one might come to the conclusion that you're being...inhospitable."

All Abbie remembered about Trellaviks from her boarding school days was this: they were major germaphobes, and they relied entirely on their tourism economy. Therefore, "inhospitable" was the worst insult you could level at them. The customs officer seemed to consider this, so Abbie pushed it a little farther. "We'll be traveling far and wide; I'd hate to think that this is going to be characteristic of your country. We'd heard so many fine things about Trella, and my friends and I were so excited to experience your wonderful inns and hotels."

"Nice try, Ms. Anderson," Officer Svoboda huffed, "but I'll be escorting you from the premises. You're being denied entry to Trella indefinitely."

# CHAPTER SEVENTEEN

AS SOON AS THE GATES closed behind them, Abbie cursed. As profanity goes, her performance was a work of art. Museum-worthy, with both nuance and substance. An older sister covered her brother's ears. A kid started taking video until his mom stopped him. Rubald had descended into furious silence and stood with his arms crossed, staring off into the distance.

"Let's find somewhere to sleep," said Rutha, rubbing her face, handing the valet their tickets. Rube handed her his phone. "Oh no," she breathed, reading the screen, which illuminated her horrified look. "No, no, no."

Abbie pulled out her phone. "We missed a bunch of calls from them. What does yours say?" she asked, crowding in to see. "Did the war start?"

"Yes," said Rubald, numbness in his voice. "But that's not it. I failed him."

"'OMW'? What does that mean?"

"On my way."

"Oh no," echoed Abbie. She barely resisted the urge to smack her forehead. *What does he think he's doing?* She groaned. "He doesn't need to come here. Come on, guys, we can figure this out. Talk to him, Rube, he'll reconsider. He's got to stay and fight. We'll find another way across."

Rubald stalked over to her, pointing a finger in her face. "This is your fault. Why couldn't we just wait for the damn doctor? You have to push people's buttons, you have to manipulate everything. And now he's coming here to mop up my mess. My whole career is in shambles, woman! What do you have to say for yourself?"

Rutha put a hand on his arm and he shrugged her off, staring at Abbie intently. Abbie's stare matched his, but she said nothing. He scoffed. "Right, of course. What could you say? Royalty answer to no one, eh? No matter how much you've sacrificed for them, they still owe you nothing."

"Rubald!" Rutha hissed through her teeth. "Stop it! You're just making things worse. Stop this now." The sun was nearly set, and most people had left during Abbie's curse-laden tirade. Abbie looked around to see if anyone was listening, and a few were. Two were whispering and outright pointing.

"Let's get out of here," she whispered to Rutha.

"What was all that talk about excrement?" Stargazer asked loudly.

"Nothing," Abbie muttered, rubbing at her temples. "Let's go."

RUBALD WOULD NOT SPEAK to her the rest of the night; a mile down the road, they set up camp in silence. Surprisingly, it had been a long time since she'd made anyone that angry. During her royal life, everyone was forced to regard her with polite deference no matter how big of a pain she was being, and she hadn't been close to many people in Gardenia. That had been intentional; being a hermit in an anti-social job was insurance. Given these circumstances, she wasn't sure what to do with Rubald's scathing wrath; she realized now that she'd acted foolishly, but what was she supposed to do in that situation, just sit there and wait forever? Now Edward was on his way because she'd screwed things up. Maybe she should text him. She pulled out her phone and unlocked it. She stared at the screen, finger poised to type but unsure where to start. The bright screen was giving her a headache, and she switched the sound off so Rubald and Rutha wouldn't hear her typing.

*Abbie: Don't come. It's my mistake. I'll figure something out. Stay at the front if that's what's needed.*

She sent it, then stared at the screen again, feeling like that wasn't enough.

*Abbie: Rubald has been great. Don't blame him for my screw-up.*

Despite the late hour, a pulsing ellipsis appeared.

*Edward: Dear A, I appreciate your candor. I'm relieved that you didn't cross the border. Trella has joined with Lincoln's forces. I had planned to come meet you to ensure your safety if your journey was prolonged, so it's not directly related to your decision to press the matter with the Trellaviks. I don't blame Mr. Jerrinson. Hopefully, I shall see you soon. Goodnight. —E*

*Read between the verbose lines, Anderson,* she thought. *He blames you, you idiot.*

ABBIE WOKE UP SWEATY. The dream was quickly moving out of memory's reach, but her heart was still racing. She'd been washing her dishes in her apartment in Gardenia, and she kept reaching up to find a crown on her head. Every time she ripped it off, another one appeared in its place. She stared down at the linoleum around her, littered with identical glittering gold circlets.

Abbie slid her feet into her untied hiking boots and quietly unzipped her tent. As she sat down onto an upended piece of wood, she heard the Jerrinsons' tent open. *Please be Rutha, please be Rutha, please be Rutha…*She turned to see a barely-there Rubald stumbling out. He trudged into the woods for a while, and Abbie heard him emptying his bladder onto a mossy tree. He returned a few moments later and paused as he was about to re-enter his tent. The older man turned, rolled a piece of wood over next to hers, and sat down hard. They sat side by side, silently staring into the coals.

"You want me to build it up for you?" Rube said at last.

"No, thank you, Mr. Jerrinson. You can go back to bed."

"No, sister. I know my duty. I'll wait until you're ready."

Abbie felt her breathing speeding up, felt the tears pushing on her tear ducts. "I'm sorry. I *am* sorry, Rube. I want to get this resolved just as much as you do."

He huffed, but his tone wasn't bitter. "I doubt that, sister." He glanced at her sideways and noticed her fighting back the tears. "Oh, come now. No need for that. I'm sorry I spoke to you as I did, and I hope you can forget every word."

"No, sir. You weren't wrong. It was totally my fault, and I told Edward so. I hope it'll make a difference for you going forward."

He put one hand on his knee, cocking his head at her. "You really did?"

She nodded and wiped her face with her sleeve, giving a snotty sniff.

"Huh. Well…" He looked around, as if he hoped the right words were hiding in the shadows.

"You're welcome." She rose from her log seat, smiled weakly, and went back to bed.

# CHAPTER EIGHTEEN

HIS AIRSHIP WAS LANDING. Edward watched out the window from the lounge as the houses began to look less like a child's building blocks and the trees more like trees and less like tiny clumps of moss. Horses and wagons moved along the straight, smooth streets, traditionally paved with stones, not concrete. He'd been to Imahara before, so he was familiar with some of their customs.

Edward scrolled through the email Gasper had sent. They were going to meet him just outside the city, hopefully avoiding the attention of passing travelers. They would head a few miles north to a guest house owned by a cousin of Rutha's: Molly Shipwash and her husband, Barnaby, who went by Pap. He had the directions for where they were supposed to meet, and he could take the train. He had cash. He felt perhaps someone should've also sewn his name and his mother's phone number into his jacket; he'd never traveled alone before. Ever.

"Ladies and gentlemen, please stay seated until the captain turns on the movement sign. Please also leave your phones in dirigible mode until notified that you can make calls, as it interferes with our communications here in the cockpit. Thank you for choosing Transient Dirigibles."

As soon as the landing gear touched the ground, passengers were getting up out of their seats in blatant disregard of the informational lights, and he heard their phones dinging with all the notifications they'd missed. He was torn between blending in and following the rules. He sighed and waited for the lights to turn. When he turned on his phone, he also had a message.

*Abbie: We're here.*

He quickly typed back. *At the restaurant?*

*Abbie: Yes.*

*Edward: You do realize I'm probably at least two hours away, correct?*

*Abbie: Oh, yes. We know. Rubald wouldn't chance missing you or making you wait. He can be very threatening when it comes to you.*

Edward snorted softly and typed his reply.

*Edward: It's nice to have them working for me rather than against me. #kinging*

*Abbie: I don't know much about social media stuff, but I don't think that hashtag's going to catch on.*

*Edward: You never know. Also, kings don't care. #kinging*

*Abbie: LOL.*

*Hey, I got a laugh,* he thought as he shuffled toward the exit.

"Sir?" A strange woman touched his elbow, and he recoiled. "Sorry to bother you, but you left your book."

"Oh. Thank you," he said, taking it, trying not to make too much eye contact.

"You're welcome."

He'd been reading up on the Unveiled. History had always fascinated him, and the Unveiled was certainly an interesting place. It was populated mostly by people who, for financial reasons, could not live inside the Veil, but there was also a large contingent of people who believed the Veil to be harmful to their personal health, something to do with radiation and it frying everyone's brains if you lived in Veiled countries for too long. There were also a good number of both permanent and seasonal do-gooders who wanted to help the poor—some more successfully than others.

Edward was curious to meet more of Rutha's family; he couldn't imagine what would make them want to live in Imahara. Although, he mused, if he had to live outside the Veil, this would probably be where he'd choose. They remained disinterested in continental politics, so it was relatively safe, despite a smattering of gang activity.

At least he didn't have to remember many details for their assumed identities: they would keep it simple. Rutha and Rubald would continue to pose as her adoptive parents because their skin matched, even though their accents didn't. They were traveling to their destination wedding in Orangiers, seeing family along the way. She was Sarafeen around strangers, but went by Abbie as a nickname. He didn't see how that was secure, but he was afraid to argue with her. He'd go by Parker Crawford, the nickname his brother had given him because he couldn't ever seem to get going as a child. Always parked in one place on his backside, mulling things over, thinking and overthinking. He knew he was indecisive. Lincoln didn't have to rub it in. Edward shrugged the thought of his brother away angrily.

He rubbed his thumb over the velvet ring box in his pocket. *Should I give it to her right away, to promote the ruse? I don't want to tick her off...* He sighed. *Woz, this is complicated.* He decided not to go for a kiss; that was too forward. But surely a hug was okay...he didn't want to pressure her, but he did want to show his affection.

After a much longer customs and immigration process than he'd imagined was possible, Edward stowed his pack above his seat on the train and slid into his seat. The stress of seeing Abbie soon was getting to him. *I just want to know where we stand, what her intentions are...*He wanted to bang his head against the window. Instead, he pulled the book out again.

*Imaharan women are very docile and easily manipulated. The people as a whole do not like to be rude, which is a worthwhile cultural endeavor in this author's opinion. Their homes are very sanitary, since shoes are removed when entering. Foreigners need not concern themselves with this custom, as our shoes are naturally sanitized from our time inside the Veil.*

Edward scowled and looked for the copyright page—it was 100 years old. He put the book away and contented himself to make observations by staring out the window and people-watching the other passengers. Before he knew it, they were calling Thahaki Station, and he was getting off.

"Oh, sir? Is this your coat?"

At least it was a different stranger.

INSIDE THE RESTAURANT, he found them sitting at a low table toward the back. Rubald stood up and gave him a hearty handshake. Edward tried to reassure him with his body language, but knew that he'd have to talk to him about what had happened eventually. Rutha stood up and hugged him like he was her own son—which, in some ways, he was.

He'd spent more time with her than with his mother, certainly.

Abbie stood up, too, but seemed to be hanging back.

He took a breath and smiled tentatively. "Hello, Abs."

"Hello...?" She paused.

"...Parker," he muttered.

"Hello, Parker," she finished, then placed her hand on his upper arm and gave him a quick kiss on the cheek. "How are you? How was your trip?"

*Well.* Edward had no idea what to think about this.

"It was uneventful, thank you. How was yours?"

"Fine."

They sat back down, and Edward noticed that Abbie was staring daggers at their waiter, who'd nervously come over to fill their waters and take his order.

"Did he kill your goldfish or something?"

"What?" She sipped her water, watching him over the rim with confusion.

"Why are you attempting to murder the waiter telepathically?"

"Because he murdered a horse and tried to feed it to me."

"Now, now," Rutha patted her hand. "There was a bit of a misunderstanding when we were ordering, and sister here found her meal quite upsetting."

"It's barbaric!" she fumed. "Just the idea. Honestly."

"Do you need to step outside again?" Rubald asked dryly.

Abbie scowled at him. "No."

He turned to Edward. "Have you seen the weather report?"

He shook his head as they put down a steaming bowl of meat, vegetables, and rice in front of him. His stomach growled.

"It looks like a large storm is moving in. Maybe even a hurricane."

"Will we be safe at your cousin's place?"

"Oh, we should be. She's lived there for forty years and she's weathered many hurricanes, so I wouldn't worry too much." Rutha stood up. "I'm off to the restroom."

"Where is it?" Rubald asked.

"Just around the corner."

"I couldn't find it."

"It's just around the corner," she said, pointing across the restaurant.

"Where, though?"

"Oh, for heaven's sake, I'll show you," Rutha said, heaving herself up off the floor with effort.

Edward couldn't stop staring at Abbie. Her face had changed in five years—her freckles were lighter, her hair darker, more like her mother's had been, even if her other facial features strongly favored her father. She wasn't as long-legged as she'd been, rounder in her hips, fuller in the chest...much fuller. Abbie noticed him staring, and he looked away quickly, feeling a dark flush building under his skin.

Before he could second-guess himself, he slid the velvet box over to her. "This is for you, to maintain the...cover story." He watched as she opened it. Her eyebrows bounced up.

"Wow. I like it."

"Truly?"

"Yes, I like it. It's really nice." She slipped it on her finger, and it fit her perfectly. The rose gold set off the highlights in her hair, and the pearl complimented her skin nicely, with a few chip diamonds for sparkle. He mentally patted himself on the back.

"How did you know my ring size?"

"I asked Rubald to clandestinely measure your finger in your sleep."

Her eyes widened for a moment before she realized he was kidding.

"No, I had Rutha estimate your ring size. She's pretty good at it, apparently."

She was staring at him, and he couldn't tell what emotions were warring under the surface. She played everything so close to the chest. She hadn't always been like that; she'd clearly had a tough five years.

"You cut your hair," she said softly.

"Yeah," he said, rubbing his hand rapidly over his cropped hair self-consciously.

"Don't—don't people in your family usually keep it in dreadlocks?"

"That's the tradition, yes. It's usually much longer than this. I cut it so I wouldn't be recognized. I feel kind of—it's kind of like I'm..." he stopped abruptly, looking around the restaurant.

"Naked?" she prompted, grinning.

His cheeks grew even hotter. "I didn't want to say 'naked' and cause you any embarrassment."

"That's thoughtful," she replied, clearly not buying the implication that she was the one feeling embarrassed. She paused and looked up at the ceiling. "I'm comfortable talking about nakedness, though. It's natural, right?"

He cleared his throat. "Right. Sure, right. It's, uh, it's normal."

"Right."

"Part of life."

"Absolutely."

"Well, I think your hair suits you shorter." She cleared her throat and flipped her hair away from her face. "Also, I can't marry you."

# CHAPTER NINETEEN

"WE SHOULD DIVERT INTO the woods, it looks like it's going to rain."

Parker looked around for something to wipe his dirty hands on, besides his pants. They'd been on the road for about three hours, and he still had no idea how to respond to her declaration. She'd tried to convince him that Paul wasn't her father, which he'd quickly dismissed, laughing. Her freckles, her thin, pointed nose, her broad shoulders: she was the spitting image of him. He didn't need a blood test to know for sure. No one would.

"You don't know for sure that it's going to rain."

Parker turned to look at Abbie. Thunder rolled in the distance, and the sky was a deep battleship gray. "I didn't say it was going to rain. I said, 'it looks like it's going to rain.'"

"It's the same thing."

"Not at all. One is a qualified prediction, the other is a surety."

"Yeah, you seem to like qualifiers. Why is that?"

Parker ducked under a low branch. "Difficult to say. I suppose I don't like being painted into a corner."

"Mmm. Neither do I. Yet here we are." She glanced at him sideways, one of her ruddy brows arched. Parker felt her eyes on him, but didn't meet her stare.

"You won't provoke me, Abelia." *I hope.*

"Is that a challenge? Great. I love a good challenge. How have you *not* painted me into a corner by attempting to enforce our marriage contract?"

"Because you yourself agreed to it."

"Yes, nine years ago, when I was basically a child. I'm pretty sure you promised me a chocolate fountain that same year, and I've yet to see that materialize."

"It wasn't a promise, it was a contract, and contracts are binding. You were of legal age. You knew the risks."

She narrowed her eyes at him. "Knew the risks? Are you joking? That's a joke, right? You're saying I should've somehow known that my sisters would die in a horrible accident and your brother would betray your father and country, and we'd end up here?"

"No, of course not. But you knew that an alternate plan of succession was a possibility."

"A remote possibility, sure, but not a surety, as you're fond of saying."

"Life is rarely a surety. You knew we were both in line. I'm not exactly tickled about it, either."

"So you don't want to marry me?"

He sighed. "At this moment or in general?"

She seemed to be losing patience, as well. "Quit dodging my questions and just answer, please. Something unqualified. Something true, for once."

That rankled. "I always tell you the truth. Can you say the same?"

"No. I'm a practiced liar, and you're only telling half the truth. Answer the question. You don't want to marry me?"

"At this moment, or in general?" The air was heavy with moisture, and it was gathering on his face. He wiped his forehead with his shoulder and took his glasses off to wipe them clean as well. This felt more like negotiating a peace treaty with a hostile nation than a conversation between two old friends.

"Either. Both."

He considered the question as their horses stepped carefully over a fallen log. "In general, yes. At this moment...while you do have an annoying propensity to argue and debate every little—"

"Nope, no qualifiers. Just answer. Yes or no." He was tired of being interrupted and considered lying rather than showing his hand, but ultimately decided that veracity would work in his favor.

"Fine. At this moment, also yes."

"You cannot be serious. Do you believe this guy?" she said to no one in particular.

"I believe whoever buys the oats," Stargazer said.

Parker staunchly ignored the talking horse. "However, if you're asking whether I find your argumentativeness attractive? Not particularly."

"Ha!"

"Ha? What, ha?"

"You admitted it! You don't find me attractive!"

"I didn't say that, I said I don't find your argumentativeness attractive. I'm sure you're not attracted to my various weaknesses, either."

"My debate skills are not a weakness. If your country valued women, you'd know that."

Parker flexed his feet in the stirrups, and he wondered if she could tell the comment had touched a nerve.

"From what I can tell, your country thinks women are good for three things: cleaning, food preparation, and procreation."

*Oh yes, she knew.*

"I'm not engaging in this. I don't speak for everyone in my country."

"Edward—"

"Parker," he hissed, glancing around. *Was she trying to expose them?*

"Parker, you literally do. You are literally the guy who speaks for your country."

"Look, I can find aspects of your personality grating and still want to marry you. Everyone who marries hopefully sees their mate's flaws in the plain light of day before they decide to go through with it. You're bending over backwards to prove to me that we're incompatible, but I find the argument irrelevant. As for your debate skills, frankly, I don't think as highly of them as you do. I can count five different logical fallacies you've used since you began."

She tipped her head. "Fine. Name them."

*She thinks I'm bluffing.* He smiled inwardly.

"Fine. Number one: A red herring. In diverting from talking about your actual contract and changing the subject to your attractiveness in my eyes. Number two: an either/or fallacy, when you tried to prove that I wasn't attracted to you just because I said I wasn't tickled about our situation. Number three: a special-pleading fallacy, when you implied that it was unfair of me to enforce the contract that you signed in good faith simply because unforeseen tragedy has befallen both our families. Number four: an ad populum fallacy, when you attacked my country's stance on women's rights. And last but not least, number five: moral equivalency, when you claimed that because I never got you the chocolate fountain I supposedly promised you ten years ago, you shouldn't have to marry me. And I didn't, by the way."

"Didn't what?" She was looking at him with an expression of morbid fascination, like one might look at a grisly dirigible crash. He sighed for what felt like the hundredth time that day. *Maybe you over-nerded that one, mate.*

"I never promised you a chocolate fountain. I distinctly remember," he said, rebounding. "We were swimming at Pigeon Lake and we had chocolate popsicles, and you said, 'Wouldn't it be fun to have a chocolate fountain at our wedding?' and I agreed, in theory. That's all."

"Well, that's not at all how I remember that."

"Why am I unsurprised?"

Abbie was quiet for a minute, absorbing this new information, flexing her hands. "Then what aren't you tickled about?"

"Ruling two countries. And if I have to do it, I'll need your help, and not just in getting to the throne. In keeping it. In doing right by your people as well as mine."

"But you *don't* have to do it! That's the whole point, Parker!"

He kept a disgruntled noise from erupting from his chest. "What, and let Lincoln win? A power-hungry narcissist who cares only for himself? Unfathomable. Ridiculous."

"No, not ridiculous, because your birthday and family of origin shouldn't dictate your every decision, no matter what we were taught about divine right."

"I won't abandon my responsibility."

"Oh, but you'll marry someone who did? Isn't that just as bad?"

"Perhaps. But I don't see that I have much of a choice." He had a headache; it was happening more often, usually related to stress. Perhaps he wasn't drinking enough water. Perhaps he could take up coffee. It was popular, after all. He dropped back and called over his shoulder. "Rutha, do you have any ibuprofen?"

# CHAPTER TWENTY

NORMALLY, ABBIE WOULD'VE felt pleased that she'd scored some points in their debate, and part of her still did. But another part was just uncomfortable about torturing this poor man who obviously cared so much about...about everyone but himself, even if it meant marrying someone as difficult as her. Despite his relentless formality and infuriating habit of taking everything literally, her respect for him was starting to grow. Anyone who could take what she'd dished out without losing his temper was obviously a skillful opponent. Was that what he was now, an opponent?

She heard a horse approaching, and she opened her mouth to ask him if he was repulsed by any of her other shortcomings, but quickly stopped herself when she saw Rutha smiling at her instead.

"Where's Parker?"

"Oh, he's going to ride with Rube for a time. They've got some business to go over, and I couldn't leave you alone up here without a companion. Surely even an old lady is better than silence."

"What am I, fishguts?" grumbled Stargazer, and Abbie snorted and patted the side of his neck, smiling at Rutha.

"I always enjoy your company, Rutha. Lead the way."

"I think we're getting close. It's been years since I was last here, but it's such a beautiful spot, I could never forget it. You're going to love Molly. She's spunky like you."

MOLLY MUST HAVE BEEN watching for them, because the minute they dismounted she was out the door and hurrying toward them across the meadow. She was the same size and shape as Rutha, but with redder hair mixed into the gray. Abbie decided to give the cousins a few minutes to catch up before the whole group descended on the house, so she walked Stargazer and Rodeo Drive over to the stables.

They had a small farm with a large lodge and equally large barn. Rutha had mentioned something about agriculture and animal husbandry for the community, and Abbie noticed several locals around, whom she waved at. They waved back.

"Abbie?"

"Yes, horse?"

"Rodeo Drive was wondering if that's the guy you're going to marry."

Abbie bit back a smile. "Oh, Rodeo Drive was wondering?"

"Yes. He told me."

"I see."

"He said it sounded like you were trying to get out of your contact. As a horse, I can tell you, if you don't want someone to contact you, just kick them. That sends a clear message."

"Well, tell Rodeo it's a *contract*, not a contact, which is a piece of paper with a binding legal promise on it."

"So you promised to marry him? Greenback's rider?"

"His name is Mr. Crawford, and yes, I did. But it was a long time ago, and we're different people now."

Stargazer whistled softly through his teeth as they entered the barn. "I'm glad I'm not a human. Mating is much less complicated for us. Say you see a filly you—"

"I don't need the details, Star."

If a horse could shrug, that's what Stargazer did. "I'm just saying. It's much simpler."

Abbie sighed, staring up at the barn ceiling, pigeons perched above her head.

"Arguing with a horse. I am so through the looking glass."

"I doubt it."

Abbie jumped and spun around. A stocky, white-haired man in overalls and a wide-brimmed leather hat was balanced in a chair in the corner, the front two legs in the air, phone in one hand. He didn't look up.

"I'm s-sorry," she said, "I didn't know anyone was in here. You know, except for the horses."

"You wanna talk about it?"

"Talk about what?"

He looked up. "Your mirror problem."

"My what?"

"You said you was through the looking glass. We don't have no mirrors out here in the stable; horses ain't got no use for 'em."

"Yes, we do!" came a voice from the far end of the stalls, and Abbie peered into the darkness.

"Don't pay her no mind, she's just vain." The man smiled. "Folks call me Pap. You must be the visitors we been anticipating. Come on, Molly's been cookin' all afternoon for you, hope y'all are hungry. And I'm sure I can find a mirror to suit you inside."

Abbie smiled back. "Sure, just let me put my horses away and give them a brush down."

"You can brush 'em after dinner, they'll keep. Come on, I'll show you the stalls. We can't put the talkers together, or they keep the others awake all night."

She allowed herself to be led back toward the house, the enticing scent of roasted chicken and cornbread making her salivate like a conditioned canine. Despite not having officially met Molly, she was about ready to kiss her on the mouth, and she didn't even swing that way. They were still ten steps away when the door opened, and Rube stood on the threshold with a mug. A mug that was steaming.

She didn't even look into the cup before she took it out of his hands and swallowed its contents in one gulp. It was. It was coffee, black as night and strong as the tide, a force of nature in its own right.

"I'm getting a cold, you know," Rube said, scowling.

Abbie smiled maniacally. "More, please."

"This time from your own mug, if you please."

She followed him into the house, where she could hear Parker, Molly, and Rutha laughing in the kitchen.

Since they'd been camping for a few days, Abbie suddenly realized she had a bit of an odor—a bit in the same way that the Orangiersian Ocean is a bit deep. She gripped the mug. More coffee first, even if it meant being contained in a room with Parker—*Edward*—smelling like this. *Maybe it would be good*, she mused. *Natural fiancé repellent.* She rubbed at her eyes with the palms of her hands. Why did she want him to dislike her? It wasn't going to nullify the contract. She heard her mother's voice in her head telling her again and again that she was just making things hard on herself. Fatigue descended on her like a sodden blanket, and suddenly all she wanted was to be horizontal—and alone.

Molly appeared in the kitchen doorway, all smiles. "Come on in, supper's ready. I was just about to the ring the bell. You must be Abbie? I've heard so much about you. I'm so tickled to meet you. Looks like you met Pap already—was he hiding out in the barn again?" The woman laughed and gathered Abbie in a firm hug, then pushed her toward an empty chair next to Parker. Pap served her up a big plate of everything, and amazingly, it all looked like things she could actually eat. She wondered if Rutha had tipped Molly off.

"So, brother, what do you like to do?" Pap directed this question at Parker.

"I like to sail," he said between bites.

"No kidding, I used to sail myself, as a younger man."

"Around here?"

"No! There's no sailing around here. In Orangiers, where I'm from. Do you do much racing?"

Parker nodded slowly, as if he were thinking about whether to lie, but it was too late. "I do, when I have the time."

"What are you racing?"

"I've got a ketch..."

"Oh, that's good for one man, but you're getting a bigger crew now," he said, elbowing Parker and winking at Abbie, who blushed. "So you can get a bigger boat!"

"Yes, I'd love to take Abbie out sailing, once we're back near the ocean again." He was smiling at her earnestly. His face had changed little since he was a boy. He still had an amazing smile; it was always his best feature. Although, his skin was still that deep, beautiful ebony color...it was a close second. His rimless glasses gave him a scholarly look that suited him without making him look like a nerd, even though he kind of was. *And those eyes...*

Molly interrupted her thoughts. "And what about you, sister? Tell us about where you come from." Abbie wiped her mouth with the cloth napkin in her lap, embarrassed that this was the first time she'd used it—her food was nearly gone.

"Well, I'm from Brevspor originally, but I've been living in Gardenia for about five years. After I left home, I started out with nothing. I lived on the street for a few months, then I managed to find a job at Fantasmic Food Mart as a produce stocker through a government program for homeless youth. That's how I paid for my first year of college at Gardenia Community College. Then I decided to take out a loan in order to finish rather than take a hundred years. I graduated a year ago with my associate's degree in environmental protection and waste reclamation systems. It's nice to be above ground at least part of the day."

The group chuckled politely.

"I bet you're glad to have that monkey off your back."

"Pardon?"

"Your debt."

"Oh, I haven't paid off my debt yet. I've still got more than $20,000 to go."

"I know. That's why I paid it off." Parker took another bite off his chicken leg and reached for the cornbread basket. Abbie quickly moved it out of his grasp.

"What does that mean?"

Parker shrugged, wiping his hands on his napkin. "I took care of your loan balance. It didn't make sense to let it sit and accrue interest when I had the money to pay it. I certainly didn't want that on my credit score once we're married." He leaned over to Pap and said confidentially, "I've got 800."

The rest of the table got very quiet and still, as though they'd just noticed a scorpion on the table. Abbie rose to her feet. She was taking very slow, controlled breaths. "Parker, may I please speak to you outside?" She quickly walked out the front door without waiting for a response. After a moment, she heard him follow.

When they were both a little distance from the house, she rounded on him.

"How dare you, Parker?"

"I see that you're upset—"

"How *dare* you meddle in my finances?"

He threw up his hands. "Who's meddling? It was a perfectly logical decision if we're to be married. I thought you'd be pleased."

"Yes, but you knew that was still an 'if,' not a 'when.' You knew I hadn't decided yet, and yet you plunged on ahead without consulting me!"

His face fell, and he reached out as if to touch her arm but she pulled away. "It'd kill me if I had to live with that crushing debt hanging over my head. Abbie, I really did think you'd be grateful."

"Well, let me be perfectly clear: I am *not grateful*. My affection is not for sale, and I'll be paying you back every golden cent." She stormed back toward the barn, then turned and screamed, "And what the Jersey do you need credit for, anyway? Pay in cash, for Woz's sake!"

SHE THOUGHT THAT BRUSHING out the horses would calm her down, but with every stroke, Abbie found herself getting more and more worked up. The horses wouldn't stand still, and she finally threw the brush into the hay in the corner with a curse.

"Abbie?" Stargazer asked timidly.

"*What?*"

"Never mind."

# CHAPTER TWENTY-ONE

AFTER SEVERAL INDECISIVE moments considering whether or not to follow Abbie into the barn, Parker decided to go back inside to finish his food. At the table, the conversation had shifted to Pap's work with the locals.

"We've helped a few of them get a real enterprise going, but it took more than farming know-how. Lots of barriers to overcome."

"Like what?" Rubald asked.

"Like thinking pigs eat mud. I endured that one for a few years before I built a stand and kept the pig out of the mud all the time, just to show them. When they saw the man-sized hog I'd grown, they finally conceded that pigs raised by Orangies didn't eat mud...some of 'em still say the pig knows its owner's a rich man."

"You'll pardon me for saying so, but you don't seem that rich to me." Parker slid back into his chair. "How long have you been here?"

"Forty years, give or take," Pap said, not seeming to mind Parker's candidness.

"That's quite the commitment. I commend you for it."

Pap raised an eyebrow. "You know, son, I don't much like to talk about it, but I'm going to tell you a story..." Molly grinned and got up to serve the pie, shaking her head as Pap continued.

"About a hundred years ago, a young man came to these parts. He was young and curious, met a lotta people, shook

**142**

a lotta hands, made a lot of observations about the way he thought things were. Wrote 'em down even, in that little book I noticed with your pack on the way in."

"You're talking about *Traveling the Undignified Road.*"

Pap nodded. "Indeed I am. What did you make of it?"

"I found it rude, racist, and prideful."

"Good. It's all that and more. And I've spent forty years trying to undo the damage it's caused."

"Did you know him?"

The older man cackled, and Parker touched his forehead. "Wait—Shipwash."

"Yes, Shipwash the Younger. The Elder, our esteemed author, died some years ago. Never realized the kind of lies he'd printed, went to his grave saying his book changed the world. Yep, he changed it all right. He changed it for the worse."

"But that's not your fault."

"Nope, but it's his legacy, and I didn't want it to be mine. So I came here with another idea...what if I came to learn, instead of coming to teach?"

Parker swallowed a mouthful of cornbread. "Don't you teach animal husbandry? Farming?"

"Yep, but I spent the first five years just living here. Just learning. Learning the language, learning the nuances of it. Did you know they've got six different words for smiling?"

Edward scowled in confusion. "Why does that matter?"

Pap gestured dramatically, chuckling once more. "Maybe it don't. But they're there for a reason, and I wanted to know the real reason why, not the reason my dad assumed it was, if he ever even bothered to find out. You know what they say when you assume, don'tcha?"

Parker shook his head.

"You make an ass of *u* and *me!*"

Parker felt himself break out in a grin as Pap cackled, pounding his fist on the table.

"That's an old joke, Pap. You're dating yourself," Molly hollered from the kitchen where she was washing up the dishes with an Imaharan woman Parker hadn't noticed come in.

"Well, he never heard it, he laughed!" He turned back to Parker. "We been married too long, see. She's heard all my jokes."

"What's the most important thing you've learned?" Parker sipped his water.

Pap regarded him suspiciously. "About marriage?"

"Well, sure, that too, but I meant about people from other countries, other cultures. About how to help, how to work with them."

"About marriage? Large doses of love and respect; beyond that, you don't need much. Though you two seem to need some help in the physical affection department, ya know? Loosen up a little, we don't bite. Don't go sneaking down that hall tonight—Rubald will end you—but loosen up." Pap finished his pie and licked his fork as Rubald, mostly silent up until this point, roared with laughter, nearly choking on his dessert.

"About cultures? That it was all important. That people don't come in a box, they come in tapestries, all woven together into experience and culture and family. You can't pull out one color and understand 'em, see. You gotta go right up to it, feel the texture, then step back for the whole view. You gotta do it humble, you see? Just because I'm not Imaharan don't mean we don't share a lot. Just because you're Orangiersian don't mean we do. Although you do like to sail, that's a point in your favor."

Parker glanced at Rubald and Rutha, who sat quietly watching him, twin looks of approval in their eyes.

"Do you think you've been able to undo what he did?"

"Depends. Can I burn your copy of that damn book?"

Parker quietly left the table, going up the shadowed stairway and returning a few moments later to hand the book over to Pap, who grinned from ear to ear.

"Good, that's one more. I've only burned 167, so I've got a long way to go. But it's a start."

# CHAPTER TWENTY-TWO

STORMING BACK TO THE main house, Abbie whipped open the door and caught Rubald by the sleeve just before he re-entered the kitchen; Rutha and Parker were nowhere to be seen. "Is there a shower? I need one." This had been true even before she'd brushed out all four horses, but was doubly true now.

Rube shook his head ruefully. "I don't think so. Molly and Rutha can take you down to the creek in the morning, sister, but daylight's fading now."

The cook suddenly appeared in the doorway, bubbles still on her forearms from washing up the dishes. "Hello, darlin'," she said with a warm smile. "You don't think we'd leave you filthy like that, do ya now? There's a warm tub waiting for you upstairs. Pap just finished filling it. You ladies can go up and use it first, then the menfolk. Go on now. Girls' bunkhouse is first door on the left."

Abbie smiled gratefully in return and thanked the woman before climbing the log staircase, where her pack was waiting for her in the first bedroom. She wondered briefly who'd brought it in for her...probably *him*. She'd treated Edward poorly, but it was totally justified, she told herself, stripping off her long-sleeve shirt and jeans. She dropped them on the floor rather than dirty the clean patchwork quilt on the bottom bunk. Rutha would likely want the bottom one, her arthritis being bad and all.

Abbie stripped to nothing and, finding no towel, she considered darting across the hallway to the bathroom rather than re-dress. Instead, she dug around until she found the silk robe Rubald had bought her.

*When did I start caring about Rutha's arthritis?* she wondered as she dipped her toe into the hot water in the claw foot tub. There were grasses and broken flowers floating in the water, and she started to back out until she caught the scent: lavender and lemongrass. Abbie felt tears coming to her eyes. It was a small gesture, but one that meant a lot on a day that had been so hard. Even though it made her feel slightly royal, she embraced the intention and not her skewed perception of it. Also, she thought, amused, it would make Rubald and Parker smell fancy.

Abbie washed first, including her tangled hair, and then intended to soak for just a minute...she closed her eyes to the rough-cut boards paneling the darkening room and imagined herself at home in her own bathtub...and opened her eyes again to a concerned Rutha leaning over her, holding a candle.

"Did you fall asleep, sister? You've been up here for an hour." The wrinkles in Abbie's fingers and toes and her chattering teeth confirmed that she'd been in the tub a long time.

"I'm so-so s-s-sorry," she stuttered as her wet skin met the lodge's cool post-sundown air. "I've ruined the b-b-b-bath for everyone. I'm s-s-s-sorry, Rutha." The round woman wrapped a rough towel around her with a smile, rubbing her arms vigorously through the cloth.

"It was a long day. I'd have done the same if not for all the cornbread I've eaten. Let's get you to bed now." She crossed the hall quickly and saw two concerned silhouettes at the bottom of the stairs peering up at her into the darkness. Rutha pushed her into the bedroom and shooed them away, closing the door. "You're lucky you didn't drown, sister. If you were so tired, why didn't you just go to bed?"

"I w-w-wanted m-m-more c-c-c—"

"Coffee. Of course, I should've guessed. Come now, let's get you warm and dry."

Still groggy and in shock from the cold, Abbie allowed Rutha to find her pajamas and towel her dripping hair. The older woman tucked her into the top bunk, adding another blanket to the foot of the bed.

"It's freezing in here," Abbie complained. The older woman put a hand to Abbie's forehead and shook her head.

"It's not the room, sister. It's you. You may be falling ill."

Abbie pushed herself up and conked her head against the ceiling.

"Ouch. No, I can't be getting sick. We don't have time for that. We've got to get out of here before—"

"Before your wedding?" Rutha chimed in loudly. Even in the lamplight, Abbie could read the annoyance on her face, and she sank back under the covers.

"The walls have ears, sister. Don't let your guard down just because we're with friends. Now go to sleep." Rutha blew out the light, and when Abbie next stirred, she had a splitting headache that pounded whenever she moved and a full bladder, which she decided to ignore.

In a few hours, Abbie woke again, this time to whispered voices near her head.

"I warned her I was getting a cold. This is just what we need now."

"This is more than a cold, Rube. She needs medicine. She needs rest. There's something...I don't know...something wrong with her. A young woman her age, an experienced horsewoman, should be able to go farther each day than Abbie has."

Abbie tried to keep her breathing deep and regular despite her rise in heartrate.

"It's raining anyway. Lousy travel weather. He's been going full tilt for weeks now. I'm sure he could use a break, too. Let's just sit tight."

Her head was still pounding, and she knew she had a fever. She stretched her sore leg muscles and rolled over, her hips and knees complaining. She was too tired to listen anymore. If they would let her sleep, it might help shorten the flare she could feel coming. The flare she knew by heart by now, could see coming a mile away.

She sucked in a deep breath and sat up, lightheaded.

Rubald and Rutha were watching her, arms crossed.

"Good morning," Rube said, "or should I say good afternoon?"

"It's that late?" she asked, looking around. The room was bright.

"Yes, it's noon. We let you sleep through breakfast, but thought we'd see if you wanted lunch."

"No. No food." She slid gingerly off the edge of the bed and winced as her feet hit the floor too hard, stinging. Abbie shuffled slowly toward the bathroom, only to bump into Parker in the hall.

"Hey."

"Hey."

"You all right?"

"Not really."

"Are you sick?"

"Sort of."

He reached toward her, and she was too exhausted to move away. Parker touched her forehead gently with the back of his fingers. "You're really hot."

"I've always thought so."

He grinned that dazzling smile, but it didn't mask his concern.

"Move, I have to pee." She slid past him into the bathroom and shut the door quietly for the sake of her head. She caught her reflection in the mirror and groaned. Her hair was curly on the side that hadn't been against the pillow and flattened on the side that had. There was a new patch of rash across her chest, and all three of them had certainly seen it. She ran her fingers across it, as if trying to probe how much it hurt and was going to spread.

Abbie peed, splashed some water on her face in the sink, and stumbled back toward her bunk. Rube and Rutha were still talking in her room, but they stopped abruptly when she re-entered.

"Oh, am I interrupting?" she quipped as she whipped the quilt over her head.

"Abbie, dear?" Rutha said softly, standing on the edge of the bottom bunk to rub her back.

"Unh?"

"Can I get you anything?"

"No. Thank you. Just sleep." She heard the older woman turn to leave, and she called, "Rutha?"

"Yes, dear?"

"Tell the men I can travel tomorrow."

"Well, we'll see how you're feeling. You never know."

Abbie sighed. "I do know. Lasts about thirty-six hours."

Rutha had returned to the side of her bed, and Abbie could hardly hear her over the steady rain beating on the roof just above their heads.

"What does, dear?"

Abbie didn't answer, and Rutha quietly left.

SHE HAD THE STRANGE dreams that always accompanied her flares, dreams that were disturbing and unusual yet not quite memorable as she tried to shake off the night's sleep the next day. She felt hungover, her thoughts thick as molasses as she tried to stir them. She was alone. Her head still hurt, but it was a dull ache now, not the throbbing debilitation of yesterday. It was still raining. Someone had left a cup of coffee on the dresser, and it was still steaming.

Pulling on her hated robe, she wandered downstairs with the mug in her hand, now only half full.

"Oh, she's alive," Rubald said, and everyone looked up as she came into the kitchen. Rutha hurried over to her.

"I knew the coffee would rouse her," she said, feeling her forehead. "Fever's gone, too."

"Oh, Woz be praised," Molly said, gesturing with her spatula. "Glad to see you up and about. You must've caught that bug that's going around." She whacked Parker on the back of the head and he jumped. "Aren't you going to greet your fiancé? Still asleep over there?"

Hiding a look of annoyance, Parker came over and put his hands on her arms.

"Feeling better?"

"Mostly." Feeling all the eyes on them, Abbie pushed up onto her toes and gave him a peck on the cheek, denying to herself that she enjoyed the feel of his stubble under her lips.

Pap cracked up. "And the winner of the most chaste kiss by an engaged couple is..." he pantomimed opening an envelope, "Abbie and Parker!"

Parker ignored him, not taking his eyes off her. "I was worried about you," he murmured as the other conversations resumed.

"Were you?"

He nodded. "Tried to wake you for breakfast yesterday, but we couldn't. Rubald even checked you for a pulse."

Abbie shifted uncomfortably. "I'm a heavy sleeper when I'm sick."

Rutha came between them abruptly, holding out a plate with eggs and bacon for Abbie. "Here you are, dear, something to wake you up and keep you on the mend. The weather's clearing up, so let's go down to the creek and wash our clothes after breakfast, hmm? I'm sure yours are as ripe as mine."

Abbie nodded, picking up the fork and shoveling a bite into her mouth, trying to ignore Parker's lingering looks over Rutha's shoulder.

# CHAPTER TWENTY-THREE

RUTHA WOULDN'T LET her help carry the clothes, so she had a chance to fully appreciate the beautiful surroundings of the farm. The leaves on the deciduous trees were fully out, a delightful frog-green, and the horses were out grazing; she could hear Stargazer talking someone's ear off between bites.

The creek was at the back of the property, behind a line of cherry trees frosted with pink flowers. They held hands down the steep incline, relying on the log steps someone had made. Rutha began to shake things out and check pockets while Abbie searched around for the washboard and the soap in the basket.

"You know," Rutha said, not looking at Abbie, "one of the advantages of having ten children is that you become a student of human behavior." She turned a shirt right-side out and stuck it into the slow-moving water that pooled by the bank. "You see a lot of lies and half-truths. You learn to see right through them, in fact."

Abbie plunged her jeans into the water, scaring away a curious fish, and began scrubbing away vigorously.

"Now, I'm not suggesting that you have to tell me what's wrong with you. We've known each other but a few days, and I wouldn't imagine I'm your closest confidant just yet." Rutha hung her blouse on a bush to dry. "But I would encourage you to tell Edward. He's a reasonable man. If you really can't marry him, at least have the courage to tell him why." They washed a few more clothes in silence. "I know you're angry with him, though why you'd be angry over being debt-free, I can't imagine. But talk to him, dear. Don't shut him out. Take it from a woman who's been married forty years."

Abbie wanted to say something, but all she could get out was, "Thank you."

"You're welcome, dear."

COMING BACK FROM THE creek, laundry left drying in the sun, Abbie found Parker sitting on the porch, finishing a phone call. Rutha winked at her and gave her an encouraging smile. Rubald was just coming out, and Rutha caught him by the arm and turned him back into the house, muttering something that stopped his complaints cold.

"Can I talk to you?"

"Of course." He was still typing something on his phone. "Give me just a moment..."

Abbie took a deep breath. "I haven't been honest with you."

Parker looked up. "Regarding?"

"Regarding me. About why I can't do this."

He set his phone on the porch railing. "But you're prepared to tell me now?"

She swallowed and waved her hands around in a vague gesture of assent. "I thought I could convince you to nullify our contract without having to put my private life on display, but now that I've met you again, I see that's not going to happen."

He nodded, then watched her expectantly. Abbie sat down quickly in the rocking chair, turning it to face him, if only to keep her knees from going out from under her. She could feel the sweat collecting under her armpits, soaking her shirt. Her heart was racing, and she tried to slow her breathing. *Best just out with it.*

"I have an autoimmune disease called lupus. Have you heard of it?"

He scooted forward to the edge of his chair, gaze intent. "Yes, I believe I've heard of it. Are you okay? Is it...painful?"

"Yes. I mean, yes, I'm okay, but yes, it's painful. It causes some of the things you've noticed me experiencing lately."

He picked up his phone and unlocked it, but she placed a hand on his.

"Just listen, okay? You can look it up online later."

"My apologies." He locked it and set it on the railing again.

"No, it's okay." She rubbed at her eyes. "I'm sorry, I just want to get through this."

"Is that why your hands are like ice?"

"Yes, they're cold when I'm stressed. And that's why I'm always tired. And why I can't be in the sun too much. And why I can't eat certain things."

"What's the cure, then?"

"There isn't one."

He met her eyes with innocent, honest concern. "Are you dying?"

"No, no, I'm not dying." She smiled, partly out of amusement at his ignorance, partly to reassure him. "At least no faster than anyone else."

"What does this have to do with our contract, then?"

She paused, twisting her fingers, looking at the rough-cut boards of the porch. "I have more limitations than most people, Parker. I can't have a high-stress job. I can't meet foreign dignitaries with a giant red rash across my face. I can't sit out in the sun watching the polo matches or stay out late attending exhausting social functions. I have strict boundaries that I draw so that I can stay functional, and the life you want me to lead is incompatible with that."

"So we'll work with your needs. No big deal. People will understand."

She stood up. "That's the thing, Parker. They don't understand. People just think you're lazy or flaky or making it all up."

He scowled. "Surely not."

"Yes, they do. That's partly why I resigned my role. They did not understand. They refused to." Pushing the sadness down deeper, she reached for the anger instead. It was so much cleaner. She'd never forgiven the harsh words, the indignation over the hours she spent in bed, the scorn and skeptical looks from physicians and family members alike; that reliable anger was still right there, like coals kept warm. Parker's voice interrupted her reverie.

"Abbie, people accept what I tell them. That's one of the few perks of being in charge of things, all right? And if I tell them that my queen can't attend their party, they'll have to accept that."

"You just don't get it at all, do you? Don't you think I tried to reason with them? Don't you think I tried to tell them all that the fatigue wasn't just my period? Don't you think I showed them the handfuls of hair I was losing in the shower every week? The weird rashes when I'd been out in the sun? You know what I got in return? Speeches. Really good ones, about how Porchenziis are made of stronger stuff and I'm a Porchenzii, so I'd better snap out of it."

"Abbie, I'm not your family."

"Not yet, you're not. And I intend to keep it that way, for your sake and mine."

Parker let out a breath of frustration through his nose and leaned further forward. "That's not what I meant. I'm saying that I believe you. I'm saying I'm not *like* them, because I believe you. Your word's not in question here whatsoever."

"Yes, I can see that...and I'm glad you do. But even so, you don't comprehend what a huge part of my life this is. And you're not getting that with a hidden illness like this, people are always going to think my absence is a power play. That's politics. They're going to be offended no matter what I do."

"So let them. They'll get over it, especially when it happens for other events besides theirs."

Abbie rubbed at her temples. "But I won't. I hate the whispers, I hate the endless apologies and explanations. I hate the judgment and the condemnation for something that isn't even my fault."

"Who's judging you?"

"Everyone!"

"Oh, come on. That's nonsense."

"And so it begins."

"Abs..." He reached for her, but missed as she started pacing, gesturing wildly.

"No, look, it's already started. I tell you what it's like to have a chronic illness, and you don't believe me."

"I believe that you do have what you say you have, I believe you that it's hard, I believe you that you've been mistreated over it. I just think it's going too far to say that absolutely everyone's judging you."

She crossed her arms. "Fine. The ones who aren't judging me pity me, which is worse."

"Look, Abs, it wouldn't stay secret for long—"

"And you think that's *better* somehow? Do you realize how we'll have to fight off the doctors trying to get at me with their magic cure-alls? Do you realize the outrage the public will have that you still decided to go through with this contract? Do you realize the suspicion, the speculation that will happen about what I was holding over you to make you marry me anyway when I'm obviously damaged goods?"

"Hang the public! When I love someone, I accept them, faults and all."

"Can you accept not having children?"

"What?" Parker's expression turned from exasperated to shell-shocked.

"I asked if you can accept not having children." Like a beach ball she'd been holding under the ocean suddenly let go, the emotions sprang to the surface in an instant. Her eyes filled with tears. "They want me to give them an heir, Parker. That's what my country wants. That's what your country wants. And you want that, too—or you will, someday soon. And I don't know if that's even possible."

He was silent for a long time, and Abbie sat back down.

"We could always adopt," he said quietly.

She shook her head. "You don't adopt a head of state. You know that. And if you did, it would be because despite your best efforts, you couldn't conceive with the wife you'd already married. You haven't married me yet, Parker. You can't choose me in good conscience."

He smiled ruefully. "You make it sound as if choosing you is a moral evil. Our contract is signed. As I see it, I'd simply be keeping my word."

"A contract made on incomplete information. And now that you have more information, I trust that you'll do what's right for your country and tear up the damn thing." Abbie jumped up and hurried down the steps, deriving no small amount of pleasure in being the last to speak, but more importantly, too terrified to hear his answer either way.

"Hang on!"

Abbie stopped, but didn't turn around. She heard his footsteps coming hard after her, and she braced herself for what would come next.

"First of all, you can drop the theatrics. Storming off isn't going to keep us from discussing this. And we will discuss it as rational creatures, not like raging loons."

"Loons rage? I had no idea. They always seem so peaceful on the pond."

"Stop trying to distract me with your wit, you're not that clever. Secondly, I do not yet have sufficient information; I'd like to hear from your doctors and see what they say. Would you agree to let me speak with them?"

"It won't do any good. They won't tell you anything I haven't."

"Nevertheless, I'd like to try. You seem to have a rather pessimistic view of...well, *everything*, and I'd like to probe whether there's another perspective."

"Fine."

"Fine."

"Is there anything else?"

"Yes, as a matter of fact," he said, moving close enough to put a hand on her shoulder, pulling her against his side, tucked under his arm. "There is one more thing."

"Which is?"

"I still think you'd make an amazing queen. Don't interrupt, I want you to hear this," he said as she took a breath. She closed her mouth and shot the unused air forcefully through her nose. "You understand what it is to feel helpless and small in a way that I never could. You understand building a life from nothing, you understand weakness and pain, and yet you're still one of the stronger people I've met in my life." He was staring into her eyes the whole time he spoke, and Abbie fought to not look down and away. "In your queendom, there are many, many people suffering, and that fact would never be far from your mind. I know you would never stop fighting for them. You would be the best champion they could ask for."

His arm dropped, and Abbie found herself with no retort as he walked back to the house, leaving her staring into the woods, the word "love" still ringing in her ears, her shoulders still warm from his touch.

# CHAPTER TWENTY-FOUR

THE NEXT MORNING, IT appeared the storm had passed, and Rubald had them all up at the crack of dawn. Abbie was already dressed and sipping her coffee when Parker stumbled downstairs, bleary-eyed.

"You didn't sleep well?"

"Nope."

"Bad mattress?"

"No, I kept smelling myself."

"Pardon?"

"I kept waking up to the smell of that bath water, I couldn't get it off my skin."

"That's with intent, young man," said Molly, lugging an armful of firewood into the kitchen, which he came over to help with. "Keeps the skeeters away."

"What's a skeeter?" Abbie asked, leaning over the stove to smell the pancakes, even if she couldn't partake in them.

"Little nasty flying buggers that bite you in your sleep. Carry disease and pestilence. Gotta keep 'em away from important guests."

Abbie and Parker exchanged a look behind Molly's back, and he cleared his throat.

"Oh, we're not important in the least, but we certainly appreciate your hospitality."

"Nonsense! The engaged relatives of my cousin's? That's a big day, that is. I gotta say, though, y'all don't act like any engaged couple I ever met. Though you do seem to holler at each other with regularity, so there is that..."

Parker ran his hand over his head, and Abbie quickly changed the course of the conversation.

"So how exactly are you related to Rutha?"

"On my sweet mother's side. The Haberchecks were Orangies for ten generations before we struck out beyond the Veil."

Abbie choked on her coffee and quickly put a hand up to keep it from squirting out her nose. "Orangies? Is that what you said? Oh, I am so using that."

Parker flexed his shoulders and the corners of his mouth turned down. "The polite term is *Orangiersian*, you know."

"Yes, I do know," she said, refilling her mug. "I do, but I find that...stuffy."

"Okay, fine. I'm off to hitch the horses," Parker said with a slap to his knees as he rose. He got three steps away before he turned back. "I, um, actually don't recall being taught how to hitch horses. Might you be available to assist me?"

Abbie rolled her eyes and followed him out the front door as Molly chuckled.

"Can't you just say, 'Can you help me?' Why do you make everyone pull out a dictionary every time they talk to you? Don't you have an informal subroutine for your robot brain?"

"I'm not certain to what you're referring."

"That." She pointed at him, descending the stairs. "That's what I'm talking about."

He gave her a smug smile.

"Don't make faces. Just speak simply when you're with simple people. When you're back with your fancy-pants friends, you can talk however you want. But here? You need to blend in."

"It seems more derogatory to call them 'simple' than to alter my vocabulary to accommodate an inadequate education—"

"See? That. That's rude."

He put his hands on his hips and stared hard at her. "What would you have me say, then? Coach me a bit."

Abbie started toward the stables, and he trailed after her.

"Fine. Let's say you need the assistance of a beautiful, intelligent young woman in hitching your horse, because your hoity-toity education has given you no real-world life skills. What would you say?"

"Abbie, would you be available to assist me?"

"No."

He scowled. "Abbie, might you have the time—"

"No. Try this: Got a minute?"

"I'm sorry, but that sentence has no subject."

"But it does have a direct object, so I'll direct you not to object."

Abbie started to pick up his saddle, but he took it from her.

"That was funny."

She smiled. "That's good! That's better. See, normally, you would've said something ridiculous like, 'That had the characteristics of an exceptionally well-structured humorous turn of phrase.'"

He chuckled as he hoisted the saddle onto Greenback.

"That's backward. The big knob goes in front, just like your pants." He laughed harder and tried to turn it around on the horse, then gave up and pulled it off, walking around to the horse's other side.

"Just use as few syllables as possible."

He walked back around to watch her attach the front cinch. "So, rather than telling you that I find your analogy vulgar, I would simply say, 'That's just wrong.'"

"Yup."

"Can I say *crass* or *crude*, maybe?"

She seesawed her hand in the air. "Borderline."

He paused, leaning on his horse. "What if I want to tell you that you're beautiful?"

"Oh, that's okay, you can say that," she said, flipping her hair over her shoulder to adjust the stirrups. "Beautiful is a long word, but it's not obtuse. It's not like you called me pulchritudinous."

"You're amazing."

"Yeah, that's okay, too. Just don't go overboard."

"Abs."

"Yeah?" She looked up from fiddling with the flank cinch.

"You're amazing." He was gazing at her, his body language relaxed, his dark eyes twinkling. *Those eyes...*

"Oh. Um, thank you, that's very...thank you." Her face felt suddenly hot.

"Am I making you uncomfortable?"

"Well, I believe you'd use the word *moderately*."

"No longer. Now I'd say a *skosh*. You've reformed me."

Any tension in the air was immediately dispelled as Abbie doubled over laughing. As she began to recover, she found he was watching her with great delight.

"A skosh? Really?"

He held out his hands defensively. "It's a short word! You said fewer syllables." He whipped out his phone and typed something in. "Look, it says, 'informal.' You indicated that I should select words that were informal."

"But it can't be so obscure, Parker! Use normal words."

"Point taken." He was watching her carefully. "Are you still angry with me about the debt?"

Abbie sighed.

"I'm sorry I didn't speak with you about it first. That was wrong of me."

"Yes, it was wrong. And I'm still going to pay you back, but at least I won't have to pay interest on it."

He nodded thoughtfully. "I'm sure we can come up with a fair rate."

She snorted in response.

"She thinks I'm joking," he said to Greenback in a stage whisper.

"I'm the one who talks, remember? Not him!" Stargazer shouted over the barrier. Abbie rolled her eyes. Parker walked around the corner and whispered something to Stargazer.

"Really? Oh, apples 'n' oats, that's great."

"What's going on over there?" Abbie called.

"Jealous?"

"Of your relationship with my horse? No." She stuck her head around the corner. "But I still want to know what you said."

"I told him about my surprise."

Abbie's eyes narrowed. "What surprise?" He waggled his eyebrows, and Stargazer gave her his big-toothed smile.

"I'm good at secrets," he said excitedly, "I won't say anything about the wagon."

"Good work, Star." She smiled as Parker put a hand to his face. "What wagon?"

"How did she find out?" Stargazer yelled as Parker offered his arm to her, then led her around the back of the stables. There she saw a large wooden wagon, big enough to carry passengers, with benches inside and a white cover over the top.

"This way, you won't have to sit in the sun. You said you can't sit in the sun, right? When you were telling me about your lupus?" He pulled her around the side, showing her all its features as if she'd never seen a wagon before.

"I have to admit, this was a good idea."

"You could even lie down in it if you have another flare."

"That's right." She glanced at him, and he looked so proud of himself. "You used that terminology well."

"Thanks."

"Speaking of getting back to the east coast quickly, have you heard any updates on my dad?"

Parker grew serious. "Not lately. I can get you his direct line, though, if you'd like it."

"Oh," Abbie balked. "I don't want to bother him."

He made a face. "Bother him? I happen to know that he'd love to hear from you."

"Oh, I don't know if that's true...but thank you, thanks for this. It'll make things much easier. Are we going to leave Stargazer here, then?"

"No. I don't think that would be wise. You two seem to have an uncommon bond."

Abbie laughed. "That we do."

They wandered back toward the house, and Parker lingered at her side like he wanted to hold her hand but didn't dare. *At least he isn't dumb.* Marrying someone who wasn't her intellectual equal would be tedious.

He went to get her pack for her; he'd been doing little things like that, carrying things for her, drawing water for her bath in the evening while she pretended to stir things for Molly. It was considerate, even when the water wasn't quite deep enough.

*Stop this,* her mother's voice whispered. *You forfeited any chance at love when you ran away. You're no queen worth having.* Abbie pushed the voice away as she hugged Pap and Molly, who wished her well. She mounted Stargazer, who sighed happily.

"Ah, that's better. Like a heavy blanket. Too much standing around lately, though I did have some nice conversations with Vivian."

"Who's Vivian?"

"The other talker. She's a lady, that's for sure; purebred Orangiersian Coastal. She had some interesting thoughts on how talking horses and humans might collaborate in the future. But I'm ready to go."

"Me too," Rubald grumped as Molly and Pap came out to say a final goodbye. "What's keeping the boy?" He lifted his voice with a sharp shout. "Your Highness! Let's go!"

Walking toward the house, Molly and Pap both slowed to a stop, turning to stare at him, then at each other, communicating something only people who have been together a long time can share.

"Highness?" Molly whispered, going pale. Rubald's face turned bright red.

"Now, let's not overreact," Rutha said, putting her hands out to Molly. "It's just a silly nickname that—"

"No, it ain't," Pap stopped her. "Even with his hairless head, I should've known."

Parker came out to the porch then, lugging both packs. He soon slowed to a stop, reading the vibe of the group.

"What's happening?"

Molly turned at his voice and hurried toward him, then stopped short, like she wasn't sure if she should curtsy to him. She looked toward Pap, and he shook his head, jerked a nod toward the group of Imaharans in the yard waiting for him to start class. Molly seemed to understand that this was a secret best kept.

"In that case," Molly said, opting instead to take Parker's face in both her hands, "let me just say that it is a pleasure to meet you in the truest sense, young man. I have heard so much about you from my dear cousin over the years, and I am so thankful that you took shelter under our roof. We look forward to great things from you." Molly suddenly tensed again, and she whispered something that made Parker chuckle softly. He let the packs slide to the porch as he embraced her with both arms and whispered something back. Abbie saw her wipe tears from her eyes.

She hadn't seen him around his people yet. No one had revered him except Rutha and Rubald, who both had more of a familiar way with him, even though they never, ever called him Parker.

Pap wouldn't let him carry the packs after that, bearing them both himself to the wagon, so Parker moved straight to Greenback.

"What did she say?" Abbie asked softly.

He started to speak, but his laughter made it too hard to talk. When his breath came back, he forced out, "She apologized for making me flush my own toilet with a bucket. I assured her she was forgiven."

Abbie found herself answering his laughter. "She'll treasure your hug forever, but can't brag about it to anyone. It's like a pastor hitting a hole-in-one on a Sunday."

He glanced at her sidelong, his expression skeptical.

"You didn't see the look on her face, Parker."

# CHAPTER TWENTY-FIVE

IT WOULD'VE BEEN BAD enough if the music had been good. She was sure she could've heard it through her dreams—that is, if she'd actually been able to drop off to sleep with that ungodly noise happening. But it was all the same. The same beat. The same chord progressions. The same fake-sounding, auto-tuned mixing. And then, just when she thought this was the most infuriating music she'd ever encountered and ever would encounter...they started over. Now it was even the same songs just played over and over. If she arrived in Brevspor with any hair left at all, it would be a miracle. Abbie beat her fists into the pillow to blow off steam, but she didn't feel any better. After a long day of travel, she was going to spend another frustrating, sleepless night in northern Imahara in a ramshackle guest house, and there was nothing she could do about it.

She heard Rutha roll over and sigh...she couldn't be asleep. The laws of physics denied the possibility. Abbie peeked over the edge of the bunk bed. She had headphones on. *Noise-cancelling, no doubt,* she thought with dismay. Abbie was putting on her robe before her feet hit the floor. Even that didn't rouse Rutha. How she envied her. Abbie stole down the hallway, feeling like she was back in boarding school and sneaking back from watching sitcoms all night in Fran Tukklen's room.

Abbie knocked softly on Rube and Parker's door. It occurred to her that Rube might not be the one to answer the door, especially if he also had headphones—but it was too late. Parker opened the door, rubbing his face.

"Abbie," he said. "What's wrong?"

He wore a pair of blue plaid boxer shorts. That was all he wore.

"Nothing, I—I'm sorry," she stammered, trying not to stare at his bare chest. "I was just trying to get my headphones from Rube."

"Oh, okay," he said, stepping aside. Rube was out cold, drooling. A skeeter was biting his face, and she waved it away. Those blessed headphones were blocking it all out. Abbie stood there, listening to that stupid music and contemplating her next move as Parker climbed back onto the top bunk. They were doing the song about how "her body is so fantastic, fantastic, fantastic" again; it was song number three of a ten-song set that she, to her dismay, knew by heart at this point. Quietly, she unzipped his pack and began to rifle through it. There were a disturbing number of knives in it. Abbie heard Parker clear his throat and she looked up.

"Do you want to borrow my phone's flashlight?"

"Sure," she whispered. "Thanks."

He handed her the phone. "I don't think you need to whisper. He seems pretty out of it."

"I know," she whispered, "but he has a *lot* of knives in here, and I'm afraid there's more under his pillow. And if he thinks I'm in here to be with you before we're married..."

Parker nodded. "Say no more," he whispered. With the help of his phone, Abbie located the box for the phone Rube had been trying to give her. She opened it. No headphones.

Abbie muttered insults regarding the genus, species, and sexual fidelity of his mother under her breath.

"Can't find it?"

"No, I found the box. It just doesn't have the headphones with it."

"Want to borrow mine?"

"Are you sure? Don't you want them?"

"Quite sure. I can't sleep with earplugs. It hinders situational awareness."

Abbie leaned on the bunk and tried to hold back a smile. "Yeah, that's kind of the idea."

"I require situational awareness."

"Okay, well, if you're sure."

"Positive," he said, reaching into the backpack at the end of his bunk. "Wait," he said, turning on his flashlight and inspecting the headphones carefully. "No, never mind, we're good."

"What's happening?"

"I had to check them for wax. But they're very tidy."

Abbie's smile would not be hidden, try as she might. "You're weird."

"Okay. Knock me out before you go, will you?"

"No way. Knives, remember?"

"Right. Good night."

"Good night."

"Close the door," he said, burying his head under his pillow.

"I will."

Abbie quietly closed the door and turned to see a perplexed Rutha, arms crossed, barring her way back to bed.

Outside, the DJ was playing song number five again, about how "the girl is fine, so fine, and she's all mine, all mine."

"What's going on?"

Abbie grimaced, holding up the phone and headphones. Rutha rolled her eyes and nodded, leading them back to bed.

"Did I wake you when I left?"

"No, dear, just keeping the thieves honest. Woz knows, no one should ever try to break into the house of an older woman on account of her late-night bathroom habits."

"I'll remember that if I ever take up a life of crime. Good night, Rutha."

"Good night, sister."

Abbie was about to put the headphones in when two gunshots sounded nearby, and the music stopped abruptly. Moments later, it started up once more. She sighed and flopped back onto her pillow. If she got shot in her sleep, at least she wouldn't have to listen to song number six again.

THE LACK OF SLEEP DID not bode well for the following day. Having spent all morning bonding with her bad mood in the wagon, Abbie decided to ride with Stargazer after lunch. They were riding in silence when it was broken by a shout.

"Wheat eaters!"

Abbie looked around and found a small child with a bucket of water balanced upright on her head. She stood akimbo, a defiant look on her face.

"Pardon?"

"Wheat eaters! Wheat eaters!"

Abbie glanced at Rubald for help, and he shrugged.

"It's a mild insult here, referring to the agriculture where you live."

Abbie snickered and turned back to the child. "Garden eater!"

The child's eyes widened before she ran away, and they all laughed.

"So, uh, how's the thing with your brother going?"

Parker sighed. "Not great. They hit two of my father's ships. It's repairable, but regrettable, especially since it was wholly preventable."

"Aren't they your ships, too?"

"Huh?"

"It's your country, right?"

"Yes, they are, and yes, it is. But technically, my father currently retains command of the navy. It's some old, obscure rule." Parker seemed tense, and Abbie wondered if she should have waited to bring up the subject of his brother's rebellion until later. "Thankfully, we've had minimal casualties, but we also don't seem to be moving toward a clear conclusion to this mess," he finished.

"So you don't think you're going to win?"

Parker shook his head. "I'm not sure."

"What were you thinking about before I asked you about your brother?"

He glanced at her, Greenback's gentle swaying not breaking his eye contact. "You caught me in a moment of sentimental reverie."

"About?"

"Our shared time at King's Beach."

She grinned. "Why?"

"Besides 'because it's a happy memory?'"

"Yeah."

He looked away for a moment, then turned back to her. "I suppose in some ways, you remind me of the ocean; you're both predictably unpredictable."

She scowled. "I'm not sure that's a compliment."

"Also, you should never turn your back to either of you," he continued, flashing her a grin. "Very dangerous."

Abbie felt her temper rising. *Can't he just flirt like a normal person without insulting me in the same breath?* "Why, because I'm going to sneak up behind you with a hammer?"

"I wouldn't discount the possibility."

"Really. Wow. That's something coming from someone who's seen attempted regicide in action."

The moment the words were out of her mouth she regretted them. Parker's head whipped around to glare at Rubald, and the other man's shoulders slumped.

"Well, I don't know what they told you about that, but it's probably not accurate," Parker said. There are a lot of rumors flying around. Just like when you left for Gardenia."

The mention of her departure due to her illness raised her hackles again, and her regret at bringing up Parker's family drama evaporated like steam from a hot cup of coffee. "So it wasn't your indecision that allowed him to get away? And you don't feel guilty about it?"

Rutha and Rubald led them into a grove with picnic tables and dismounted while Parker and Abbie continued to bicker.

"Attack me all you want, but there's plenty in your life that doesn't add up, too," Parker said. He waited until she dismounted to do the same, so they were eye to eye.

"Like?"

"Like Gardenia, speaking of. Why pick a country that would be so willing to extradite you? Why pick the one place that's known for harboring fugitive royals? You had to know those things before you chose to set up there." He took a step closer to her, eyes intent. "There's only one reason I can think of. You wanted to be found."

"What?" she scoffed. "That's ridiculous."

"Kids," Rubald said in a low voice, "let's not do this here." They both shot him a look intended to firmly remind him of his place in this argument—that was to say, no place at all.

Parker turned back to Abbie. "Is it ridiculous?" He came even closer. "Do you know how long it took Rubald to find you?" He held up three fingers. "Three days. That's it. Yet in five years, no one ever located you. No one found you, even though you barely changed your name, even though you didn't change your appearance. No one found you...because no one came looking, right? You can't tell me that didn't hurt."

"Sure I can," she said, summoning the most patronizing voice she could muster. "See, Parker, the reason you run is to get away; why would I give a burnt brownie if anyone came after me?" She turned back to Stargazer's saddlebag to dig around for her lunch.

He was silent for long moments—so long that she turned back around to see if he was still there. He was. "Because you wanted to know who loved you for you," he said softly. "Despite your illness. Did they want an heir, a ruler? Or did they want *you?*"

Abbie blinked back sudden tears, furious at herself. How was he doing this? Was he really that perceptive, or was she that transparent?

"You know what? I don't have to listen to this pathetic analysis," she said, whipping back around to the distraction of the saddle bag and its jumbled contents.

His voice was so soft Abbie could hardly hear him with her back turned. "I want you around, Abs. You can't run so far that I won't come looking. Just try it."

She spun to face him once more. "You've got some nerve standing there, picking apart my life, acting like you've just got my best interests at heart. You're a damn liar." Parker's fists clenched at his sides, and she felt pleased at finally getting a reaction out of him.

"I am not a liar." He spat out the words, drawing his shoulders back.

"Oh, really? So you don't need to put a wedding ring on my finger to end this conflict between you and your brother?"

He shook his head and had the grace to look away. "Yes, I do."

"Yes, you do. So don't stand here and act like you care about me, *Edward*. You and I both know it's not true. I will not be manipulated."

"No real names!" Rutha called.

"I'm not trying to manipulate you! It's not mutually exclusive, you know. I can actually care about you and need your help at the same time!"

Abbie rolled her eyes, still holding back tears. "That's convenient," she muttered.

"No!" Parker shouted, making her jump. "No, it's really damn inconvenient is what it is! It's tearing me apart!" He swiped quickly at his face, but she couldn't tell if it was at tears or sweat. "And the worst part is that you think you're so broken, no one would want you. You don't even see what a wonder you are."

"More manipulation. Nice." She turned and walked toward the Jerrinsons at the tables, hoping to end the conversation with their proximity.

He paced ahead of her to cut her off, relentless. "No, you're wonderful. You *are.* You're strong and you're brave, and you're beautiful even when you're covered head to toe in dirt. I don't care if you don't want to hear it. You care about people who need help. You'd be ten times the sovereign your mother was."

Abbie inhaled sharply. "You don't know one thing about my mother."

"I know she bullied you. I know she misunderstood you. I know she doubted you and made you feel inferior. What more do I need to know, really?"

She took a step closer to him, coming into his personal space. "You cannot be serious right now. She ushered Brevspor into an era of political influence and economic prosperity like we'd never seen before. Before her reign, we were an afterthought, we were just like Imahara, like Descaret. Now we're a world power." She held out her arms dramatically. "She's the only reason your parents would ever entertain the idea of a contract with me."

"Ugh, stop selling yourself short!" If he still had his hair, Abbie had no doubt he'd be clutching at his dreads right now. "So you want to be loved for you—who doesn't? Why is that such a crime in your mind? Did she so thoroughly convince you that you're unlovable?"

Abbie crossed her arms, breathing hard through her nose but saying nothing. She looked past him to Rubald and Rutha, who were eating their lunch and pretending they weren't listening to every word.

"Woz, you're such a know-it-all. It's insufferable." She moved toward the table again, and again he cut her off.

"Fine," he said, ignoring her barb, "if you think you're unlovable, I guess it's my job to prove you wrong." She thought he was going to go back to his horse, but instead he wrapped her in an unexpected hug. Shock kept her from squirming away. His scent was a mixture of horse and something gingery, and his strong arms pinned her own to her sides, leaving her no possibility of reciprocation even if she'd wanted to.

She wanted to stay mad. She wanted to keep yelling at him, to keep pushing him away. Instead, all the tension and anger inside her began to dissolve under the steady pressure of Parker's awkward, earnest embrace.

After a few seconds, his phone started to ring, much to Abbie's relief. He let go and walked away without another word.

# CHAPTER TWENTY-SIX

"I'VE HAD NEWS," PARKER said, walking into the picnic area just as Abbie was finishing. He didn't appear to have eaten anything. "The armed engagements we've had so far with Lincoln's forces haven't gone our way. Lincoln has rallied considerably more troops than we anticipated. And more importantly to Abbie, her father has taken a turn for the worse." He looked at Abbie, then looked down at the ground. "He'll be entering hospice care any day now."

"Is Gratha completely out of the question?"

"We were never able to confirm the rumor about the bounty on Abbie's head. So, in my mind, it's still our worst option...except it is faster." Parker crossed his arms. "There is one more possibility regarding Gratha," he said, "but it's not one I'm excited about."

Rubald nodded slowly. "I thought of him, too, sir, but it's a risk. He may not even be in the country, or we may not be able to get to him before the raiders find us. He's a wild card."

Parker shrugged his broad shoulders. "We're out of viable alternatives, I'm afraid."

"Um, hey, anyone want to fill me in?" Abbie asked. She hated it when they spoke in code. They were so used to leaving women out of the conversation they didn't even realize they were doing it.

"Blair Moreau, the Silicon King," said Rubald. "He lives in Gratha."

"He's not a real king," Parker said, his brows knit. Even if Abbie hadn't known this was a sore subject for Parker, his body language would've made it obvious: shoulders high, arms crossed tightly across his chest, pacing like a caged animal. But she did know. The Silicon King had been a real king in Descaret. Unexpectedly, he had given up his title, abandoned his wife and children, and disappeared. A few year later, he'd popped up again in Gratha with his own palace. She'd actually considered going to Blair for refuge when she left Brevspor, but she didn't know how to find him.

Abbie watched Parker with grudging sympathy. Despite their earlier fight, she wanted to get up and massage his tight shoulders. She felt like slapping herself—these conflicting emotions were getting old. Abbie the Erstwhile Best Friend was warring with Abbie the Never-Wife.

"I'm familiar with the Silicon King," she said. "How does he fit in?"

"He's my godfather." Parker spit out the words as if they were sour.

"Would he shelter us?" Abbie asked, choosing to let the godfather thing be for now.

Rubald shrugged. "Your guess is as good as ours."

"What's the downside?"

"If he turns us away, we're in the middle of the desert with no shelter for a hundred miles. Grathan raiders on every side. Sandstorms. All manner of wild creatures who'd likely eat us."

"And what's more," Parker added, "we'd have to do the run in one shot. We can't stop. We leave at nightfall and push through the next day. Some of us can try to sleep in the wagon, but someone will have to steer the horses, and some-one will have to help keep a lookout for leeching lizards and smoldering snakes."

"Well." They all stood in silence, staring at the grass.

"I say we go." Abbie felt their gaze on her, but didn't look up. "More than likely, he'll want to help. But we can't afford to offend the Silicon King."

"He's not a real king!" Parker yelled at the sky.

"See, that's what I'm talking about!" Parker had all the charm of a wildfire as he stalked around the grove, kicking at loose pinecones and muttering under his breath. *Where's the calm, composed prince now, huh?* Abbie thought with a jab of guilty pleasure. "Okay, are we going?" she pressed. "I vote yes. Rubald?"

"Yes."

"Rutha?"

"Yes."

"Parker?"

He heaved a sigh. "Yes, all right, we're going."

"Everyone, get out your warm layers," Rutha mothered, and Abbie cocked an eyebrow.

"I thought Gratha was a desert?"

"Yes. A desert formed by a high mountain range, which we'll need to cross tonight."

EVEN FROM INSIDE THE wagon, Abbie could feel the air getting colder. Rube had picked up the pace; she knew from eavesdropping that they were concerned about snow. And indeed, about an hour before they stopped for dinner, despite her bones feeling like they'd been rattled clear out of their joints, Abbie sat, delighted, and watched as the snow began to lightly fall. It had been years since she'd seen it—Gardenia was too warm for snow.

*You can't do this.* Her mother's voice was so clear, she almost looked around to see if she was there. *He deserves better.*

*Look,* Abbie fought back, *I told him the truth. I laid it out for him—I even tried my best to offend him out of caring about me. But he still wants me. He still wants to make it work.*

*He has no idea what life with you would be like. The rigid schedule, the medications, the strange diet, the fatigue, the excuses—*

*Shut up, Mother. You may have been a great queen, but you were a crap parent.*

Surprisingly, that did shut the voice up. Abbie breathed a sigh of relief and shook out the tension that had accumulated in her shoulders and neck. Parker dropped back to ride directly behind the wagon and peeked in at her.

"You all right in there?"

She nodded.

"Warm enough? I think we've got another blanket up front if you need it."

"No, I'm fine."

"I, uh...I apologize for shouting at you. Back at the picnic site."

Abbie shrugged. "You didn't say anything that wasn't true."

"But the manner in which I delivered the information could have used some refinement." He sighed. "I seldom lose my temper, but you seem to evoke strong emotions in me."

She smiled at his slide back into his formal speech patterns. "I always have."

He smiled back. "That's true. So, what about you?"

She cocked her head. "What about me what?"

"Is there anything you want to apologize for?"

She narrowed her eyes. "Is there something you want me to apologize for?"

"Not what I asked."

She stared at him hard, noting the infuriatingly adorable way the snow was accumulating on his lopsided wool hat. "Fine. I apologize for calling you insufferable. You're not. You're quite...sufferable."

His smile brightened, then faded. "And I'm sorry I criticized your mother. I know that's a sensitive subject, and I'm sure she was doing her best. Parenting probably isn't as easy as it looks."

Abbie fingered the fringe of the blanket on her lap. "It doesn't look that easy to me."

"That's what I meant."

She swallowed hard. "And I'm sorry I called you a liar. I said it to upset you, and that was a low blow."

"Thank you. I appreciate that." He cleared his throat. "And you mistook my meaning before, about you being predictably unpredictable. I know you're not a threat to me, but you do keep me on my toes. And for someone as boring as I am, that's actually a favorable trait." He wiped his nose. "One of many, actually."

"Oh." Abbie didn't know what else to say, and she shifted on the hard wagon bench.

"All right. I'll check on you again later, Abs."

"Okay," she said. She still didn't know what to say, but she wished her traitorous heart would quit beating out of her chest every time he called her that.

WHEN THE WAGON STOPPED, Abbie jumped out. Rubald was bowing to an amber-skinned Imaharan man, who thankfully seemed to speak the Common Tongue. It appeared they were negotiating letting them stay on their land for the night. She hoped it was going well. Traveling was easier with the wagon—a lot easier—but it was still tiring, and she was ready to be done for the day. They were bowing again, and she noticed two little boys, about eight and twelve, hanging out around the side of the house, watching them.

Rubald came over. "He says we can stay here for tonight, as long we promise to bury our waste." Rutha was getting out cooking pots with a deep sigh when Rubald put a hand on her arm to still her. "And he says that his wife can cook us dinner for a small fee."

Her eyes lit up. "How small?"

"It's nothing this one can't afford," he said, gesturing to Parker, who put on a show of sighing in a tortured way.

"I suppose that would be acceptable."

Abbie was wandering into the woods to look for dry firewood under the canopy when she heard footsteps behind her. Parker fell into step with her a moment later.

"Mind if I join you?"

"No, that's fine."

They walked in silence, both pausing to gather sticks.

"See how casual I was there?" he said after they'd both collected a small bundle. "I used small words."

Abbie chuckled. "Yes, I noticed that."

"I'm learning," he said, nudging her with his elbow.

Suddenly, Abbie felt something cold and wet hit her in the back. "Ow! Hey, what the..." She turned to see the two dark-haired Imaharan boys, now armed with snowballs, grinning from ear to ear. Her mouth dropped open in mock outrage, and she looked at Parker, a mischievous grin claiming her face. "You ready?"

"Oh, it's on." He dropped his stack of firewood and immediately began scooping up snow and flinging it in the general direction of the boys, who laughed hysterically.

"No, no," Abbie snorted. "You have to pack it into a ball first, beach boy," she said, demonstrating, then she lobbed a perfectly formed ball in a high arc at the oldest boy, who successfully ducked.

Parker took a snowball to the side of the head and shook it off. Abbie pulled him behind a fallen log by his sleeve and quickly began supplying him with snowballs.

"You're stronger, so you can throw farther. Here, use these ones." She ducked down to avoid another frozen projectile. Abbie barely even peeked over the log to see how they were doing until she'd made fifteen balls, then she began lobbing them as well. Parker began gathering the remaining snowballs in his arms with a glint in his eye, and she saw where he was going with this. She scooped up the rest of the pile, and he gave her a nod. The two of them ejected from behind the log, firing like crazy, running closer and closer until the two boys held up their hands and kept repeating the same word over and over between bouts of breathless giggles. If she had to venture a guess, it meant the Imaharan equivalent of "uncle."

Abbie and Parker were laughing, too, and she held up her freezing bare hand for a high five. He responded immediately, then wiped some errant snow off her braided hair.

"We make a good team, Abs." He held her gaze for a moment, breathing hard, before stumbling back toward his firewood pile, still laughing. The kids came running over, wanting high fives, too, which Abbie gladly gave them. Parker was beaming at her, and she knew without a doubt that he was in love with her.

She also knew that she was going to break his heart if she broke it off now.

# CHAPTER TWENTY-SEVEN

"PARKER?"

The prince rubbed his eyes, reaching for his phone automatically. It was 2:13 in the morning.

"Parker!" came the voice again, and he saw a shadow against his tent. He sat up. He opened the zippered door. Abbie stood outside, shivering, her hair soaked, snow accumulating on her shoulders.

"Come in, come in. What's wrong?"

She tumbled inside, dragging her sleeping bag behind her. "Branch. Heavy with snow, fell on my tent. Got a big rip now, can't sleep there." She sounded mostly asleep. She sat up, tipping to one side, looking like she was about to go over again. Parker rummaged through his bag and found a cleanish flannel shirt and long underwear.

"Here, you should get out of those wet clothes. I'll just turn my back."

Abbie raised her arms over her head.

"What, you think I'm going to do it? You can forget that. Absolutely not."

Abbie groaned and shook her arms insistently. "Soooo tired," she whined. "Knock off the proper nonsense, just help."

It was tempting. She probably wasn't wearing a bra...he'd get to see her breasts in all their cold, perky glory; that'd be good. But then he'd still have to share his tent with her the rest of the night...that'd be bad.

"Get ahold of yourself," he said, more to himself than to her. "I'll help you dry your hair, but that's it." He pulled a towel out of his bag and heard her rustling behind him, pulling off her wet shirt, her teeth chattering. Out of the corner of his eye, he could see that she'd turned her back to him, and he was at once somewhat grateful and extremely disappointed. He checked his phone as she tried to get her damp pajama pants off.

"You know, you could have hypothermia. It's a classic situation. This says your clumsiness and drowsiness could be part of it. You could also become confused so as to engage in risky behaviors." He glanced over at her warily. "You're a bit mad even on a normal day, I'd like to see that—Abbie?"

She'd stopped moving. Her wet pants were still around her ankles, clinging to her pale skin. Parker reached over and put a hand on her forehead. Ice-cold. He quickly pulled the pants off and got her into the long underwear, still trying to rouse her. "Abs, I know you're tired, but you've got to get into your sleeping bag. We've got to warm you up."

She groaned as he tried to wrestle her limp body into her sack. She snuggled into the warm, dry covering and sighed. He touched her face, the only part of her left exposed. Still too cold. He put a hat on her head and lay his coat over the top of her bag, but he knew it wasn't going to help much. "Oh, socks," he said aloud...but that would mean wrestling her out of her bag and then back in—unless he could get her to wake up a bit more.

"Abelia," he shook her by the shoulder. "Abs!" He said loudly, and she sat up, dazed. "Put these socks on, okay?"

She nodded, took the socks, then lay back down.

"No, no, come now. Cooperate. Put them on your feet. You'll thank me tomorrow when you can still feel your toes." He sat her up, then squeezed in behind her, leaning her against his chest, their heads almost touching the roof of the tent. "Put them on your feet," he repeated firmly. He gently pulled her knee up toward her chest so she could reach her foot better, and miraculously, she complied. "Good, darling, that's good. Now the other."

Abbie giggled and pivoted sideways to look at him, her side resting against his chest. "You called me *dahling*," she said, mimicking his accent.

"Is that humorous?"

"Yes!"

"How so?" He meant to keep her talking, keep her awake so he could finish warming her up, maybe dry her masses of red hair a bit more.

"We haven't even kissed."

"That's right."

"So how can I be your darling if we haven't even kissed?"

"Put on the other sock. And I can't care for someone I haven't kissed? That seems absurd."

"Well, it's not, it's a rule." She pulled on the gray wool sock, nodding ponderously to herself.

"I see. Well, thank Woz I have you to enlighten me." He took off her intarsia knitted hat and pushed her loose hair away from her face. He was reaching over to his area to get the towel when she took his face in her hands and kissed him.

He knew he shouldn't, but he found himself dropping the towel, wrapping his arms around her, pulling her closer.

All those things about "increased risk-taking" and "confusion" he'd read earlier went out the tiny tent window. New thoughts, which tried to suggest that he had been sending her mixed signals by touching her face and her hair, were pushed aside for later analysis. Right then, he only heard what he wanted to hear, what his heart was telling him with every beat: *She wants me. She wants me. She wants me.* In the dim light of the tent, he felt her fiddling with his shirt buttons. The physical shock of her freezing fingers trailing across his stomach brought him back to reality.

"Stop," he gasped, grabbing her cold fingers, and she pulled away, smiling a groggy smile.

"*Now* you can call me darling," she said, and she promptly crawled back into her sack and fell asleep.

"A mad woman," he muttered, inserting himself gingerly back into his own sleeping bag. "Completely mad. I suppose I asked for it, really. Should have just let her freeze to death." Yet, for some reason, he couldn't stop grinning.

"YOUR HIGHNESS?"

Parker was getting tired of being woken up like that, even by Rutha's soft, kind voice. Phone check: 6:11. *Oh, it was going to be a long day.*

"Yes, Rutha?" he rumbled.

"I'm so sorry to disturb you, sir, but have you seen Abbie? Her tent is empty, and we're quite concerned."

"I'll be right there." He pulled on jeans over his long underwear, laced up his boots, and grabbed his coat back from Abbie, who still had it covering her sleeping bag. He felt her head gently—nice and warm. Her skin was pinker, too. He sighed with relief. As quietly as he could, he unzipped the tent, but she rolled over and blinked at him, not quite awake.

"Hi."

"Hi. Go back to sleep." It worked with his brothers and sisters if they were half-awake.

"Okay."

"I'll bring you coffee in a bit."

"Mmm. Okay."

"You all right?"

"Yeah. Close the door, it's cold." She flipped the sleeping bag over her head.

He stepped out and zipped the flap shut. Parker gestured silently to Rutha to move away from the door, and she led him across the hard earth of the snowy campsite toward the fire.

"So, she's in your tent, then?"

He nodded. "As you saw, hers was uninhabitable. I assume she didn't want to wake you. I'm surprised you didn't hear it."

Rubald piped up. "Neither of us did. It was quite a shock to find that this morning and her gone."

"It was a shock in the night, as well. She had a bit of hypothermia, but I think we've got it under control now. Her color was better this morning, and her skin felt warmer."

Rube and Rutha exchanged a meaningful glance, and Rubald coughed.

"You zipped the sleeping bags together, then? Huddled for warmth and such?" They were both watching him carefully.

Parker paused, his coffee mug halfway to his lips. "What? No." He scowled, partly because he resented the implication, and partly because he wished he'd thought of it at the time. Rutha wandered toward the horses, and Parker knew her well enough to know that she was giving them space so he could be honest.

"All right, tell me truly now," Rubald said, sitting down shoulder to shoulder with him.

"Honestly, uncle, it's all right. I just warmed her up with fresh kit, tucked her back into her sack. It was dry inside. She was half out of her mind, anyway. Delirious."

"Delirious, eh? What, nonsense talk?"

"Yeah, a bit. She wanted me to take her shirt off. I refused, of course."

"Naturally."

"Kissed me, too."

A slow, wide grin spread across Rubald's face. "Did she now?"

Parker quickly swallowed his hot coffee. "But like I told you, she was nearly mad, bonkers. Didn't know what she was doing."

"But you didn't..." Rubald's voice dropped away, and he gave him what Parker had come to call The Eye.

"Didn't what?"

"Didn't kiss her back. Seeing as she was out of her head."

Parker cleared his throat. "Well, I may have...but I stopped there."

Rubald leaned closer and slapped him on the back. "Good man." He stood up, stretched, and was still grinning when Abbie stumbled out of their tent.

"Morning, sister," he called, sending the crows in a neighboring tree to flight. "What can I get you? Coffee? A warm blanket? Sounds like you had quite a night! Rutha, is there food yet?" He walked off quickly in Rutha's direction.

Abbie shook her head, her hair flopping into her face, and sat down hard next to Parker, close enough that their shoulders were touching.

"What's he so happy about?" It was more indictment than question.

Parker shrugged and took another sip of his coffee before passing it to her. She accepted with neither comment nor complaint.

"You warming up again?"

She nodded. "Thanks for your help."

"I wasn't sure if you'd remember..."

"I remember." She sipped the coffee and Parker, suddenly uncomfortable without something in his hands, wished he had gotten her a different mug.

Abbie took a deep breath. "Sorry if I was too...forward."

"No, it's fine." He winked and draped a blanket around her shoulders. "*Darling*."

Abbie reddened. "Parker, I hope I didn't give you the wrong impression. I can't...I mean, it's not that I don't..."

"I'm just ribbing you. Besides, I've always suspected you were wildly attracted to me; now I have proof." Parker stood up to add another log to the fire.

"I am not."

"That's not what the tongue you slipped me last night indicated."

"Oh Woz, please stop, Parker."

"Sitting in my lap, unbuttoning my shirt...how far would you have gone if I hadn't—how did you call it?—shut it down?"

She was hiding her face behind her coffee now. "I'm sorry, okay? Will you just shut up?"

"You're sorry? What's the problem? We're engaged. It's just a kiss."

"But I...I led you on. I enticed you. That was unfair."

Parker turned to look at her and saw the solemnness in her eyes. He squatted down in front of her and put his hands on her knees. "You think I'm enticed by that? I'd like you fully present the first time we're together, thank you very much. You were barely conscious last night. I knew you were delirious, I told Rubald so this morning."

She covered her mouth with one hand. "You *told him?*"

"Of course I told him. Look at him. He's fairly skipping around the campsite." It was true. All that was missing was a friendly woodland creature on Rubald's shoulder for him to sing a duet with. Rutha brought them each a plate of eggs and bacon, though where it had been cooked was unclear to Parker.

"Here's a spot of eggs and rashers for the happy couple after an eventful night."

"We are *not* a couple, Rutha."

"Oh, right." She winked at her, and Abbie balanced her plate and coffee on the log beside her as she stood up, gathering the blanket around her shoulders.

"Everyone, listen up."

Parker stood up, arms crossed, a small smile on his face.

"Yes, Parker and I shared a tent last night. It was a purely practical decision. And the kiss we shared was simply an effect of hypothermia. Nothing more. Is that clear? It changes nothing."

Parker grinned wider, enjoying her discomfort immensely. "If you say so, darling."

Rubald raised his hand, and Abbie pointed at him. "Why didn't you use the wagon, then?"

Abbie paled at the question. "What?"

"I said, why didn't you just crawl into the wagon? It's warm and dry."

Abbie's blush raced back to her face, though she said nothing.Parker's grin grew by degrees, and he quickly changed the subject. "By the way, where did you cook this, Rutha? It's delicious, as always."

Rutha swallowed hard. "Oh, I set up the stove some way off to give you two a bit of space to snuggle over here by the fire."

"Not snuggling, just sitting," Abbie muttered, shoveling eggs into her mouth.

"I just know couples like a bit of privacy sometimes, especially when things are new—"

"Not a couple!" Abbie shouted as she stormed off into the woods, leaving her breakfast behind.

"We're leaving in twenty!" Rubald called after her, his usual gruffness still absent.

"You think she's coming around, then?" Rutha asked once she was out of earshot.

Parker shrugged, rocking on his heels. "Time will tell. Let's not push her too hard, eh?"

The older couple nodded but couldn't hide their smiles as they began to break camp.

# CHAPTER TWENTY-EIGHT

"ALL RIGHT, YOU TWO, here's the situation," Rubald said, handing them each a fishing pole, "There's very little food in Gratha that's desirable. We need to take stock with us. That means fish, meat, berries. I've set up a few traps, Rutha's off collecting what she can find, and you two are on fishing duty. See what you can do."

They nodded dutifully. It was like they were back in scouts again. Abbie led the way down the trail, feeling strangely excited to be alone with Parker. When had she stopped calling him Edward in her head? He seemed completely divorced from the enemy she'd built him up to be now. Renaming him felt right.

The lines were already rigged correctly for bobber fishing, and she cast out into the lake and sat down on the dock, enjoying the wind on her face. They sat in silence for a long time, both lost in thought, both tired. It felt good to just sit. After a while with no luck, Parker reeled in his line and began to re-rig it to cast and reel rather than use a bobber, which earned him five nice rainbow trout. Abbie lifted one eyebrow at him.

"Will you re-rig me? You seem to be having better luck."

"Certainly." He dug through the tackle box for a moment, then took her pole. Abbie crossed her arms.

"For a guy who likes to sail, you're better at lake fishing than I would've thought."

"Your dad takes me."

Abbie's head snapped around. "What?"

"I said your dad takes me."

"You've been fishing," Abbie spluttered, "with *my* dad?"

Parker nodded.

"Um, what? Why?"

"We meet monthly; the activity was his suggestion, preferable in his mind to just eating lunch at the palace. I politely declined the first few times, but his persistence wore me down. That's a trait you share, by the way." He looked at her over the top of his glasses as he cast her line and passed back her pole. "You seem surprised."

"Yes, I—I am surprised. I guess I'd assumed you stopped meeting when I left."

Parker shrugged. "Why would we? You didn't formally abdicate. We assumed you'd come back."

"Yes, well, why did you keep meeting when I didn't?"

"We enjoyed each other's company. Your father doesn't have a lot of male friends."

Abbie sniffed. "My dad doesn't need your pity."

"Don't misunderstand me—it wasn't pity. He's advised me well in many areas where my formal education fell short."

Abbie raised an eyebrow. "Like what?"

"How to convince someone to follow you when they don't want to. How to get information from someone while appearing to make small talk. Coping with living in the spotlight when it gets tedious. Marriage, sex. Subjects like that."

"You talked to my dad about...that?" Abbie tried not to show how horrified she was by this admission, but the high blush in her cheeks gave her away immediately.

"Yes." He grinned at her. "Would you like me to relay the information he shared?"

"You can't be serious."

"Of course I'm serious."

"Oh Woz, please stop. Just stop."

"That's not a no..."

"Yes, it is absolutely a no! No! No! No! A million times no!"

"Hey!" Rubald called from the top of the ridge. "You're going to scare the game away!"

"Sorry, Rubald," they called back.

"That's okay," Parker said, lowering his voice. "I can show you later."

"Oh Woz," Abbie said, her face getting uncomfortably hot.

"Yeah," he muttered, "that's just what you'll say when I show you."

Abbie's mouth dropped open, and she whispered for fear of being overheard by the Jerrinsons, "Edward Kenneth Keith Francis Benson Broward, when did you get such a dirty mouth?"

He grinned again and winked at her. "It's all right, darling, you can picture it."

"I'm not!" She was, though. Abbie shivered, imagining his hands sliding under her shirt.

"Are you cold?"

"Yes," she lied.

"Should've brought a coat."

She turned to face him. "What's wrong with yours?"

"My what?"

"Your coat."

He shook his head, chuckling. "Forget it, I'm using it."

Abbie sighed dramatically. "I guess it's true what they say."

"What's that, then?"

"Chivalry really is dead."

"This isn't a lack of chivalry, darling, this is poor planning on your part. You knew the sun was going down. Good try, though." It was indeed going down, and the frogs and cicadas were warming up for their evening chorus.

"What if I pay you for it?"

"No, thank you. I've got loads of money. I'm the Second Son, you know." There was a hint of bitterness in his voice, which Abbie noted.

"I wasn't thinking of money."

He glanced at her sideways. "Oh? What were you thinking of?"

She shrugged and reeled in her line, slowly scooting closer to him. "I was thinking of something more...experiential."

"Oh?"

"Yeah. Something more...personal." Abbie put down her pole and rested her hand on his leg. In the weakening light of twilight, she could see his pupils were dilated.

"Like a kiss?"

Abbie nodded slowly, not looking away. She wasn't sure what she was doing, really. She *was* a little bit cold; she wanted that coat, partially just for the joy of the conquest. But that wasn't all she wanted.

He reeled in his line and set his pole down next to him, turning to face her and pressing her hand to his leg before she could attempt to remove it. "How do I know you'll give it back?" He asked with mock seriousness, rubbing the back of her knuckles with his thumb.

"Your coat?"

"Yes, my coat. This is a very nice coat; it's fleece. I bought it myself, online."

"I'll give it back when we get back to the wagon. Deal?"

Parker held very still, holding her gaze. Impatient, Abbie reached up behind his head and brought his lips down to hers. She was surprised at how wet they were. But as he wrapped his arms around her waist, she felt herself relax...until the tongues came into play. There was too much of them, both of them. She tried to pull back a little, but he took it as playfulness and leaned in to follow her, until she turned her head away and wiped her mouth.

He looked put out, and as a reconciliation she scooted nearer, wrapped her arms around his neck to bring him close to her again, then whispered, "More gently, okay?" She could feel his breath warming her face as his cold nose brushed her cheek, and he nodded, serious now. Their next attempt was much better, even if it was still a bit sloppy, and she let her fingers tug at the short, spiraled hair at the nape of his neck.

"Ha," he said, breathless, when they pulled apart.

"Ha?" she asked, smiling.

"I never said 'deal,' and due to your impatience, I got two free kisses."

She snickered. "Not very good ones, though."

He nodded, thoughtful. "You're right, they were terrible. I'd be willing to put in more practice if you'll commit to the effort of improving the quality. After all, this is a very nice coat."

She feigned offense. "Me? You're the one using too much tongue. Honestly. Virgins."

Parker chuckled as he slipped out of his coat and drew it around her shoulders. His hands went quickly back to her waist, and he leaned forward to murmur in her ear.

"Is that what you wanted?"

"Not exactly, no." His light beard scratched against her cheek, and he smelled like ginger and cedar. Her heart was fixing to beat out of her chest. What did she want? Why was she leading him on like this? His fingers threaded into her hair, and he tipped her head to give himself better access to her neck. Suddenly, Abbie didn't feel like the one doing the leading, after all. Parker trailed light kisses down her neck, and it made her shiver despite the coat. The encroaching darkness made it too easy to just close her eyes and enjoy his closeness. That's when she moaned.

"All right," Parker said, standing up without warning, "that's enough. We should be returning to the wagon."

"What? Wh-why?"

Parker stood on the dock, running one hand over his face. He took in one big, gulping breath, held it, then let it out slowly. "Abs, I don't want to push you away, believe me. But if I don't push you away now, I'll be forced to pull you much, much closer. And I haven't yet made the requisite commitments in order to do that." He turned and strode down the dock, leaving her to gather up the fish, tackle box, and poles and feel her way down the dock as the stars above her began to make themselves known.

"Can you at least lend me your phone so I can see where I'm going?" she called, but he was already too far away to hear her.

# CHAPTER TWENTY-NINE

THEY TALKED THROUGH their strategy for making the night run across the desert: the ladies would stay in the wagon. It grated against her feminist sensibilities, but it seemed there was no convincing the men otherwise.

Rubald held up his phone. "I sent Pap a message. He warned us strongly against this, but said if we're dead set on it, hide the women. That's the one thing he said. Hide the women. Also, everyone take care of bodily needs before we leave, we're not stopping until morning."

Abbie rolled her eyes, resisting the urge to bite her nails lest she show how nervous she actually was. "Of course he did. But think of it this way: What's less innocuous than two women who don't appear to know what they're doing?"

"Abs, it's not about you seeming non-threatening to them," Parker said, "that's a very Brevsporan way to think about it. You need to make yourself a hard target. Overpowering the two of you would be nothing for these bands of raiders."

"It's not ideal," Rubald said, stroking his beard, "but the fact that so many mercenaries have been called to the war may work in our favor."

Abbie shook her head and was about to offer another rebuttal when Rutha spoke up. She so infrequently offered up her opinion in these discussions, the other three fell silent.

"What's the proverb about the prudent see danger and...?"

Abbie wanted to glower at Rutha for trying to manipulate her, but she couldn't muster the ire required.

"The prudent sees danger and hides herself, but the simple go on and suffer for it."

"Hmm. Wise words," Parker said, rocking onto his heels, not meeting Abbie's gaze.

"Oh, knock it off, all of you. You're lucky I'm too tired to argue," Abbie muttered as she climbed into the back of the wagon. "I can't wait to get back to a civilized country where I'm not treated like a crystal vase."

"It's not personal, Abs," Parker said as he led Greenback toward the tongue. "We just care about you."

"That's small comfort when I'm back here, bouncing around, getting wagonsick, with no idea what's going on. I feel like cargo."

"I'll let you know what's going on, Abbie," Stargazer offered. "Let's see; Mr. Jerrinson's climbing up to the wagon seat now, a bit ungracefully. He's adjusting the reins; Rodeo Drive is already hitched, and Mr. Crawford is trying to get Greenback hitched, but he doesn't really know what he's doing. Now Mr. Jerrinson's getting down to help him. Oh, that's better, now they've got the breeching sorted out. Mr. Jerrinson's much better at this than Mr. Crawford, isn't he?" Abbie put her index finger to her lips to stifle a laugh, and she heard both men grumbling under their breath.

"Okay, Star. Thanks for the update."

He winked. "Anytime." She was never going to get over that.

The moon was already up, and without the beating sun, Abbie was freezing. She pulled the wool blanket around her shoulders—it had been nice to have the wagon, if only to carry more supplies. The two women were still arranging their packs when the wagon lurched forward at a breakneck pace. Abbie reached out a hand to brace the older woman, and she clung to her until the horses eased into a matched pace on the packed-earth road. Abbie was exhausted, and she lay down in the back of the wagon, but sleep didn't come. She queued up *The Final Nightmare* on her phone and watched it for a while until a message came in.

**Parker:** You're unable to sleep?

**Abbie:** What gave me away?

**Parker:** I can see your screen glowing in the back.

**Parker:** Would you care for a bedtime story?

**Abbie:** ...

**Parker:** Once upon a time, there was a pulchritudinous princess. Her wicked family treated her dreadfully, so she ran away, but she never forgot the fantastic man she was engaged to. And he never forgot her...

**Abbie:** Go on...

**Parker:** He thought about her every time he looked up at the stars. Every time he ran a foot race with his sisters. Every time he saw a woman with the same coppery red of her hair...even though his princess's was far prettier.

**Abbie:** Naturally.

**Parker:** It goes without saying, really.

**Abbie:** Of course.

**Abbie:** Now back to my story.

**Parker:** My apologies. So deep was his longing to be with his princess, the prince wrote her long letters that he didn't know where to send. He worried about her often. He dreamed about her. Her fantastic, creamy skin, her throaty laugh, her propensity for deep discussion...

**Abbie:** And her? Did she feel the same way?

**Parker:** He wasn't sure, but he thought she would if he could only see her again. He didn't want to give up on her just because he couldn't find her. Then one day, he walked into an Imaharan restaurant, and there she was. He couldn't get over what a beautiful, brilliant woman she'd become.

**Abbie:** How does the story end?

**Parker:** I was hoping you could dream up a good ending for me...but you'll first have to turn off your movie and close your eyes...

**Abbie:** What? No HEA? Lame.

**Parker:** HEA?

**Abbie:** Happily Ever After. Hey! I finally knew an acronym you didn't!

**Abbie:** Did you

**Abbie:** I mean, did the prince bring the letters?

**Parker:** No, he didn't. Sorry. Go to sleep.

**Abbie:** I don't take orders from you.

**Parker:** That's just what my pulchritudinous princess would say! Remarkable.

**Abbie:** Good night.

**Parker:** Good night.

**Parker:** I love you.

Abbie stared at the screen. Her thumbs hovered over the keyboard. Her throat was dry from the arid air, and she wanted a drink, but she didn't want to have to try to pee in a bucket in the swaying, rolling wagon. She could make a joke, but that felt unkind. But saying nothing, just allowing it to hang in the virtual air between them...how could she say nothing? What could she say besides "I love you, too," which she absolutely should not say? *What is wrong with him? THIS is the moment he picks to say THAT for the first time? Really? In a text?* She resisted the strong urge to glare at his back through the forward gap in the wagon canvas and chewed on her nails instead. She ignored her bursting heart. She ignored the tears in her eyes. Apparently the silence was unbearable for him as well, because her phone vibrated in her palm moments later.

**Parker:** And she can read the letters on our honeymoon in La Bonisla.

Abbie started breathing again, and her head dropped to her makeshift pillow as she wrote back.

**Abbie:** Who says we're going to La Bonisla?

**Parker:** But you concede a honeymoon? I'm chuffed.

**Abbie:** Shut up, I'm trying to sleep.

**Parker:** Bring a bikini.

**Abbie:** Stop.

**Parker:** Please?

**Abbie:** NO!

# CHAPTER THIRTY

PARKER GLANCED BACK into the deep dark of the wagon. She'd finally fallen asleep, phone still in her hand. He read through their interactions one more time before putting his away as well, if only to make their presence less obvious to anyone who might be observing them. Too bad they couldn't do anything about Rodeo Drive's dappled white coat. Rubald had covered his skin well. They'd taken reasonable steps; it would be fine as long as they kept moving.

He scanned the horizon with his binoculars. Maybe they should've started their run during the day after all. He'd read that some people thought the heat kept raiders away better, and there were fewer creatures out. They should swap the horses before dawn to minimize their exposure during the light. It would be fine.

Why, why, why had he chosen to say I love you for the first time *by text message?* He'd intended to tell her soon, just not in such an impulsive, cowardly way. He knew it came off as desperate. She'd just been giving him so many good signals lately: he kept catching her staring at him when his back was turned, hiding her amusement at his jokes behind her fist and a cough. And then, of course, there was the kissing. Tender, passionate kisses that made his hair stand on end and kept him awake at night...Granted, neither of them had had very much practice, but Abbie seemed keen to make up for lost time, ever since that night in the snow.

Out of the corner of his eye, he noticed Rubald nodding off. Parker elbowed him tactfully, giving the impression that he'd been jostled by the wagon's movement. The older man looked around, disoriented, then his head seemed to clear quickly as he recognized his future sovereign sitting on the bench next to him.

"Need more coffee?" Parker asked, reaching for the thermos.

"Sure, sure," Rubald said, clearing his throat. Parker poured the cap half-full and passed it over carefully, still trying to scan the horizon at the same time. Rubald took a sip and passed Parker the reins.

"You might as well get used to the feeling of holding the reins. Soon enough, you'll be doing so for all of us as king."

Parker looked up at the stars. "Maybe."

"Maybe? What's that supposed to mean?"

He shrugged, mildly amused that Rubald had dropped all deference. "I'm not sure...what Abbie's going to do yet. I don't think she's going to sign."

"So?"

"So if she doesn't sign, I have to fight—"

"And you'll win. You've got to." Rubald passed the cap back and Parker swapped him for the reins. A deep sigh escaped from his chest. He should've known better. He'd tried to have the same conversation with his father earlier in the week with the same level of success. *No one wants to talk about the alternative, even though they should.*

His eyes drifted back to the incredible display of stars overhead. If Lincoln hadn't gone off the rails, he could have waited for her to come around. He'd have waited until those stars fell out of the sky, and eventually, she'd have come back on her own. Instead, here he was, like a caveman dragging her back by her hair. If he made her sign under penalty of imprisonment, what kind of marriage was that? And if she still refused, what would a prison stay, even a cushy one, do to her health? It was absurd to even consider it.

Parker's chest felt tight, and he rubbed it with one hand. He closed his eyes—just for a moment—and found himself sailing off the coast of King's Beach, whipping along, the wind tearing at his jacket, the spray kissing his face. The sun was setting behind the castle on the bluff high above. He knew the scent of the wild roses couldn't possibly carry to him at that distance across the water, but it was. Seagulls called to each other overhead. He tacked across the wind, and suddenly, he noticed another boat coming up alongside him, and the leisurely evening sail turned into a race. He couldn't quite make out the other captain, until he saw his dreadlocks flying out behind him. Lincoln. He was grinning at Parker—not maliciously, but just as a brother who's winning a friendly race would. The sky, which had been sunset mauve, turned gray, and the sudden drop in wind temperature chilled him. Lincoln was laughing. He heard his name on the wind: his real name, which Lincoln never used...

"Sir? Wake up, sir. I don't want to have to get one of the ladies up here."

"No, I'm awake."

"You've got *emu*," Rubald said, grinning. It was a game Parker hadn't played in years until this trip, and he narrowed his gaze thoughtfully.

"May I say *unicorn*? Does that count?"

"In the Unveiled? Sure." They both chuckled. "I'll say *nutria*, then."

Parker stroked his chin, the bristles of his rapidly thickening facial hair a pleasant prickle against his fingers. "That leaves me with *a*, then?"

"Unless there's another way to spell *nutria* of which I'm not aware."

"Just for that, I say *antelope*, leaving you with an impossible *e*."

"*Elephant*."

"Nope, we've used that."

"Um..." Rubald looked around. "*Iguana*."

"That starts with an *i*, I believe."

"Really?"

"Unless there's another way to spell *iguana* of which I'm not aware."

Rube elbowed Parker and they both laughed again, an edge of giddiness emerging in the sound.

"I'm so tired."

"Me too."

"*Echidna*."

"Fishguts, another *a*..."

"What's that?" Parker's senses suddenly snapped out of their soft-focus haze. Rubald was pointing. "You see it?"

"I see it." Parker lifted the binoculars. The moon was illuminating a moving shape halfway between them and the horizon.

"Stop the wagon."

Rubald pulled the horses to an abrupt halt, nearly throwing Parker from the seat. The shape was moving north across their path. It could be one giant animal, but he felt it was more likely a pack of animals. Were wild animals or raiders worse to run into in the middle of an inhospitable desert in the dead of night? There was no time to debate it, even in his own mind.

"Do they see us?"

"I'm not certain."

"May I see?" Parker passed the binoculars, still staring in their—or its—direction.

"Nightstallions."

"So there's more than one of them?"

"Yes, it's a herd." Hearing this, the horses began to paw the ground nervously.

"Easy, easy. They haven't seen us."

"Which way is the wind blowing?"

"Toward us. That's good."

"We'll wait here until they've passed by." Parker's leg began to bounce. Sitting still felt wrong, exposed.

"Until who's passed by?" Stargazer had wandered up from behind the wagon, still breathing hard, his breath visible in the cool night air.

"That herd of nightstallions."

"Whoa."

The herd suddenly shifted, turned...and started coming directly for them.

"What's happening? Why did they turn?"

"It's me," Stargazer panted. "They're calling to me. They...they want me to join them."

The two men looked at each other, eyes wide in the dark.

"Go!" roared Parker, and Rubald snapped the reins. He held on as Rubald veered them off the road and through the scrub, trying to avoid boulders and cacti. The deep sand was slowing them down, and one glance over his shoulder at the dust cloud the nightstallions were kicking up told him that they were still tracking them easily. Rubald was driving the mares hard, and Parker wasn't sure how much longer they could go at this pace. He peered into the night; there was something else in front of them. He saw the ravine just before it was too late. Lunging for the reins with a yell, he yanked the horses to the right, away from the nightstallions, away from their destination, and most importantly, away from the gaping hole in the earth they'd been hurtling toward.

Parker craned his neck around toward the back of the wagon. Stargazer was still there, but he was now actively pulling against his tether, whinnying and kicking his back legs.

"We're not going to outrun them, they're still gaining," Rubald bellowed.

"Tie him tighter to the wagon!" Parker ordered. "We're not giving up so easily."

"What's happening, why did we stop?" Abbie was rubbing her eyes, peering into the darkness.

"The nightstallions are coming for Star."

She didn't miss a beat, wide awake in the space between one blink and the next. "Like Jersey they are."

Despite his racing heart, Parker shook his head and smiled. *This woman, I swear to Woz...*

"Okay, how do we stop them?"

"We have to convince Stargazer to stay with us," Rubald barked. "They won't take him against his will. They'll just break it with their lies."

"I'd be free. I'd be the wind," the horse muttered, straining against his bonds so hard the ropes were creaking.

Abbie wrapped her arms around his neck, careful to avoid his pawing hooves.

"You can't be the wind, Star, that job's taken. We love you. We don't want to lose you. Stay here with us. It's better here with us."

The stallions were racing closer now, and Parker tore his gaze away from them just in time to see Abbie swing herself onto Stargazer's unsaddled back.

"No!" He yelled, but he was too late. Stargazer's eyes were wide, white, wild. He was tossing his head to be free of the ropes. Abbie's face was hidden as she clung to his neck, her legs pressed tightly against the horse's sides.

*Please*, Parker silently begged. *Please, Star, don't take off with her on your back. We'll never find her.*

He knew that time was passing normally as the black cloud of spirit horses enveloped them. He knew it, but he couldn't feel it. He could feel his voice vibrating in his throat, screaming for Abbie to hold on—he had no idea what would happen if she fell off. He could feel it, but he couldn't hear it. They did sound like the howling wind, and their little band was in the center of the storm as they circled the wagon.

Their chalky mist hid Abbie and Stargazer from his view. Could she be trampled by a cloud? Maybe in the Unveiled. Then, finally, the cloud began to part, and Star and Abbie were still there. The herd was moving off.

Getting Abbie to let go turned out to be the hard part. Parker and Rubald both rushed over to her, both yelling their commentary about what a boneheaded idea that had been with varying levels of politeness or lack thereof. But their shouts died on their lips when they heard what she was murmuring under her breath: "Not again. Not again. Not again."

Stargazer was still breathing hard, but seemed to have regained his right mind. Parker put a hand on Abbie's back and she fell silent, but didn't move.

"You can get down now, darling. You saved him. He's safe."

After a few minutes of gentle back rubbing, the ex-princess sat up slowly, swiping at her face. Parker held out a hand to help her down, and to his surprise, she accepted it as she slid from Stargazer's back. He pulled her to his chest and found no resistance to his embrace.

"Thank you, Abbie," Stargazer nickered. "Without you on my back, I would've totally gone with them. But I knew I couldn't go with you."

Rube cleared his throat. "Princess, I think I speak for all of us when I say, you're not right in the head, and I'm very grateful for that."

Parker found that his voice was stuck in his throat. He knew she was ready to be released from his grip, knew they should keep moving. But seeing as she'd almost just disappeared forever right in front of him, he didn't have it in him to let go.

"It's okay, Parker," she choked out. "I'm okay. I love you, too."

He did release her then, but only to kiss her soundly and help her back into the wagon. The prince decided the next model would definitely have a locking mechanism on the back; a keyed lock, not a combination. She'd almost certainly crack that.

# CHAPTER THIRTY-ONE

ABBIE FELT THE WAGON come to an abrupt halt just as the sun was beginning to tint the morning sky with subtle pinks and oranges. She lay with her eyes closed, breathing in the scent of her own musty clothes, Rutha's soap, and the earthy horse-smell that lingered from her adventure the night before.

Did he think she'd been trying to escape? The thought never occurred to her until just now. It would have been an idiotic plan, for there was no telling where the nightstallions would've taken her. He probably realized that...but maybe she should say something. Then again, her big mouth had been getting her into trouble lately.

*I love you, too.* What in the world had gotten into her? It's not that it wasn't true; it was completely true, but it was ultimately irrelevant. Attachment was not an option. Her health had made that decision for her. *So why did I say it?* Abbie sighed. *Because he was so scared and he held me so tight. Because he needed to hear it. I wanted him to be okay. I wanted him to feel better.*

Caring about someone she wasn't allowed to love was proving tricky.

She heard Rutha stirring, and she rolled over.

"Good morning, dear. How did you sleep?"

Abbie propped up her head on one elbow. "For a woman who's usually awake more than the mice, you sure were zonked last night."

"Beg pardon?"

"We ran into nightstallions. It was pretty wild."

Rutha's eyes went wide. "Oh my. But all went well, I trust?"

"Wife, it's better if you don't know." Rubald was doing his best faux-stern face through the rear opening of the wagon as he untied Stargazer.

"Yes, it all went fine."

"Well, I'd better be about breakfast. Mind lending a hand?"

Abbie's phone emitted a muffled *bee-dunk*, and she rummaged under her pillow until she located it. "Sure, I'll be right there," she said absentmindedly as she unlocked it.

*This is Kurt. We need to talk. Call me on this number ASAP.*

*My brother? What's my brother doing texting me? I assumed he never wanted to speak to me again...maybe he has news about Dad. Bad news.*

"Uh, I have to make a call." Abbie stuck her head out the back opening. "Where's Parker?"

"We're not stopping, sister, just swapping the horses. He's watering them from the pump. Stay in the wagon."

"I just need ten minutes."

"You've got two."

"Leaving without me? Hmm. Guess I'll get my exercise running to catch up."

She ignored his quiet yet perturbed gesticulations and Rutha's failed attempts to calm him down and stalked toward the pump and trough where Parker was working. Nervous as she was about calling Kurt, watching him work that pump from behind was doing something for her. Like, seriously doing something for her. She stopped a few feet away, her throat dry. He didn't notice her, and she coughed. Rodeo Drive looked up from drinking and nickered. Stargazer looked up as well.

"Abbie wants you," he sputtered.

Parker glanced over his shoulder at her, wiping the sweat off his forehead with his sleeve. It was already blazing hot out. So was she, especially when he smiled at her like that despite his obvious fatigue.

"Good morning, darling. You look lovely. Fancy a drink?"

She shook her head, ignoring the compliment and the endearment. "Kurt texted me."

"Did he indicate what he desired?" Oh good, he was slipping out of fiancé mode and back safely into prince mode. She still felt sweaty.

"Just to speak with me. Will you...could you please..."

Parker lifted an eyebrow. "*Please*? Oh my, you are nervous."

"Stop."

"I'll gladly stand by while you speak with him."

"Thank you."

"Not sure I can stomach this sudden politeness, though. Could you restore the attitude for me?"

"Oh, knock it off."

"That's my girl."

Abbie motioned him out of range of the horses' hearing; she didn't want Stargazer asking awkward questions. Her stomach felt like a brick. What could her brother want? Had her father died? They'd barely tolerated each other when they'd lived in the same household...

It was ringing.

"Abelia?"

"Kurt."

There was a long pause.

"Are you alone?"

"No, I have Edward here with me."

"Hello, Kurt," Parker chimed in, and Kurt's voice went from stone cold to spring thaw.

"What a nice surprise! Hello, old man. How are you?"

"Doing well, doing well, and yourself?"

"Eh, I've been better."

"I can imagine."

Abbie shot Parker an annoyed look. "Would you two like to be alone? I can leave."

"Sorry, mate, she's not had her coffee yet."

"Ah. She never was a morning person." Kurt cleared his throat. "I'm calling about the vote on Thursday."

"What's today?" Abbie swiped her phone's screen. "Tuesday. Woz, I'm so upside down."

"Sorry, what's this vote? We've heard nothing."

"The Brevsporan Parliament has decided to hold a vote of no confidence regarding my qualifications as an heir on Thursday. I'm hoping you both can come and speak in my defense."

"I'm not sure we'll be across the desert by then," Abbie said. "But if I am, I will certainly be there. I don't want the job."

"Yeah, I figured that when you took off five years ago and never looked back."

Abbie clenched her free hand into a fist. "Bitter much?"

Parker elbowed her. "I'll do my best to get her there, mate."

"It's not going to make any difference, though, will it?" Abbie continued with a sigh.

The frosty edge was back in Kurt's voice. "Why is that?"

"Well, we've had a matriarchy for sixteen generations. You don't change something like that overnight."

"It's not overnight, I've been studying under Father for years."

Abbie huffed out an impatient breath. "Yes, but you didn't study under *her*, and that's what they'll care about. That's what the parliament will argue. You didn't have the right education under the potentate."

"They weren't offering it for boys, now were they? Forget second class citizens, we're lucky you offer us citizenship at all!"

"Now, now, children, you can debate your country's flawed institutions at another time. Not when we're sitting still in Gratha."

"Woz, you're in Gratha? I'll let you go."

"Thanks, mate. We'll be in touch."

"Goodbye, Abelia. And...thank you," Kurt snipped.

She sniffed. "You're welcome."

"Woz. I didn't miss you."

"Right back at you, haystack brain." She emphatically pressed the red button and looked up at Parker, who had his hands on his hips.

"Haystack brain? Really? I've heard you insult your pack with more panache when you can't find a hairbrush."

"Well, his mother was off limits for obvious reasons."

"Certainly."

"And as you so astutely observed, I haven't had my coffee." Abbie pursed her lips to hide a smile. "Does *everyone* like you? I'm not jealous, mind you, just curious."

His hands went from his hips to hers, but his eyes were on her lips, and she was once again aware of the heat. *Woz, it is so hot.*

"No, not everyone likes me. But those who don't, I work hard to win over. I can be quite persuasive." He leaned forward.

"Children, let's *go!*" Rubald hollered from the wagon seat.

"How're you going to leave without the horses?" Abbie hollered back, and Parker winced at her volume.

"Yeah!" shouted Stargazer. "How are you going to leave without us?"

"We're coming, uncle." Parker laced his fingers with Abbie's as he tugged her back toward the wagon and she raised an eyebrow at him, gesturing to their joined hands.

He shrugged. "You love me. I can hold it if I want to."

Abbie made a *hmphing* noise, but didn't pull away.

# CHAPTER THIRTY-TWO

THE PALACE BEGAN TO rise above the horizon around noon. Rube spotted it first; Parker's eyes were dry as the sand and playing tricks on him. He was fighting exhaustion with every blink. The building was angular, stair-stepped on both sides, the roofline v-shaped. It backed up to a bluff that rose into a mid-sized mountain range; his godfather could undoubtedly see for miles from this location, but he didn't know why he hadn't placed the palace on the bluff instead of below it. All he knew was that Blair had built the place after he abandoned Malieka and Crescena.

Parker could still hear his father's voice raging behind the closed door when he'd gotten the news. The nannies had shooed him and Rhodie away from the den, but his father's fury at his closest friend was still ringing in Parker's ears. And more than that, his tears. Even the carved oak hadn't blocked out the man's sobs and his mother's gentle words of consolation and comfort. Maybe that was why Parker still took Crescena's calls on his private cell. He felt a kinship with her over the whole ordeal, a brotherly protection for this abandoned girl and her mother. Even Malieka, who had been left to rule Descaret alone, still leaned heavily on Parker's father at times.

They were still three miles away when they were stopped by his guards, a group of men with skin the color of copper clay in flowing garb that matched their surroundings. They were heavily armed, but their faces were friendly.

"His Majesty has been expecting you, sir," said one of the men with a nod. "You are all welcome here. We hope you enjoy your stay."

It was all Parker could do to not mutter under his breath. If he'd wanted to be a king, all he had to do was stay in Descaret. This? This windswept desert was no kingdom. Just a wasteland nobody wanted.

They proceeded down the road, which was professionally paved in cobblestones. Vegetation had been planted alongside, providing shade. From what he could see between tall hedges, there were lush gardens for acres in front of the palace. Parker wondered absentmindedly how he watered the plants, but nerves were beginning to push out all other thoughts. He wanted to punch him in the face; he shouldn't do that. If he could keep from doing that, he'd probably be okay. They needed his cooperation, but he didn't have to like it. And he didn't have to hide that he didn't like it.

Rubald pulled the wagon up to the massive front doors. Up close, Parker could see that the roof was actually alive, with all manner of vines trailing off the edge. *Unbelievable. What a waste of water,* he thought sourly. He turned to Abbie to commiserate but found her starry-eyed, clearly impressed by the design of the place.

"I bet that's to keep the palace cool; they say that a living roof insulates the structure and reduces the temperature by as much as fifty degrees. I read about them in college, but I've never seen one, even in Gardenia. So awesome."

The prince bit his tongue as they walked up the front steps, where his godfather was coming out to meet them.

"Godson. I wondered if you'd show up here." Smiling, the king moved to embrace the younger man, then noticed his firm rejection.

"Blair."

The older man crossed his arms, his aging but still handsome face falling into a frown. "I heard you were in trouble."

"Why else would I come here?"

"Perhaps you wanted to see an old friend."

Parker felt Rutha shift uncomfortably, and he could tell she wanted to chide his rudeness but didn't dare. Parker glared at the man, making his contempt plain on his face. He'd aged well—unless his long, loose robes were hiding more than they appeared to. Besides the gray at his temples and in his beard, his face was the same as the man who'd taken Parker crabbing for the first time.

"I'm Abbie," she said, stepping between them and holding out her hand with a smile.

The Silicon King took it, turned it palm-down, and brought it to his lips. "Lovely to meet you, Abbie. My, your hands are cold. Well, we shall warm them up quickly here."

"May we come in?"

"Certainly. This way." Blair moved aside for the group to enter, then moved for the guard to close the door. "My spotters saw you far off, and the staff is preparing a feast for you tonight, as well as quarters. I was not sure what your preferences were, so I gave each of you a room, except the Jerrinsons, of course."

"How incredibly gracious of you, sir," Abbie said, threading her arm through his as he offered it. "I never could have imagined such lush accommodations in this wasteland. We just can't thank you enough. Isn't that right, darling?"

Parker grunted his disgruntled agreement.

"I realize it wasn't your first choice to come here, Parker, but I'm so glad to—"

"Edward."

"Pardon?"

"You may call me Edward. Or His Highness the Second Son. And I'm only allowing Edward because of that business with you and my father in Wellwood Forest."

Blair's steps slowed, and he turned to face him, dropping Abbie's arm. "What do you know about that?"

"I know you saved his life. And I know it's why you're my godfather, because he believed you'd come through for me when I needed you."

"That's true, Edward."

"Time will tell. You know what they say: the desert has no king."

# CHAPTER THIRTY-THREE

THE FIVE OF THEM STOOD awkwardly in the main corridor of Blair's mansion. The older man's eyes had gone distant. *Pity.* That's what Abbie felt. Pity toward Blair, irritation toward Parker, who was usually the controlled one. Check that: always the controlled one. She'd never seen him like this, so angry, so filled with disdain.

"Please excuse me," Blair murmured. "I have some work to finish before this evening, and I'm sure you'd like to rest after such a long journey. My stewards will show you to your rooms." When Abbie glanced over her shoulder, he was still standing in the same place, watching them go.

When the steward stopped, Abbie opened the carved wooden door to her room and gasped. A steaming cup of tea and a chocolate chip cookie was waiting next to the overstuffed chair overlooking the gardens. She had a private bathroom with a jetted soaking tub, a steam room, and two vanities. There was a plush, white cotton robe waiting for her on the bed, which appeared to have silk sheets. A stack of romance novels sat on the nightstand.

"Goodbye," she said happily as she closed the door on Parker. He pressed his hand against the outside to keep it from latching.

"Abs, you know I have to check your room."

"What, this place? Are you joking? It's amazing."

"Right. And what better way to lure you into a trap than to make you extremely comfortable? Don't forget, you are still in Gratha. We don't know what his relationship is with the Warlord." She pushed her hair away from her face and allowed him to push the door open and enter her new favorite room in the universe. He stared at the bed for a moment, then swallowed hard.

"No comment on the sheets?"

The prince shrugged, one hand on his knife, his eyes scanning everything. He moved slowly through the bathroom, poking his head into the steam room briefly.

"Seems like something you'd normally complain about." He leaned against the bathroom door jam and cocked his head at her.

"You'd like me to complain?"

"No, not—I just mean—you're not your usual, practical self, who would hate the idea of silk sheets because clearly, cotton is more easily washable and has more traction."

"Ah." He was staring past her out the window. A few moments ago, all she'd wanted to do was push him out the door and dive into this space and all its luxury and comfort, but now...the deadness in his eyes and the tension in his body had marred it for her.

"All right, sit down on the bed."

His eyes narrowed as he looked around. "Why can't I sit in that overstuffed monstrosity of a chair?"

"Because I can't get to your body there."

He gave her half a surprised smile, and she felt her face flood with color.

"Your shoulders—I meant, I can't massage your shoulders."

He reticently walked to the edge of the bed and sat down. Abbie knelt behind him on the down comforter, ignoring the dust they were both casting on it. She started running her thumbs across the back of his shoulders, dragging them down to the inside of his shoulder blades.

"What if I don't want my shoulders massaged?"

"Oh, hush! It's okay to let your guard down once in a while, you know...you can't be 'on' 24/7."

"24/24," he muttered.

"You know what I mean." She kneaded the knots in his taut muscles with her knuckles. "We're safe here. It's okay to let loose a little."

He grunted. She put her left hand on his forehead and tipped his head forward.

"Rest your head in my hand, please." She felt the weight in her hand increase as he released control to her, and he let out a deep sigh. She massaged the back of his neck, watching him for a response, as it was sometimes a sensitive area. His eyes were closed, and he didn't seem to be fighting her anymore. In fact, he didn't seem to be...conscious.

"Does that feel okay?" Abbie laid her right hand on his shoulder. "Parker? Parker..." Well. This was unexpected. Her feminine pride was only mildly wounded, though he might've been at least a little excited to be alone with her, getting rubbed down on her bed. But then again, he'd been up for two days. Yeah, that was it.

Abbie slid her hand across his back to his other shoulder so that his head rested on her shoulder, then she eased him down flat onto the bed. He barely stirred when she removed his weapon and placed it on the nightstand. She pulled off his boots and swung his legs up onto the bed, noting his desperate need for clean socks as soon as possible.

Throwing the lock, Abbie headed to the bath, delighting in what she imagined Rutha would say when she found her freshly bathed and the Second Son passed out on her bed. She'd been in the bath about an hour, devouring a new novel as she sipped her tea, the cookies long gone, when she heard a quiet knock at the door. She tried to hurry to get out of the tub; if they woke up Parker, she'd—

"Yes?" she heard his groggy voice mumble from the other room.

*Fishguts.* She sat back down. "Parker, can you get the door?"

"What's the magic word?"

She rolled her eyes. "Please?"

"Certainly." She heard him throw the lock and the door creak open. She made a mental note not to try to evade her guard that way. After a few moments of muffled conversation, she heard the door close and Parker knocked at the bathroom door.

"You decent?"

"Never."

"Can I come in, then?" Since she knew he was one hundred percent joking, she called,

"Sure, come on in, the water's fine."

There was a long pause, and Abbie chuckled to herself. Okay, so maybe he was only ninety percent joking.

"Who was at the door?"

"Your lady's maid. She was quite scandalized to see me, but when she'd composed herself, she asked me to convey that dinner is at six and there's appropriate attire in the closet. I'm not sure you're going to be pleased with what they consider appropriate, however."

Abbie pressed her lips into a thin line, sighing. "I'm coming."

"Don't drain the bath."

She made a face as she stepped out of the tub and slipped into the thick, fluffy bathrobe. The water was practically gray, and there was a layer of sediment at the bottom. "Why?"

"I'm going to use it."

"No, you're not. Go use your own bathtub."

"Water's scarce here, Abs. I'm not wasting a full tub just because it's a bit nippy." Ah, there he was. She smirked, then yawned, wishing she could slip under the covers for a few hours instead of wedging herself into an uncomfortable evening gown. And she'd had far more sleep than Parker last night.

"Well, I'm not sure you'll actually get cleaner, that's all." *And you can't be naked in the next room, because I totally want you naked in the next room...or the same room.* She opened the bathroom door to find him rifling through the dresses, sneering at them skeptically. "Hey, don't touch them, you're filthy."

He grinned for the first time in days as he looked her over. "You're not."

"No," she said primly, "I'm not. Now go take your bath. We're going to be late."

He paused. "Someone told me I should let loose a little. I can't think of a better moment to start." He stepped toward her and she put out a hand defensively, the other holding her robe shut at the chest, stifling a giggle. Her previously wounded feminine pride was grinning smugly.

"You wouldn't dare."

"We've got a contract."

"I don't give a burnt brownie what we've got, you keep your grubby hands off me."

"Come on, darling, give us a kiss."

She grinned at the use of the word, her face warming at the memory of kissing him in that freezing tent, the tender way he'd taken care of her. "Forget it."

Parker advanced slowly, eyes twinkling, and Abbie tried to circle away from him toward the closet. Her mouth dropped open as Parker casually took off his shirt, never taking his eyes off her. Her eyes immediately fell to the floor as she carefully inspected the intricate, hand-painted tile. It was chipped or otherwise damaged in five places, including one of the tiles that was now obscured by his dirty shirt.

"Hey." Parker stopped moving, and she could see in her peripheral vision that he'd put his hands up and his shoulders were slumped. Abbie glanced up at him.

"I was just playing. I'm sorry. I'll stop. All right?"

She could hear her own heartbeat. She wanted to say out loud that it was okay, that he'd just surprised her, that she wanted to kiss him. All she could do was nod.

"You should wear the green one." He grinned as he disappeared into the bathroom, and she heard the lock turn.

Abbie kicked herself. Why did she go on lockdown so fast these days? He'd always liked to tease her, and it'd never bothered her before. *It's because it's real now. It's not a game anymore. It's because I might actually say yes. I'm not scared of him—he's only ever been a gentleman. And now, I'm scared he'll actually stop.*

"Oh, motherf—" she heard him catch himself as he started to curse at the cold water.

"Don't waste water, you said. Don't mind if it's nippy, you said. I warned you," she sang through the door.

"Yes, thank you," he said, his voice an octave higher than usual. "I don't know if I'll be capable of siring an heir after this experience."

Abbie laughed and headed to the wardrobe.

Which dress did he say? The green? Her natural inclination was to be contrary, to pick anything but the green one, but she'd shut him down so completely a few moments before...She pulled out the green one and held it at arm's length. It was made of an emerald georgette silk so thin it would have been see-thru if it hadn't been layered. The ruffled keyhole halter neck with open shoulders appealed to her, as it wouldn't give the Silicon King her chest to gawk at, thereby hopefully preventing Parker from stabbing him with a butter knife at the dinner table. Not that she thought Parker's godfather was a letch, at least based on what she'd seen of him so far—but her boobs were one of her best features, and few men could resist a peek. She had no necklaces to wear anyway. The color would bring out the red highlights in her hair...but that slit up the middle was quite high. She'd have to see it on. Parker was still splashing around in the bathroom, so it was safe to disrobe and try it on.

She stepped into it, zipped up the back, and brought the clasp to meet around her neck. Abbie backed up from the closet to see herself in the mirror. It wasn't bad, really. The slit was still high, but she was tall. It might be a tad more suggestive than she'd like, but it wasn't obscene. The middle was cinching up her belly quite nicely. The bathroom door opened.

"Abelia, I—" Parker suddenly fell silent, taking in the sight of her. "Whoa." Though she could guess his thoughts, Abbie decided to fish for compliments, feeling smug.

"Oh, you don't like it after all?" She crossed away from him toward the closet. "I guess I could wear the blue one instead..." She reached for the blue dress, but he reached out and grabbed her arm.

"Don't you dare."

*He's breathing hard for someone who was just sitting in a bathtub...*"Just wait until you see what I'm going to do with my hair." She slipped her arms around his neck and suddenly noticed he was only wearing a towel. "You should go get dressed."

"I'm clean. Where's my kiss?" he husked.

"Will the towel stay on?"

"I don't know. Do you want it to?" He asked with a guileless expression. His deadpan wit had only grown into a more deeply entrenched facet of his personality since they were kids, and Abbie resisted the desire to roll her eyes.

"Yes."

"Then it'll stay on." He was rocking forward and back on his heels.

"You're not great at hiding your excitement," Abelia chuckled.

"Why should I hide it? Embracing you, touching your soft skin..." he brushed his fingers against her bare shoulders, "hearing you laugh, even at my expense, kissing you...I've dreamt about this for years. I can't be aloof when it comes to you. Never have been."

Abbie knew she should pull away now. That would be the smart thing to do, the kind thing. But she'd never stared into the eyes of someone who was head-over-heels in love with her before, and it was more powerful than she was prepared for.

"I..." Her mind went blank, and seeing his opportunity, he pounced. Abbie would later describe the kiss he gave her as, well, *assertive*. He was uncharacteristically confident with her. Completely unhurried, yet there was a definite insistence in the way he savored her, pivoted them to press his chest against hers as he backed her against the closet door, brought his hands up to cradle her face.

A soft knock at the door startled them both, and Abbie was glad her tongue wasn't in his mouth at that exact moment or it might have been half an inch shorter.

"Yes?" Abbie called, trying to slow her breathing.

"Your maid, Highness. I wondered if you needed help dressing."

"Could you come back in five minutes to help me with my hair?"

"Of course, Highness." As her footsteps receded, Abbie's nose wrinkled at the moniker.

"Well, *Highness*, I'll be going now." He winked at her, and she rolled her eyes.

"I should've let your unclothed body scandalize her again." He started for the door, but she grabbed his hand. "One more thing." He turned to face her, grinning.

"Does it involve more kissing?"

"No." She dropped his hand and crossed her arms. "Be serious for a moment."

He mimicked her defensive stance. "Okay, fire away."

"I want you on your best behavior tonight."

He shrugged. "Of course."

"You said that before. Yet your antics when we arrived fell far short of my expectations."

"Antics?"

"Refusing physical contact, disallowing the use of your nickname, implying you only came here because you had no other choice?"

"He deserves every bit of that and more."

Abbie held up her hands. "I'm not saying he doesn't. I'm saying you can't treat him that way. We're guests here, Parker."

"Is this a scolding? What am I, five?"

"No, you're not." She stepped closer to him, let her hands fall to his crossed arms. "You're an adult, and I'm treating you as such. I'm on your side. I know he gets under your skin, but you've got to hide it better. Open contempt will have us sleeping in the wagon tonight, listening to Rubald's snoring. I'm looking forward to those silky, scorpion-less sheets too much for that."

His eyes narrowed, but the tension left his posture and he let out a breath. "Fine. I'll do better." He turned and opened the door, then added, "Also, in addition to being impractical, silk sheets are dry clean only, and I don't have to tell *you* how harmful that is for the environment."

Abbie stared at the bed, knowing her disappointment was plain on her face. "Damn it."

# CHAPTER THIRTY-FOUR

RUBALD AND RUTHA WERE already at the table by the time he arrived. He'd waited outside Abbie's door for a few minutes, assuming they would find their way together since his room was just around the corner. Just as Parker pulled out his phone to text her, a passing servant informed him that she'd already left. Striding down the hallway, he found the dining room quickly, but no Abbie. Where in the world was she?

Behind him, he heard soft laughter as his fiancé came down the hall, once again on the arm of the biggest traitor he'd ever known. Well, second-biggest. Woz, he needed new friends. Possibly a new family. They had stopped to admire a large still-life of a bowl of oranges. He didn't see what could possibly be so funny. *Does she have to stand so close to him? Doesn't she comprehend what kind of havoc this man has wrought in my life? What he's capable of?*

He stormed into the dining room, taking his place across from the Jerrinsons, both of whom were freshly washed as well.

"How's your room?"

Rube cleared his throat. "More than adequate. Yours?"

"Fine." Parker snapped his napkin open and put it in his lap. Abbie and Blair waltzed into the dining room, still laughing. He'd never seen her schmooze anyone, and seeing it now was like a front row seat to his worst nightmare. She slipped into the seat next to him and gave him a wink as she handed him his knife under the table.

"You left this in my room," she whispered. He accepted and sheathed it without comment. "You okay?"

"Yeah. Fine." He looked her in the eye for the first time, and he tried to soften his demeanor. "I do like that hair." Her maid had helped her to braid her long waves into a crown around her head, curling a few trailing pieces to frame her face. She touched her head lightly, clearly pleased at his mention of it.

"I thought you would."

Parker winked at her. He loved seeing her blush. His blushes never showed on his skin, and it was his favorite thing she didn't know she did. Maybe he could get her alone in the garden later and whisper a few things that would make her positively glow...

"Well," Blair said, standing at the head of the table, "shall we eat?" He motioned to the servants standing by, who came in with chilled gazpacho in shot glasses followed by spinach salad with strawberries, blueberries, and goat cheese. He hated goat cheese.

"This is good," Parker muttered. "Do you grow it here?"

Abbie gave him a small smile. *Good.* At least she saw he was trying to be civil.

"Yes, we have extensive gardens. There's a perched aquifer that supplies us with all the water we need, most seasons. Of course, we also have a large cistern under the house, which helps keep it cool."

"Yes, it's a very comfortable temperature," Rutha agreed, and they all nodded. Where the Jersey did he get all this money? How did he support such a huge staff? It was just him here, right? Where did they all live?

"Did you finish the work you needed to do?" Abbie asked, and Blair nodded.

"I owed my publisher another draft of my latest work-in-progress; I just needed to put the finishing touches on my edits."

"You're an author? Since when?" Parker tried to come off as simply surprised but couldn't keep the edge of annoyance out of his voice entirely. Blair chuckled.

"Yes, many times over. I needed a source of income to support myself for the first time in my life. Like Abelia, I also went to Gardenia at first, but found that I drew too much attention there. So, when my fifth book hit the bestseller list for twenty-five weeks straight, I bought this land and began to build."

Abbie swallowed her bite. "What kind of books do you write?"

He smiled a cagey smile. "I'm hesitant to say."

"Yes, I'm also curious," Parker pressed. "I consider myself a fairly voracious reader, and I don't recall your name ever hitting the bestseller lists." *What would he gain by making this up? Inveterate liars don't need a reason, I suppose.*

"I write under an assumed name." *Ah. More lies.*

"Really?" Now they'd piqued Rutha's curiosity as well.

"Out with it already," Rubald said with a laugh.

"I write as Nancy Blake." Both women gasped, and the two Orangiersian men exchanged glances.

Parker hesitated. "Is it...literary fiction?"

The three in the know burst out laughing.

"No, darling." Abbie put her hand over his on the table. "Nancy Blake is the most popular, prolific romance novelist on the continent."

Well. That explained the house, and the artwork, and possibly the spell he'd clearly cast over his normally rational Abbie, who was now going full fangirl.

"Oh my Woz, I've read everything you ever wrote. A friend shared a copy of *The Duke's Intended* when I was homeless and it gave me such a beautiful escape from my harsh reality. From then on, I was obsessed with finding the rest of them. The library only carried the tame ones, not the real..." Abbie flushed and gesticulated vaguely.

"Bodice rippers?" Blair finished, chuckling. "Lots of fans have complained about that. And it's a double standard, because you know the librarians are reading them, they just won't buy them for the public."

*A romance author?* Parker's mind was spinning. Someone who believed so little in the sanctity of marriage was now making his living by filling women's heads with fantasies that the average man could never achieve? His opinion of the Silicon King had not improved with these recent revelations.

"Who handles your social media, then? Because I swear the picture on your author page is a lady."

"I found a lady on Tennerr who was willing to represent me and keep my secret. She has also stepped up to do live social media events. Blanche knows the books forward and backward, and people are less intimidated at the idea of reading a romance written by a middle-aged white lady than a middle-aged black man."

The Jerrinsons tittered, nodding. A servant put down a plate of tilapia topped with chili-lime butter in front of him, and Parker sniffed. He did like fish.

"Where did you acquire fish?"

"I have aquaponics in the rear. I would be glad to show you after dinner."

"I think Abbie and I were going to explore the gardens," she glanced at him, "if that's okay with you."

"Of course, of course. You are my guests, please feel free to explore, rest, enjoy."

*Impossible.* The nap Abbie had gifted him with her massage had been a fluke. Exhausted as he was, he expected to be up half the night staring at the ceiling, resentment ringing in his ears like a bell at being under this roof. *I shouldn't have come here.*

His phone rang, and he pushed back from the table. "Please excuse me. Hello?"

"Edward, thank Woz. Are you all right? No one's been able to reach you since you entered Gratha."

"Crescena. Good to hear from you." He gave Blair a pointed look as he walked out, and was surprised to find pain on his face. "Yes, we're all fine. We made a call earlier today, so I'm not sure if it's a problem with the networks, but we're fine. Thanks for checking on us."

Her voice was shaking. "Did you find him?"

"Yes, we did."

"How is he? Is he...well?"

"Yes, he's fine. More than fine, actually. He's rich and powerful. But he doesn't seem entirely...happy." *And I'm probably contributing to that.* "How are you?"

"Mama and I were so concerned for you, Edward. You have got to call your mother, she is sick with worry."

"Yes, I will—I will call her directly. Would you also send her a message in case I can't get through?"

"Of course, of course." Woz, she sounded just like her father when she said that, and it stung.

"Do you want to talk to him? Either way is fine, don't feel beholden, you owe him nothing."

There was a long pause. "No," she whispered finally. "No, I do not."

"All right, darling." *Oops. How did that slip out?* There was a vulnerability to Crescena that just brought out all his protective instincts, but he didn't feel that way about her. Parker checked over his shoulder through the open door and saw Abbie still talking and laughing at the table. "Don't worry about us, we're fine here."

"We are prepared to send troops whenever you want them."

"I don't want to involve Descaret in this unless I have to."

"It is not an imposition, truly. They could do with the experience. And of course, we believe wholeheartedly we are aligning ourselves with the winning side."

Parker smiled. "I appreciate that. I'm going to call my mother now, Cress."

"Goodbye, Edward."

"Bye." He dialed his mom, and she picked up on the first ring.

"Oh, Edward." He could hear the tears in her voice. "I'm so glad you're all right."

"Hi, Mum. Yes, I'm fine." He was used to this facet of her. Lily was born to worry; she'd been International Worrying Champion twenty-five years running with no clear competitors for the title. He'd resented it as a teenager, but he understood it better now that Abbie gave him plenty to worry about. "Sorry I gave you a fright. I think our phones weren't working."

"Just please be careful, all right? I can't lose another son."

"All right, Mum, I hear you." *But either way, before the Brothers' War is over, you're likely going to.* "Please excuse me, I'm supposed to be eating dinner with my host."

"Did you find him?"

"Yes, I did."

"How is he?" Sometimes he forgot that they'd also been friends. Parker noticed that both women avoided his name; he didn't know if that was to avoid the curse he'd brought on them all or simply the deep emotion of his betrayal.

"He's fine. He's the same."

He heard her gentle smile in her voice. "Is that a good thing or not?"

"Not."

"Mind your manners, son, for my sake. For history's sake."

"Very well. I've got to run. Kiss everyone for me."

"Yes, I will, love."

"Bye, Mum."

Parker went back to the table, where they were all talking and laughing like old friends. Abbie turned to him and asked under the conversation, "Everything okay?"

He nodded. What was this now? Quail? Roasted with bacon, tomatoes, and basil. His mouth watered, but his stomach wasn't used to such rich food anymore. He pulled off a leg and nibbled at it, pushing around the other food with his fork. He'd retreated from the conversation entirely, but no one seemed to miss him, especially Abbie, who was animatedly telling a story about someone who bought so many cigarettes from the grocery store they had to get an extra cart.

Dessert came; chocolate lava cakes. His stomach complained and he pushed the plate away. Parker stared at the ceiling. Might as well get a jump on it.

# CHAPTER THIRTY-FIVE

ETHEREAL PAPER LANTERNS lit their path into the garden as the sun gave one final sigh and retired for the night. Fireflies floated through the fading lilies. Abbie pulled him deeper into the garden, into a large grassy area hidden by a hedge. She kicked off her shoes and flopped down onto her back, sighing. Parker smirked. You could put the woman in a dress, but she was still just holding her breath for you, uncomfortable, waiting for the formalities to cease. She was the most casual person he knew; he had an admittedly formal friend circle. Occupational hazard.

Parker unbuttoned his shirtsleeves and rolled them up, lying down next to her and enmeshing their fingers.

"Are you okay?" she asked, and he brought the back of her hand to his lips.

"I am now."

She laughed softly. "Yeah, you didn't look okay during dinner. But I know you were trying."

"Love, it took all my strength. I'm spent."

"Really? Not a bit of energy left?" A smile played at her lips as she rolled toward him, tossing a casual arm across him.

"Well, maybe just a little bit."

He brought his arm around her shoulders and snuggled her to his chest. *This is good,* he thought. *This is what I needed. I could fall asleep out here. Maybe I will...*

"Crescena doing all right?"

He nodded. "Just checking on us. They'd been trying to reach us."

"This must be weird for her."

"Heartbreaking is what it is. All of it. He's such a bastard."

"So he just up and left them? No explanation?"

Parker shrugged, trying not to jostle her. "I guess things had been tense between them for a long time, but my parents thought they were trying to make it work. Turns out one of them was trying harder than the other."

"You should've seen his face when he knew Crescena was on the phone. The agony. He looked like you'd just ripped his heart out."

"He deserves every bit of pain he gets."

Abbie propped herself up on one elbow, and he tried to ignore how her dress hugged her shifting curves like a second skin. He swallowed.

"How can you forgive me and not forgive Blair?" He yanked his attention back to her voice and face, hoping she hadn't noticed his distraction.

"Simple. He betrayed his country. He betrayed his family. You didn't."

"Parker..."

"Abs."

"You can't be serious."

"You say that frequently. Most often, it's patently untrue."

"There's no difference between what I did and what he did."

Parker shook his head vehemently. "No, there's a world of difference, Abbie, can't you see that?"

"He couldn't do it," she said, her voice dropping to a whisper. "For whatever reason. He got scared. Don't you see how he wants your forgiveness? How he's reaching out? You're choosing to forgive me. It's always a choice. Nobody deserves it. Least of all me."

"You had a valid reason."

"And his wasn't? I find that hard to believe."

Parker rolled away and sat up. "He just didn't want to be married anymore. He ran away from his commitments! A real man doesn't do that!" This wasn't the kind of hot-under-the-collar experience he'd been hoping for tonight.

"Good men and women make mistakes all the time!" She pushed herself up to sitting, her knees curled in. "Why can't you see how he hates himself now? How deeply he regrets his choice? How badly he wants to make amends?"

Parker wasn't listening. His own words were ringing in his ears, vibrating like a cymbal crashed too close. *Aren't I doing the same thing? Running from the battle I should be fighting, selfishly trying to solve this without confronting him?* His doubts had been nagging him louder and louder lately. He'd tried to push them aside after the hypothermia incident, but...maybe there was no hope for them. And if there was no hope for them, he was committed to go out to meet his brother in battle. *The more time I waste trying to change her mind, the more people die. I shouldn't be here.* His anger surged like a rogue wave inside his chest.

"I thought you were on my side."

Abbie scowled at him. "I am."

"Doesn't seem that way. You're working awfully hard to defend a terrible man. Do you think I haven't noticed you two laughing together, the way you cling to his every word? Does the Silicon Queen have a nice ring to it?" He could see he'd overstepped as she quickly got to her feet, and he immediately regretted it.

"Grow up, Parker." Abbie left her high heels behind as she stalked out of the gardens on the grassy path.

"Wait..." He scrambled after her.

"Screw you!" she called over her shoulder, and his steps slowed, letting the breeze swirl around him, envying the way it played with the silk that trailed off her lower back. He saw the moonlight reflect off something small that hit the bushes—she'd just thrown her ring away.

Abbie had shut her door by the time he caught up with her, but her light was still on. He knocked softly.

"Who is it?" Her voice was oversaturated with singsong sweetness.

"Parker."

Silence.

"May I come in?"

"Sorry, no, I'm not decent." The fake sweetness was almost worse than her wrath. This Abbie was holding him at arm's length. At least when he bore the brunt of her anger, he knew it was really her talking, unfiltered and real. He gently tried the door but it was locked.

"Okay, fine, but unlock the door when I leave so we can access your room in the case of a medical emergency."

"I'm not an invalid. And you're the one who told me there could be assassins in the steam room. Now go to bed."

Hmm, at least this was edging closer to honest. He wanted to be indignant at her tone, but he knew he deserved her anger.

"I'm sorry. I never should have thought that, let alone said it."

Silence.

"Did you hear me?"

"Yes."

"Isn't there a saying about going to bed angry?" That did it. He heard her stomping across the room, and she unlocked the door and threw it open. She was dressed in a matching lavender camisole and boy-shorts, and hadn't even bothered with that ugly robe. Parker bit his cheek to keep himself from reacting, knowing it would just provoke her more. But holy hellbats, she was gorgeous.

"It isn't about going to bed," she snapped, "it's about the sun going down, and it was already down when you accused me of cheating on you with your godfather!" Her shouts echoed off the stucco, but he knew better than to ask her to calm down.

"Oh, I see. Well, thank you for correcting me."

"And since we're correcting misapprehensions, I would never cheat on you. When I make a promise, I keep it."

"Yet you're seeking to break our contract." He cringed. What the Jersey was wrong with him? Why would he say that now? Why did he have to argue about everything? He'd only just got the door open, and he had a feeling it was about to be slammed in his face.

"Seeking? Oh, it's broken, buddy." She stabbed a finger into his chest. "I wouldn't marry you even if you were common. I'll never marry a king, Silicon or Orangiersian. Sleep on that tonight, Your Highness."

The slam reverberated in the corridor, and a moment later Rutha's head peeked out of their bedroom, an unspoken question in her expression.

Edward stood there, heart still hammering in his chest but feeling oddly hollow, like all the tempestuous questions of the past day had just been answered by Abbie's last words. Rutha cleared her throat, and he started to wave her away, then stopped. "I need to speak to Rubald," he murmured. His voice sounded strange to his own ears.

"Now?"

"Yes. Now. Right now."

# CHAPTER THIRTY-SIX

ABBIE WOKE TO BLINDINGLY bright sunlight across her bedspread. It must have been past nine o'clock in the morning. Despite their argument, she'd gone right to bed, clutching her righteous indignation to her chest like a stuffed animal. She hadn't slept that well in weeks, but instead of being refreshed, the heavy sleep stayed with her like a hangover. Abbie groaned. The healing process was going to be long, and this trip's effects were going to last. Emotionally, certainly, but the physical part scared her just as much. If she couldn't go back to work right away, she might lose her job. She was already maxing out her vacation time.

Throwing on casual clothes from the closet, she shuffled down the hall, massaging her temples with one hand and knocking softly on Parker's door with the other. *What am I going to say when he opens the door? Maybe I should've done coffee first...* When there was no answer, she tried the door handle and pushed it open a crack.

"Parker? Are you dressed?" Maybe she could offer a reconciliation snuggle in his bed—she shouldn't have ended the argument that way, even if most of it had been his fault. The bed was perfectly made; it didn't even look slept in. *Well, military men tend to be that way. He must be having breakfast. Good, I'll get some coffee and we can talk.*

Hearing voices, Abbie went down to the dining room, but all conversation stopped abruptly when she walked in.

"Morning, all."

Rube and Rutha said nothing.

"Where's Parker?" Neither would meet her gaze. Her heart went double-time. Though she hadn't done so in years, she did her best impression of her mother: throwing back her shoulders, she stood at her full height, hands on hips, and growled, "Someone better start talking, *now*."

"He left," Rutha whispered, and her expression told Abbie it was the truth.

"He wouldn't leave without us. That's ludicrous."

Rubald pulled out an envelope and slid it across the table to her. A maid poured her some coffee, but she was trembling so hard she was afraid she'd burn her lap in an attempt to bring it to her lips.

"He said this should help explain things."

Abbie had already spent most of the morning replaying last night's argument in her mind. He'd been wrong. He was wrong to insinuate that she had feelings for Blair. She was star struck, that's all. How often did she get to meet one of her favorite authors? As she rewound the tape a bit farther, she replayed a few more scenes...ones where Parker had been watching her giggle over Blair's wit too long. Ones where she followed Blair around like a lovesick puppy. And, of course, the ones where she'd led Parker on, kissing him, staring into his eyes, only to pull away from him when she remembered she wasn't supposed to have fallen in love.

Worst of all was her parting shot. She hadn't meant it, of course—it was the hurt talking. The hurt that went deep because he valued her body and her wit and her title, but not her influence. She'd just been trying to help, and he took it so personally. *I should've known he wasn't ready to hear that,* she thought as she ripped the envelope open.

*My Darling Abelia,*

*I want to once again apologize for our argument last night. I was in the wrong. In fact, I've been in the wrong this whole time. It seems my own desires have blinded me to your true feelings. I'm sorry for putting you through this.*

*Given this new insight into your decision, I have realized that only one course of action remains: I leave to meet Lincoln in battle. I remember you asking in Imahara why I wouldn't marry someone else, and I couldn't admit it just then. But the truth is that there is no one else for me. Patriotic duty be damned—it's always been you. And my love for you has never been impacted by the agreement we made in the slightest. I've loved you since I pushed you into that glacial lake and you came up spewing insults. I love your relaxed way with people you trust, your realism with people you don't. Your willingness to talk about things at length, even silly things, perhaps especially silly things. Your leadership. Your burning heart, especially for the weak and vulnerable. Your tenderness and passion.*

*I doubt I shall see you again anytime soon, so I shall close this letter with best wishes for your future, wherever it takes you. Thank you for the time we spent together. I treasure it.*

*Yours,*

*Parker*

Abbie held in her tears valiantly until the last line. She'd killed him. He was marching into a battle he had little hope of winning, because of her big mouth—no, because of her pride. Abelia Olivia Jayne Venenza Ribaldi Porchenzii silently dropped her head to her arms resting on the table. The snot was flowing now, too. She dropped the letter, realizing she might dirty it. She was still wiping the tears away as she sat up.

"Let's go after him."

"No, Abbie." Rutha had tears in her own eyes, and she reached out to hold her hand.

"We can do it. He listens to us, he'll change his mind. Marry someone else."

"Our orders are to get you to Brevspor to say goodbye to your father, if that's what you still desire." Rubald spoke robotically. He turned to her briefly, then seemed to change his mind and turned quickly back to the window.

"We cannot let him do this! We are morally obligated to change his mind. We have to catch him! Come on, who's with me?"

"What would be the point?" Rubald asked, shaking his head. "He's got a half-day's start on us, we don't know which route he chose, and we'd be traveling in the heat of the day, which, as I recall, is most difficult for you."

"Screw my health! I don't even care anymore! My body's wrecked already, let's just go!"

"You had your chance to prevent this, sister." Rutha spoke just above a whisper. "You chose differently, and now, he must make his choice as well."

Abbie withdrew her hand and crossed her arms. "You won't help me? Fine. I'll go alone. But I'd rather die than see him mount a warhorse." Abbie snatched the letter from the table and swept out of the room dramatically, only to run squarely into Blair's chest.

"You must not do this to yourself," he said, gently grasping her arms.

"Do what?" she snapped, pulling away. "Save my best friend from a potentially life-ending decision? You'll pardon me if I disagree."

"I know what it is that you want. The run to the train station. The valiant princess who scoops up her prince and spirits him away to safety. But that will not work here, Abelia. That is not what makes love work."

Abbie tossed her hair out of her face. "So what am I supposed to do? Stand by and watch him die? I don't think so."

"He may yet surprise you. He seems to have surrounded himself with wise counselors. He may do well. In any case, the handmaid is right. You had your chance to save him."

Abbie's temper sparked and she lifted her chin angrily. "You have no idea what marrying Parker would've cost me."

Blair nodded once. "That is true. But I do know love, and without sacrifice, it is an empty vow, no matter how pretty the poetry of it. I was not willing to sacrifice for the one who loved me, and I have regretted it all my lonely, windswept days. Do not rule your life like the Silicon King, my dear."

"Thanks for that little speech, it was nice. Now get the Jersey out of my way. I've got a phone call to make."

# CHAPTER THIRTY-SEVEN

ONE RING. TWO. THREE. Four. Voicemail.

"Hello. You have reached the voicemail of Edward Kenneth Keith Francis Benson Broward. Please leave a message and I'll get back to you."

Abbie packed tomorrow's clothes on the bottom, her glass coffee pot, her toothbrush, her hairbrush, her meds, and finally her pajamas on top. Just like she'd been doing for weeks. She could sleep under the stars. Or in a tree, maybe.

*What are you thinking? You can't do this alone. Your illness will put these plans of yours in the ground before you get five miles from here, and he could already be twenty miles away by now.* Abbie brushed away the voice of her mother—or perhaps the voice of reason—and stalked off to the kitchens to find food, redialing as she went.

One ring. Two. Three. Four. Voicemail. "Hello. You have reached the voicemail of Edward Kenneth Keith Francis Benson Broward. Please leave a message—"

The kitchens were quiet as the breakfast dishes sat drying in the rack, and Abbie helped herself to some cheese, a salami, a bag of mixed nuts, a pear, and after a good search, coffee.

One ring. Two. Three. Four. Voicemail. "Hello. You have reached the voicemail of Edward—" She ignored Rubald and Rutha, who were on her bed waiting for her when she got back. She carefully packed the food in, figuring that on horseback, she could make it last a few days at least. Then a new thought occurred to her, and she stood up straight.

"You're not going to let me take Stargazer, are you?"

Rubald shook his head sadly. She expected curtness from him, severity. Pity was something new. She hated it. "Don't pity me. I don't need it. Keep it for your king. He's about to die unless someone can talk some sense into him. I can't believe you just let him leave alone like that."

Something hardened behind Rubald's eyes, and he looked like he was about to speak. Then he stood up and quickly walked out, not looking back.

"Can I help you with anything?" Rutha asked, hands clasped, her face pinched and anxious.

"No, thank you."

"I'd go, but I know I'd be no help to you. An old woman whose hips are failing. I'd just slow you down, and you need speed if you need anything."

"I need a team. I want you to come."

Rutha shrugged with one shoulder. "I can't..."

Abbie let her pack slide to the ground. "All right, I have to say this." She cleared her throat. "Look at me, Rutha." Abbie waited for Rutha's eyes to find hers. "The way your husband treats you sometimes..." She paused. "The way he treats you would never be tolerated where I'm from. But more than that, I can't believe *you let him* treat you that way. That's what bothers me most. After all this time, you don't know your own worth. If he loves you, and I believe he does, he'd learn to handle your opinion when it matters."

Shock painted Rutha's face. Shock, but not dismay or sadness. Shock, but not regret or remorse. Rather, shock that slowly, slowly melted into something like resolve.

"You know, dear, when you are married a long time, it's not always so simple as you'd think. We have trust between us, but someone has to be in charge. I have learned to follow his lead and reaped the benefits of it. However, on this occasion, I find my heart at odds with his decision. I believe I will go with you."

Rutha helped Abbie lift her pack to her shoulders. "I'll saddle Carnival." Even with one horse, they could perhaps take the wagon as well. It would slow them down, but it would be nice to have shelter from the wind. Abbie hurried out into the hallway, intending to waste no time getting down to the stables. As she passed Rutha's room, she heard raised voices and paused.

"Why bring me, then?"

"As a support to me!" Rubald was shouting. "Someone to help along the way!"

"Someone to cook your food and wash your clothes, you mean."

"Yes!"

There was a tense silence.

"I love you, Rube, but I love Edward, too. He's my sovereign, but he might as well be my son. They put him in my arms too the day he was born. And the girl, she's got more guts than any of us. I won't let her leave alone. Foolish or no, husband or no. She's earned my loyalty as well. Suffering the way she does, I can't imagine..." She heard Rutha's voice catch, and a lump rose in her own throat.

"He forbade it, Rutha. I have my orders."

"Well, Rubald Jerrinson, I love you with all my heart, but his orders didn't extend to me. You'd be wrong to accept this order, anyway, and if you can just look past your own stubborn fear and pride, I think you'd see that, too."

Rubald's voice was rumbly. "His orders may not extend to you, but mine still do. You can't do this. Two women alone in the desert? You'll be eaten by some wild creature within a day."

"Any other time, I'd gladly comply. You're a good husband, and I have all the respect in the world for you. You've protected me all these years, fed and clothed me. Loved me when I didn't deserve it." She gave a shaky sigh. "But I can't obey you this time. It's too important. Now, will you help me with my pack?"

After a few moments of silence, Rutha came out, her face a thundercloud, straining as she dragged her pack behind her. The older woman's eyes met the younger's, and Abbie could see the hurricane of emotions swirling in them. She pulled Rutha into a strong embrace, and a gentle sob came bubbling out, as if her feelings had been squeezed to the top. After a moment, Abbie held her out by the shoulders and said, "I think you're brave, too, woman. I know that wasn't easy."

Rutha shook her head. "It'd be harder in the long run, knowing I did nothing to help Edward. Let's go. Time's wasting." Abbie helped Rutha quickly shoulder her pack, and they hurried down the hallway together.

"Just a moment!" Abbie knew before she turned that it wasn't Rubald's voice. She wasn't sure what he would do next, but she knew he wouldn't come around that quickly. The two women's mouths fell open as the Silicon King stalked toward them, dressed in his sailing uniform.

"Please allow me to see you safely to the border. I have a fleet of sand cruisers that I use when I travel, and I would like to help you on your way. I see now that you both have a deep resolve in this matter." He turned to Abbie. "It has occurred to me that there's more than one way to sacrifice for love."

Abbie nodded, not trusting her own voice. They both turned to follow Blair as a silent Rubald watched from his doorway, arms folded across his chest. Abbie pulled out her phone and texted Parker three letters:

*OMW.*

# CHAPTER THIRTY-EIGHT

TWO HOURS LATER, ABBIE and Blair met at the gangplank. Rutha's horse had been brought aboard one of the ten sand cruisers he'd mustered. "Cruisers" turned out to be modesty on his part; these were huge ships. She figured there must be a magical element to them as they floated above the sand, their canvas sails flapping in the wind.

"I have to go say goodbye to my horse," Abbie said, handing him her pack.

"He talks?"

Abbie nodded.

"Those are special. Take your time. We will make good progress—the wind is with us."

She trudged over to the stables through the sand. At least he'd be well cared for here with Blair. Maybe she could come back for him someday. As she approached the tall, open door, she could hear Star's voice.

"And then, out of nowhere, here comes this *huge* bear, like, the *biggest* bear you've *ever seen*."

One of the other horses nickered and whinnied.

"What do you think I did? I ran for my life! Thankfully, my girl held on very tightly. Oh, there she is now! Is it time to go?"

Abbie shook her head. "I'm afraid not, friend." She cleared her throat. "Listen, Stargazer, you've been a great help to me. I don't know what I would've done without you through all this, but now, I can't..." Her words felt choked out, and she looked away.

He walked through the horses crowded around him and nuzzled her shoulder with his soft nose. "You can't what, Abbie?"

"She can't wait to get you on her ship. We're sailing to the border, let's go." Rubald had appeared in the doorway, standing with feet spread and arms crossed.

"Oh, goody! I was sick of sand, anyway. I didn't want to say anything, but—"

"Now, beast."

"Touchy, touchy," Stargazer muttered as he passed Abbie and walked toward the doorway.

"Are you coming, too?" Abbie asked without turning around, not ready to see his thunderous expression again so soon.

"You haven't left me much choice, have you?" His voice was flinty. "Once again, you've thrown your royal weight around." He paused, and she turned to face him. "You asked me while we were still in Gardenia what my favorite proverb was, and I didn't answer you then."

"I remember."

"An excellent wife, who can find? She is far more precious than jewels." He cleared his throat, his voice now thick with emotion. "Blair can keep all his fancy food and desert aquaponics and jetted tubs. My Rutha is a far greater treasure. But my second favorite is 'A friend loves at all times, and a brother is born for adversity.'" He kicked at the straw on the floor of the barn, then lifted his eyes to her. "You were born for this. Perhaps not the way we thought, but as his friend, you ought to try to help him. As your friend, I ought to help you."

"Thank you, Rubald. I don't deserve it."

"Make no deals with Blair. Let him help if he wills it, but promise him nothing." He stiffened. "Let's go."

The noonday sun was baking the top of her head, and Abbie put on her hat as they boarded the cruisers. "Why are we taking all ten?"

Blair's eyes narrowed. "I haven't made it this far without a few tricks up my sleeve. We'll send them off in pairs to determine which path he took. After that, I understand that Lincoln's forces are partially made up of many Grathan mercenaries, are they not?" Abbie nodded. "They do not call me the Silicon King for nothing. I will call them home."

"What if they won't come?"

He glanced down at her from where he was scanning the horizon. "Then I will make their lives a living Jersey. Parker's still my godson, whether he likes it or not."

"What about Lincoln? Isn't he your godson, too?"

"Lincoln can go jump off a cliff for what he has done to Ignatius."

Blair stalked up to the forecastle deck, and she followed him. If she hadn't been so nervous, Abbie would've really enjoyed being on the cruiser. Whipping along over the sand, despite brilliant blue sky above them, she watched the horizon for a black man on a horse and nothing else. She couldn't eat. After a while, Rutha convinced her to let the spotters do their jobs and the two women went below decks. Abbie lay down, but the motion of the ship was getting to her stomach. She closed her eyes. That was not better. Rutha left for a few minutes and came back with a novel...a romance novel.

"I borrowed it. I hadn't read this one yet. I was going to send it back with him, but..."

Abbie gave her half a smile and accepted the book gratefully.

When she woke up, they were stopped.

"What's happening? Where's Parker?"

"They didn't find him, sister." Rutha sat on the edge of her bed. Had she been there watching her sleep the whole time? Abbie got up too quickly and had to steady herself on Rutha's shoulder. Her head was pounding, her hands were cold. *Not now, body, we don't have time for this.* She mounted the stairs and headed straight for Blair.

"Status."

Despite the situation, he grinned and met her with a mocking salute. "Highness, we have reached the southern border, commonly called the Crossroads, where Trella, Attaamy, and Gratha meet. My cruisers cannot cross the rivers; they do not exist within the Veil. We need a way to communicate to the mercenaries that I am here for them."

"What do you suggest, sky writing?"

Blair shrugged, as if this were not entirely out of the question.

"Why didn't we find him?" Her voice was smaller than she intended, but it matched her mood.

"He must have called one of his commanders to come and pick him in a dirigible or ship. That is all we can surmise. He could not have made it to the border that quickly without help."

"Unless..." Her throat tightened.

"No, we are not going to entertain that thought yet. We would have found his horse if something unfortunate had happened to him."

Abbie sighed, massaging her temples. "Okay, then let's focus on solvable problems. How do we contact the mercenaries? Could we send me in as an emissary?"

"That is too dangerous. You'd be killed almost immediately. They're not good listeners. And Edward will ask why we did nothing to stop you."

"Parker knows me well enough to know I'm difficult to contain."

She pulled out her phone to text Parker, then stopped. He hadn't texted back the first ten times she'd tried; why would he text back now? *But I know who does want to talk to me...*

"What if I didn't go directly to the mercenaries? What if I went to the Warlord instead?"

Blair's head started shaking before she'd even finished her thought. "You cannot. He wants to bargain with your life."

"Exactly. He wants me alive. I'm in no danger in his hands."

Blair began to laugh, softly at first, then building the longer he considered her words.

"Sweet princess, you have no idea what you are saying."

"I'm not sweet."

"You are compared to him. So is an Imaharan snow tiger." *Fishguts, there were tigers in the mountains they'd crossed? No one mentioned that at the time.*

"All I need is leverage. He doesn't know my engagement is off."

"He can smell lies. His magic is untamed, but effective."

"That would matter if you didn't have the leverage I need."

His eyes narrowed. "You want a favor from me?" The Silicon King took a step forward, his boots shuffling against the boards of the cruiser. "Do you know what that means here?" Rubald's words in the barn echoed in her mind, but Abbie brushed them away. Parker needed this. He had a shot at winning against Lincoln if the mercenaries retreated.

She swallowed. "Yes, I want a favor. Do they know about your secret identity?"

"Yes. Everyone around here knows about it. They're big fans, actually, especially since I've had all my works from the third book on translated. Their wives were very..." he winked, "grateful."

"And in turn, I suspect the mercenaries were grateful as well."

"Anthropologists say the birth rate shot up at an unprecedented rate. They called it the Blake Effect. I was flattered." He crossed his arms. "What does that have to do with recalling the mercenaries?"

"Everything." Abbie paced as she talked. "The way I see it, you have an army of fans that we need to put to good use. If we can put pressure on them to retreat by threatening to withhold future translations..."

He barked out a laugh. "This is madness." Blair paused, looking at the deck. "But it might work." He looked her up and down. "The Warlord does have a weakness for redheads."

She glanced toward Rubald and Rutha, who were talking nearby, oblivious, and said, "Set it up...quietly."

# CHAPTER THIRTY-NINE

BLAIR PULLED OUT HIS phone and walked away to make the call, veering away from the Jerrinsons, his voice low, carried away by the wind. Abbie gazed out over the border, trying to see what was going on, but it was all too far away.

She pulled out her phone and stared at it. *Would I answer if I were him?* She put it away again. *What if it wasn't working in the Unveiled, though, and now it is? What if he didn't get my calls before?* She took it out again and unlocked it. No new messages, no missed calls. *What if my phone isn't working? Maybe he did call me back, and I just didn't get it?* Lying to herself was unsatisfying; he hadn't called back. He wasn't going to. She'd save her next call for when she had real news to report.

Blair came to the rail at her side. "He's on his way." He looked slightly surprised at this fact.

"How long?"

"He just said 'soon.'" Blair muttered something to one of his aids, who called something in a language unknown to Abbie to the ships on either side of them, and men began to line up along the railings. They had arrows notched to their bows. They had crossbows, bolts in place. They had knives and machetes. They were literally armed to the teeth; there was not an open place on their bodies that didn't have some sort of weapon strapped to it.

Naturally, this caught Rubald's attention. "Sister, what's happening?" She wiped the sweat off her brow, thinking that she was stupid to be standing in the sun all this time.

"I called a meeting."

Rubald paled. "With whom, may I ask?"

She turned to look into his eyes, and he knew.

"Oh, you can't be serious." He turned to Blair, who gave a single nod. He spun back to face Abbie. "What's the one thing I said? What's the one thing I asked of you?"

She lifted her chin but didn't answer.

"*Abelia,*" he roared, "favors in the Unveiled are *binding.* Whatever he asks of you, you'll be obligated to give him, in one form or another, if you can't dissuade him from asking. Why can't you ever—"

"He is here," Blair interjected.

"...listen." Rube's voice dropped to a whisper as his eyes snapped to the horizon. Abbie's mouth dropped open.

The Warlord of Gratha was coming, and he was riding a nightstallion, a contingent of fifty soldiers behind him, all on nightstallions as well, followed above by a thunderstorm, lightning scorching the ground perilously close to his men.

He stopped thirty feet from their ship, and she rubbed her eyes. As she approached on foot, Blair and Rubald both trailing her, she noticed immediately that he looked like he was younger than her, but that wasn't possible—he'd ruled here for close to thirty years. His heavily freckled face was well-proportioned, his skin lighter than Parker's or Blair's, his head shaved clean. His feet hit the ground, and the wind suddenly died, the desert sounds stilled, even his feet on the sand seemed quieter than average. He spoke Common Tongue without any discernable accent.

"Most people who request an audience with me have the sense to bow."

"The way I see it, you should be here to thank me." Abbie heard a rumble of nervous muttering behind her, but she held the Warlord's gaze, refusing to waver.

He cocked his head, amused. "And why's that?"

"I saved you a million-dollar reward by not getting caught."

"I'm sure I have no idea what you're talking about."

"What shall I call you?"

"Warlord is fine."

"You don't have a true name?"

"My true name is too old for your young tongue."

Abbie put on a show of being unimpressed. "Fine. Warlord, here's the situation: recall your mercenaries."

He pulled out a knife from the arsenal hanging from his belt, and Abbie gave Rubald the hold signal.

"I see your companions have not told you how things are here. They are not my mercenaries. They are Gratha's mercenaries. And if she wants them back, she will recall them herself."

"Oh, she will, when she learns what our friend Nancy Blake has planned if the mercenaries don't walk away now: no more translations."

The Warlord considered her words, twirling the knife slowly in one long-fingered hand. "What would withdrawing from an active conflict do to their reputation, though?

Nations will hesitate to agree to upfront payment if they turn their backs on the First Son now."

"Oh, I see. No refund policy, huh? Well, what are they going to read on those long, cold nights away from their wives if they stay? Who's going to bear the brunt of their anger when they learn who's responsible for taking away their favorite pastime? I can't see that going well for you."

He strolled closer, still spinning the slender knife, and she mentally willed Rubald to play it cool. The Warlord leaned close enough to whisper in her ear. "You really are an interesting princess, Abelia."

Against her will, she shivered. "Ex-princess."

He frowned slightly. "That's...not a real thing."

"It is now."

A large, dark cloud appeared five feet above her head, startling her and Rubald both. "A bit of shade for our delicate flower. Your rash will be worse the longer you're out here, won't it?" He smiled, but it was without warmth. "You know, if you had no contract, if you were well, I would make a bid for you." She swiped at her face to cover a snort at his patronizing confession, trying hard not to think about how he'd gotten all this information about her. "Your mother was an impressive leader, and I'm in the market for a bride, as you may have heard," he continued.

"No, I hadn't. I'm off the market anyway. Have been for nine years."

"Are you truly, though?" He pulled back to look into her eyes, and something flickered in his own, a cruel flash that made her stomach drop and her knees press together instinctively.

"Yes, I am."

"If I whisked you off to my palace right now, who'd come looking? Who'd care?" He drew a line down her cheek with the sharp tip of the knife, and she felt a drop of blood roll down her face. She wasn't sure what hurt more: the wound or his words.

She heard Blair's men drawing weapons from their sheaths behind her and Rubald's grunt of barely suppressed rage, but she once again held up her hand to stop them.

"He didn't even kiss you goodbye, did he? Just disappeared into the night. Walked right out of your life without looking back." Abbie clenched her fists to keep from slapping him.

"I'm sure I don't know what you're talking about."

"I could heal you, you know. I have the power. I've done it for others. It would be..." he cocked his head again as he took in her body from head to toe, "a unique challenge." She tried to take a deep breath, but the still air was choking her, stifling. He gave a casual shrug, as if to say, "take it or leave it, princess."

*This is just a game to him, a diversion,* she realized. *He doesn't really care either way.* She took a deep breath and let it out, steeling herself. *All right, Mr. Warlord, if it's a game you want, let's play.*

"Warlord, we have an expression where I come from: What good is it to gain the whole world and forfeit your soul?"

They stared at each other in silence for long, tense moments. He didn't blink. Neither did she, despite her stinging eyes.

Finally, the Warlord stepped out of her personal space to see her better. "I will call them back...if you beg me."

Abbie hardened her stare, and his eyes gleamed in challenge. Her lips twitched, and she struggled to hold back the acerbic curses that begged to blast into the still air like a winter storm. She glanced at Rubald and Blair, both of whom gave her a nod; apparently, they approved. *Perfect.*

"Warlord, would you please recall—"

"On your hands and knees, Abelia," he corrected quietly, and his men chuckled.

Abbie swallowed hard, her stomach churning. *Of all the debasing, degrading, disgusting, unreasonable, uncouth—*

"Oh, yes," he murmured, "I can just imagine what you'd like to say to me right now. Let it out. Just let those curses fly, and let's be done with this farce. Your young princeling is not worth it."

And just like that, Abbie suddenly saw laid out before her all the ways Parker had sacrificed his pride in the last few weeks. *Cutting his hair. The endless phone calls, unanswered. Trudging across Imahara in the snow. Sleeping on the ground. Calmly discussing the contract when he had every right to simply demand that she keep her promise to obey it. Having all his decisions questioned by her. Staying awake to keep watch while she slept. Meeting her criticisms and barbs and belittlings with his unique mix of calm debate and flirtatious challenge.*

*Oh, Parker.*

She fell to her knees in the deep sand, the weight of Parker's love and sacrifice making it suddenly easy. She lifted her eyes to the Warlord's as she stretched out her arms in front of him, pressing her palms into the sand, giving him exactly what he wanted.

"Exalted Warlord, I need your help. I beg you for it. I am less than nothing, unworthy to even bow in your presence. Yet if you will, please grant my request and remove your mercenaries from this fight." He stared down at her, the delight plain on his face...but delight wasn't agreement. She waited, not moving until he sheathed his knife with a gusty sigh.

"Request granted." He offered her a hand up, which she ignored.

"How soon?"

"All in due time, princess."

"Ex-princess. How soon?"

He chuckled. "Have a pleasant journey, and I'll see you soon."

"I doubt that."

"Then I'll enjoy proving you wrong at our next meeting."

Abbie merely inclined her head at this. "I hope you and your mercenary friends enjoy the next installment of *The Duchess's Dalliance*, Warlord."

# CHAPTER FORTY

THE AIRSHIP LANDED just north of the front. Parker disembarked quickly and found his friends waiting. They saluted quickly for appearances, and he returned it. Parker tossed his phone to Saint.

"Figure out how to block her number on this thing, will you?"

The phone started to ring and before Parker could stop him, Saint answered it.

"Edward's phone."

He listened.

"No, ma'am, that was Lieutenant James, I'm Lieutenant Saint. Yes, ma'am, he is a cheeky bastard." The men chuckled, and it galled. They shouldn't be enjoying talking to her when he couldn't. Wouldn't.

"Just hang up," he growled. The three other men glared at him reproachfully.

"Yes, ma'am. I'll tell him. Thank you, ma'am." He started to hang up, then caught Parker's eye. "Oh, one more thing, ma'am: let me give you my number in case you need to get a message to us. You probably won't get him on this number for a while...no, ma'am, he asked me to block—"

"Give me the phone." Parker held out his hand. He didn't wait to hear her voice before he launched into his speech. He laced his own words with a steel resolve. "Abelia,

278

please don't call me. Do you understand? Don't call me. Don't text me. I don't wish to speak with you." He hung up and handed it back to Saint. "I said block her," Parker said through gritted teeth. His head was pounding as he walked away, and he headed to the mess for some water; he hadn't brought enough with him as he'd crossed the desert, and he'd gotten dehydrated. If he went to sleep now, it'd just be worse when he woke up.

Saint was behind him now, jogging to catch up. "Sir, I know you don't want to hear this, but you should."

"Not now." The deep grief that he'd carried across the sand had melted to molten anger, threatening to erupt all over whoever happened to be nearest. Saint was in the blast zone, but at least he seemed to know it. There were always a few who wouldn't evacuate.

"The Silicon King took her to the border in his ships. She successfully negotiated calling back the mercenaries with the Warlord-in-Chief. They should be leaving soon."

Parker whirled. *What?* So that's what she'd meant by *OMW*.

"I have no idea how, but she convinced them both to help. Sir, if we attack the contingent from Op'ho'lonia, they'll have no chance to call for reinforcements. We could drive them back—all the way back."

"Get Gasper in here."

"Yes, sir." Saint handed him his phone. "Good to have you back, sir. And I'm sorry."

"For answering her call?"

"That it didn't work out with—"

"Stop." He wouldn't listen to her name on another's lips. He knew it was petty and jealous. But if she was determined to be alone, to make her own way, then it was all he had left.

"Are you all right, mate?" Saint asked quietly, dropping the military formalities.

Parker nodded, softened. "Of course. Get Gasper in here, will you?"

Saint nodded once, then backed out of the tent as if he didn't dare turn his back to Parker in his current mood. Parker threw back the water like shots, and it sat heavy in his stomach. He thought he might throw up. His head spun, and he braced himself against a long table. So tired.

Gasper came blasting in with all the advisors in tow, and the next hour was all strategy sessions, followed by briefings he'd missed while he was with Abbie. The weather wasn't conducive to an offensive, but a high percentage of the mercenaries were already leaving. Everyone was attributing the move to involve Blair to Parker, not Abbie, and his attempts to correct them were seen as false modesty. Despite the rain, he decided to go ahead and have his forces cross the river tonight, before Lincoln could rally more troops from Trella. Between the ground forces and the fleet, they had a good chance at victory.

"Sir," Gasper said under the conversation, "you should get some rest."

"I'm fine."

"Just get a few hours. We'll wake you." Gasper put a fatherly hand on Parker's shoulder, and it nearly knocked him over.

Parker nodded, barely able to keep his eyes open. He trudged across the camp, avoiding eye contact, the rain just starting to pepper the canvas tents. He fell into bed, not bothering to kick off his boots. Suddenly, tears came with the pounding of the rain, and he fell asleep between one exhausted sob and the next.

GASPER LIED. DAY WAS dawning when Parker opened his eyes and stretched, and he charged out of the tent to find his right-hand man, the random soldier standing watch outside his tent hurrying after him.

"Status," he barked at the collection of officers in the mess, all bent over maps. They threw him a salute that he didn't bother to return.

"Sir, the offensive was a huge success. Without the Grathan mercenaries, the Op'ho'lonian forces panicked and beat a hasty retreat across the border of Attaamy. Thanks to the darkness, Trella didn't realize we were on the move until it was too late; we took out five of their ships before they even returned fire. Three got away, and six we damaged beyond repair."

"Casualties?"

"Our losses are estimated at fifty."

"That few?"

"Your plan was a good one, sir. We owe it all to you. Knowing that the mercenaries would abandon Lincoln like that, knowing how to manipulate them—it made all the difference."

Parker nodded, tired of correcting them.

"Assemble a strike force to find my brother and arrest him immediately."

General Tybald piped up. "Hear, hear."

The room cascaded into a cacophony of overlapping voices, and Parker held up a hand.

Lieutenant Paris cleared her throat. "Sir, Op'ho'lonia may not cooperate..."

He leaned forward, placing his hands on the table. "I don't give a damn what Op'ho'lonia will or won't do. It's time to shut this down, once and for all." He drew himself up. "This is the only way to end this. With my impending marriage now on hold indefinitely, there's no other way to ensure peace. I'm tired of dancing around my brother's power-hungry machinations. I'm tired of politics. This conflict cannot reach our shores. It will not."

Parker thought Gasper was going to burst his buttons he looked so proud.

"Yes, sir."

"I want an update on candidates in an hour."

An hour; that was probably long enough to shower and eat...he rubbed his chin, feeling his need for a shave. Maybe he'd let it grow. There was no one to impress anymore anyway.

Lieutenant James fell into step with him.

"Sir."

"James."

"Send us."

Parker shook his head. "No way."

"We'll find him. You can trust us."

The prince stopped, his arms crossed at his chest. "It's not about trust. I can't afford to lose you."

"You won't. Simonson, Saint, and I talked it over. We want this assignment. Let us do this for you, sir. You won't regret it."

"No." His phone rang, and they exchanged a look. "It's Rhodie. Why is she calling me?" He focused a glare on James. "You wouldn't know anything about this, would you?" His friend shrugged benignly.

Parker answered with a smile. "Dr. Broward."

He heard her smiling back. "Second Brother. A little birdie told me you were back at the front." He liked how she twisted Second Son into something kinder.

"That's correct."

"Are things going well?"

"Yes. As much as things like this can go well."

James began to edge away, but Parker caught him by the arm, shaking his head.

"Good, good. Everyone's really missing you."

"Everyone at home?"

"Yes, we'd like a video call sooner rather than later, please. How's Abbie?"

Parker swallowed hard. "I couldn't say. We've parted ways...but something tells me that's not news to you. In fact, I've got your co-conspirator here by the arm. He'll be drawing kitchen duty in the near future."

"No, no, don't punish him, it's all my doing. We'd heard so little from you, so I pumped him for information. He told me you were a bit broken up about it all. I just called to lend my support."

"Well, thank you." Parker glared at James, who smiled like a fox. When it came to Rhodie, few men could say no, and Arron was especially susceptible since he'd had a huge crush on her since the day they'd met.

"I'm sorry," he said under his breath. "She makes me weak. Don't put me on dull duty, sir, send us to Op'ho'lonia."

"What was that?"

"Nothing."

"Not nothing, little brother. What was that about sending Arron south?"

"Nothing, stop worrying, you're as bad as Mum. Give everyone my love."

"Parker?"

"Rhodie?"

"All kidding aside, it's okay to not be okay. I'm here for you—we're all here for you. We love you, you know. However it all turns out. You're doing great. We know you did your best with Abbie. Brevsporan women are the worst."

He wanted to make a joke, but he could hear the genuine concern in her voice. "Thank you, Dr. Broward."

"Okay, I'm off."

"Bye." Parker let go of Arron's arm and punched it, but not too hard.

"Ouch!"

"You're a dunce, and a wimp." It wasn't true; Arron was one of the most intelligent people he knew, even though he hid it behind stupid jokes most of the time.

"What was that for?"

"That was for taking my sister's call."

"What, you expect me to send a gorgeous doctor-slash-princess to voicemail? Not likely."

He punched him again and he yelped. "And that was for saying she makes you weak. Be a man for Woz's sake."

"This doesn't feel like a fair fight, sir."

"Man up, James. You brought this on yourself. Go talk to your C.O. if you want Op'ho'lonia." The prince sighed at his grinning friend's back as he turned to go find his commanding officer. At least he hadn't talked to his mom.

# CHAPTER FORTY-ONE

BLAIR HAD DROPPED HER off up north toward Brevspor. In her mind, Abbie felt the stream of foreignness begin to abate, and just as it did, a new stream took over. This was home, or at least it was supposed to be. Many things were familiar—it was especially soothing to understand the language of people around her with ease. The paranoia she'd lived with for the last month that she was being talked about or found out began to ebb away, just as a new one surfaced. She had no idea what she was doing.

At the border, the kiosk asked for her R.E.A.L. Identity Card; she didn't have one, and they scrambled to find an officer to help her. All the nonsense they'd dealt with in Trella was abated by a simple shot of air from her nose into the waiting tube: In the surprise of the century, she did not have Squealing Nose Malady. The money they changed for her had her father's portrait on it instead of her mother's, the bills crisp and the coins shiny. Rubald and Rutha were watching her closely, asking a lot of questions, but she didn't hear most of them.

She wasn't home. She'd never intended to come back here, and now that she had, it wasn't hers anymore. She kept picturing her little flat in Gardenia City, her thrift store furniture, her plants, her photos, the tired staircase up to her door. Hers.

She passed an ad for football, and her mind flitted to Parker. He would've said something funny about that nose tube. *His quiet, steady presence in the midst of all this turmoil would've been so...*how did she want to finish that sentence? He felt strangely necessary now, this person she'd pushed away. Even his pompous vocabulary would've given her comfort going through customs. He probably could've worked in "rudimentary" or even "bothersome" easily.

"We'll leave you here, then." Rutha lifted her voice above the steady hum of conversation around her.

"You're leaving? You're not coming to the palace?"

Rubald shrugged with one shoulder. "You've seen one, you've seen them all."

"But I'm sure my father wants to thank you himself for all you've done for us."

"Thank us?" Rubald scoffed. "Why? We failed."

"You got me here safely, in time to say goodbye. Didn't you say yourself that that was your primary objective? I'm sure he doesn't see that as a failure."

"You're in good hands now, dear," Rutha said when Rube didn't answer. "You don't need us tagging along. Your people will ensure that you get to the palace."

In a moment of impulsive affection, Abbie held her arms out to Rubald for a hug. His crossed arms fell, his shoulders relaxed, and he pulled her into the tightest hug she'd ever had.

"If you are a failure," she whispered to him, "it is entirely my fault. Thank you for bringing me here. You've fulfilled your mission." Rubald coughed and cleared his throat, then patted her back hard and released her. He sniffed, looking away, turning to gather up their backpacks.

Rutha was standing playfully akimbo. "Don't think you can get away that easy. You can't give him one and not me. I deserve it more." They both laughed through tears and Rutha embraced her with such tenderness that Abbie choked back a sob.

"You've given me so much. Much more than you know. Thank you."

Rutha said nothing, but nodded and gave her a wobbly smile. Abbie stepped back, watching them gather their things and walk back toward the check-in gates.

"Your Highness, this area is not secure. At your pleasure, let's move toward the carriages." She turned and was quickly ushered toward the doors and out onto the street, where the traditional carriage was waiting for her, including the dogs.

THE SPEED OF LIFE INSIDE the Veil—that was a surprise. She knew it shouldn't be since she'd only spent a month outside it, but somehow, trains seemed bullet-fast compared to Stargazer. And it wasn't just the speed of the transportation—the conversations, the fruit-buying, the street-crossing, the tax-paying: it was all so damned efficient. There was no time to talk to anyone. The expectation of speed and fluidity everywhere they went left her feeling even more dizzyingly lonely.

Pulling up to the palace gates, their carriage was let through without question or delay. A crowd of about 100 people had gathered; how they'd known she was coming, she couldn't fathom. She leaned away from the windows to avoid cameras, and suddenly, she was thirteen years old again, driving home from her sisters' funeral, the media's fickle attention now suddenly latched onto her as she tried to hide her tear-stained face.

The palace itself hadn't changed. They were flying her colors on the north turret, but other than that, it looked exactly the same from the outside. Abbie wanted to be aloof about the whole thing, but the memories that kept flooding back were warming her heart like cocoa by the fire. That's the window they'd broken when Eliana tried to show them how to surf down the stairs on a sled. That's the waving balcony where they'd done public greetings; one time, Allegra had drawn mustaches on all the big girls and they couldn't be scrubbed off in time, so they'd had to wear makeup over them, and Abbie had bawled the whole time because she didn't get any. It couldn't be heard over the crowd, but her mother had still been furious with all of them. Abbie tried not to think how furious her mother would be with her now.

As soon as the carriage doors opened, Abbie gasped. Her father's personal valet, Warner, was standing there. He was as close to a grin as she'd ever seen him, which is to say he was sporting a small smile despite an overall somber demeanor. She'd never seen this guy break in the sixteen years she'd spent here, and it wasn't that it hadn't been tried—half of the dinnertime antics they'd been spanked for had been in pursuit of just one snicker from Warner.

Next to him stood her mother's former private secretary, Mrs. Braun, who was still serious as a heart attack. Unlike Warner, who privately played jokes on the kids—albeit with a straight face—Mrs. Braun was the hammer, and she left nothing but bits and pieces in her path when she rolled through. No infraction, however minor, from unmade beds to cookies pinched from the kitchen to a tongue stuck out at a sister's back, was ever left unreported to Her Majesty. Abbie had met her children once, and they were shy, wispy things that looked like a stiff breeze might knock them over, shivering and shaking like birches. It was no wonder.

She didn't know why she'd assumed they'd retired, but as Warner helped her from the carriage, she couldn't help but return his small smile with a super-sized one of her own.

"Good afternoon, Your Highness, welcome home. Your father is waiting for you in his study," Mrs. Braun said, and just the tone of her voice made Abbie cringe inwardly. The crispness. The utter deference. She could see why her mother had liked it, but she wasn't her mother. Never had been. It seemed neither staff member was willing to acknowledge that a significant amount of time had passed since her disappearance, so Abbie played along.

"Thank you, Mrs. Braun. Warner, will you walk with me?"

"Certainly, Highness."

As soon as they were out of earshot and visual range of Mrs. Braun, Abbie took Warner's arm, and the older man covered her hand with his protectively.

"How is he?"

"He's very ill, Highness. He won't last much longer. You came just in time. How was your trip?"

"Our journey was complicated and long. I'm sure you'll hear the details in due time, and I'd enjoy hearing about your children and your wife..." Abbie trailed off as she watched him react to her last statement.

"My dear Petra passed away two years ago. Breast cancer."

Abbie put a hand on her chest. "I'm so sorry."

Warner patted her hand but said nothing as they arrived at the doors to the study.

"I'll announce you." He cleared his throat. "Her Majesty, Abelia Olivia Jayne Venenza Ribaldi Porchenzii, rightful heiress to the throne. Long may she reign."

Abbie was shaking. She couldn't see into the study but she knew it by heart: the deep-pile crimson carpeting, the fireplace lit, his high wingback chair in the corner by the front window. Everything would be just as she'd left it. Except for her father, who was in the process of dying. The man she left five years earlier would've sprung from his seat to scoop her up in a tight embrace and kiss the top of her head. The gaunt man who sat before her could barely raise his eyes from his book and smile. Abbie's trembling hand flew to her mouth. His once-broad shoulders seemed bony and bent like a bow, and his sunken chest was slow to draw in breath.

"They didn't tell me *you* were coming." He held out a hand to her from his overstuffed leather chair by the fire. She crossed to him quickly and held him gently as Warner brought her a chair.

"Don't blame Warner, they didn't know until I'd already arrived at the border crossing. They accommodated me beautifully." Good Woz, where was this sweet, refined voice coming from? Abbie wanted to slap herself back into normalcy.

"You sound so regal," her father teased, and Abbie relaxed. "You must have been practicing on the journey for your new role." Abbie tensed, and she could feel the sweat gathering on her forehead.

*Best to just tell him.* She braced herself. "Unfortunately, Dad, that's not why I'm here. I just came to say goodbye and make peace."

Her father merely continued to regard her with steady patience. Abbie shook her head; there was no point in putting off the truth.

"I'm sorry, Dad." Tears began to fall, and for the millionth time she was so glad she rarely wore mascara. She stared hard at the crimson carpet. "I can't take the throne. I know you wanted me to fix things here, and I tried, I wanted to help, but I just can't. I'm so sorry to disappoint you, I wish there was another way, but I—"

"Disappoint me?" His hand covered hers, and she looked up nervously.

"You're my daughter, Abelia. You're *mine*. And we both tend to jump into things first and think later, and we're stubborn, and we love too deep. I know you would've done this if you could. You'd have done it out of sheer love for me, if you could. But you couldn't. So the only thing that disappoints me is that we missed out on the last years of my life together, just because you were afraid to tell me the truth."

If she thought she was crying hard before, it was nothing compared to what came then. *How could I think that he'd ever agree to disown me? How did I forget who he was so completely?* She couldn't tell what were tears and what was snot and in what direction it was all going. It was most unladylike, which pleased some part of her immensely.

"Your brother wants to see you."

Abbie chuckled as she wiped her face. "That's a lie, and not a very good one."

Her father shrugged his bony shoulders and smiled sadly. "Okay, so it's a lie. He's mad as Jersey. He's hurt that they don't want him. More than likely, they'll vote in a new family, and then he'll have time to think and heal and come to his senses."

She sighed. "I'm sorry I broke our dynasty." Her father's large laughter turned quickly into a hacking cough, and he waved away the physicians who hurried toward him from the corner of the room where they'd been hovering.

"How did you leave things with Edward?" he asked when he'd recovered.

Abbie looked out the window. "I told him I'd never marry him, but I didn't mean it. I mean, I did mean it—I meant I can't rule a country with him, and there's a lot of reasons for that. But I didn't mean to hurt him, and I did. I...I screwed things up."

Her father nodded—a listening gesture, not agreement. "What will you do now?"

She heaved a shuddering sigh. "Well, he ought to marry Crescena or someone else. Really, anyone else..."

He leaned forward, his voice low and kind. "I didn't ask what he would do, dearest. I asked what you will do."

"Go back to my life. My other life, the one I built in Gardenia. Hopefully I still have a job."

"Can't you speak with him? Make things right, just for your own peace of mind?"

Abbie looked away before answering. "I don't know what to say, Dad."

"You don't think he'll marry someone else?"

She shrugged. "He says he won't...You know how he is about promises..." She felt so stupid. So stupid sitting here with her dad, after all this time, who clearly had bigger things to think about since she wasn't going to fix their queendom, going on and on about her personal problems. It was just what she needed, but it felt selfish.

"Yes, I've known Edward—Parker—a long time, and I know integrity is very important to him. Did you know I've been mentoring him?"

"Yes, he mentioned that. Talked about you at length. We had a lot of time to kill on the road."

Paul nodded. "In all that time, I've never known him to lie to me. Even when he had the opportunity. Even when I couldn't have known. He always, always told me the truth, even at the expense of his pride or his reputation. So if he tells you something, I'd believe him."

Abbie massaged her temples. "Why did you choose him for me, anyway?"

The old man burst out laughing again, and Abbie jumped.

"I didn't choose him, silly goose."

"Mother, then."

"Mother didn't choose him, either."

"Sorry, Dad, if this is a joke, I'm not getting it."

"Abelia, every summer you came home from Orangiers, all we heard about for the next nine months was Edward. Edward said bats aren't mammals so it must be true and Edward said no one knows how many stars there are, but we got ten million when we counted and can I have swimming lessons instead of croquet lessons so I can beat Edward across the lake next year? Your mother wanted Lincoln for you, but we could see it wasn't going to work, a fact I've thanked Woz for more times than I can count of late." He reached out and took her hand. "Abbie, you'd already chosen each other. Trying to keep you apart would've been futility, not to mention cruelty." He looked into her eyes. "Take that for what it's worth."

Abbie withdrew her hand gently. "That...that can't be true. Mother always got her way."

He chuckled. "Not always. Seldom, in fact, when it came to you. She spent many nights fretting over your future, and then once you left..."

"I know, I broke her heart."

"No, dearest—she just realized how wrong she'd been, but she had too much pride to tell you so." Her father seemed winded, his breathing becoming labored. "Warner?"

"Yes, Your Majesty?"

"I'd like to lie down now." He turned to Abbie. "We'll talk more later, all right?"

"Of course, Dad." She kissed him gently on the cheek, and she saw tears gathering in his eyes as they wheeled him out of the study.

# CHAPTER FORTY-TWO

ABBIE WAS UNPACKING when Kurt came in. No one announced him; it shouldn't have surprised her as men were never announced in Brevspor, but it somehow now felt wrong. She turned to find him leaning against her door frame, arms crossed, staring. She jumped, then scowled.

"You startled me. Say hello, for Woz's sake." Abbie crossed to him and gave a quick curtsy before offering him a friendly kiss on the cheek.

"You don't have to curtsy. You're the heir." The stench of his bitterness filled the small room.

"Can't you hug me before we start arguing?"

A tight smile appeared on his face, and he gave her a brief embrace. To say that he looked tense was like saying an elephant is decent-sized. She stood back, arms crossed, and he went back to his preferred station by the door, as if he'd need to make a quick getaway...or maybe prevent her from making one.

"I'm here to testify and say goodbye. Nothing more. But I'd like it if we could be a bit closer going forward. You'll likely need my help if things go your way."

"Why would you help me? You don't care."

Her eyes narrowed. "What, exactly, don't I care about?"

He shrugged with one shoulder as he drawled, "Me. Brevspor. Anyone but yourself."

"I came here to help you, not be attacked. I left because I was sick and no one would believe or help me. So I helped myself. I stood up for myself, which is more than I ever saw you do with her."

He surged forward, pointing. "I've had to stand up for myself every damn day since you left, trying to prove why I was good enough to stand in your high-heeled shoes, and it's never been enough. Never. Just because I'm not a woman."

His bright blue eyes flashed with pain, and Abbie knew she should feel sorry for him, but it wasn't in her. After the last month traveling through some of the poorer parts of the Unveiled, her sympathy tank for spoiled royals was running close to empty.

"Oh, poor baby. Isn't your life hard? Living here in luxury, the world open to you, except the one highly exclusive career path you've chosen? What a tragedy."

He stood up straighter. "Someone had to step up. Why shouldn't it be me? Who's better suited?"

"No one's better suited, but Kurt—they don't want you. They want me."

"That's why I need you to get onto that podium tomorrow and tell them there's no way that's going to happen and endorse my claim."

"I said I would, didn't I?"

"Just making sure there's no surprises. Edward says you're still a wild card."

At the mention of his name, she paused her unpacking and tears pricked, hot and unexpected, at her eyes.

*Don't cry in front of a male.*

Oh, her mother's ghost was so much louder here. Abbie sniffed haughtily and stared him down.

"Well, it's over with him, so don't worry too much about his opinion. As soon as I do this for you, I'm gone, and you'll never have to deal with me again."

"Good."

"Good? I'm breaking my contract, and you just say, 'good'?"

"I meant good that you'll be gone again. We don't need you."

"Woz, your insecurity is heartbreaking, Kurt. Seriously."

"Screw you."

"No, thanks. We're related. That'd be weird."

"Shut up."

"You shut up."

He blew out an angry breath and pulled two envelopes out of his coat. "These are for you. Read the briefs for my claim hearing first, then you can read the letter from Mother."

Her heartrate sped up. "What letter?"

"Before she died, she wrote everyone a letter; we didn't know where to send yours."

"Not interested. You can take it with you."

"Burn it yourself, I don't work for you."

"Goodbye, Kurt."

"One o'clock tomorrow at the State House."

She pushed him out and closed the door.

THE HEARING WAS UNUSUALLY well-attended due to her presence. She'd chosen her own outfit, avoiding the pantsuit the staff had laid out for her in lieu of a knee-length navy blue pencil skirt and a white blouse: she could at least wear their colors, even if she couldn't wear their crown. She let the staff do her hair, perhaps lulled into it as normal by Rutha. *Rutha.* She hoped they'd made it home okay. Maybe she'd text them later. Though the staff did an excellent job, she'd have exchanged their boring upswept bun for one of Rutha's elaborate gathered braids down the back of her head, if only for the calming conversation that always went with it.

She'd rehearsed Kurt's talking points the previous evening after dinner with him and her father. They'd eaten outside, enjoying the spring breeze; the staff had prepared a meal that rivaled their Christmas feasts, and she and Kurt had tried to keep things civil until her father laughed at them. Then they argued like old times, and he seemed to relax. He'd closed his eyes.

"What are you listening to, Dad?"

"My kids fighting. Evening birdsong. The river. The breeze in the pines. All as it should be."

She'd tried to share a smirk with Kurt, but he didn't return it. It couldn't have been easy for him, watching both his parents die, alone. She swallowed her guilt with her chocolate peanut butter pie.

They finally called her name. "Her Royal Highness, Abelia Olivia Jayne Venenza Ribaldi Porchenzii, rightful heiress to the throne. Long may she reign."

She cleared her throat and the room fell silent. Such attentiveness, such respect, even after all these years away. Hopefully it would make them more open to what she had to say.

"Gentlemen and ladies, I come before you today, not as your heir, but as a sister. As many of you know, I abdicated my role in this government long ago, despite my remaining title. Though I cannot share with you all the details of that decision, I assure you that it was wholly necessary to my continued wellbeing." Her formal vocabulary made her thoughts drift to saddling horses with Parker, teaching him slang, and she forced them back to the present moment.

"At the present time, I know that you desire me to rule, to fulfill my commitment to Brevspor. Though my heart still burns for the glory of our great nation, I am not the one to lead you, despite my birthright. But Kurt shares that same burning heart, my friends. He has lived and breathed it for years. He can steward this queendom for future generations." She swallowed, not daring to glance at him across the room. The literature had been clear: she was to advocate for a king-dom, not a stewardship. But they'd never agree to that, no matter who was asking for it. This was the smart move, but he was going to be livid.

"With my father's passing near and events in flux in Orangiers, our closest ally, we need stability. We need expe-rience. We need Kurt. He is the obvious choice for steward, and without him, I fear what may befall us."

Brief, to the point. Good enough. She hadn't stumbled or cried...but even though she'd never really been a crier, it was as easy as breathing these days.

An older man she didn't recognize stood. "Your grace, thank you for joining us today. We are honored by your pres-ence and we will heed your wise words. You have the same strong spirit of your mother, and we mourn that you cannot lead us."

"Thank you, Chancellor." She stepped down, still not meeting Kurt's gaze. The hearing went into recess, and he caught her just as she was entering the carriage.

"What the Jersey was that?"

"If you want to rule, you must steward. It's the only way."

"No, it's not! Francis rules! Parker will rule! There is no reason—"

"There is to them. I'm still alive. And that's everything."

"Then I wish you were dead." He shut the door on her, and Abbie felt all the air leave her lungs.

"Wait!" Someone behind Kurt was calling out, gesturing wildly. He ran up to the carriage and motioned them both inside.

"Your Highnesses, there's no easy way to say this. Your father has passed away."

# CHAPTER FORTY-THREE

THE CHURCH WAS FULL. Abbie would be seated first, her brother second. Their conversation from the previous afternoon was still hanging between them, crusty and blackened like a scorched pot. It was functional, like their relationship, but that needed some elbow grease before it would be worth something again. Kurt was standing next to her, dressed like a king. She wore no tiara or crown, just pearls and three-inch heels, but she felt beautiful.

Abbie had walked into her dressing room ready for a fight. She had stayed the night in one of the guest rooms again; her old room just felt too quiet without sisters nearby snoring, giggling, jumping on beds. And all the beds were twin-sized, anyway. It didn't help that she felt three breaths from crying all the time since...since her dad...died.

She was ten minutes early, yet Mrs. Braun was already waiting, hands folded in front of her, a tailor with a ribbon of measuring tape around his neck standing at her side. She was dressed all in black, as always, no jewelry. Her body reminded her of Rutha's, comfortably round in the middle, but she had no twinkle in her eyes, no color in her cheeks. She'd dyed out all her gray, and her posture was straight as a board. Unyielding. No matter. Abbie was just as tough. Just as hard. No way was this woman going to get the better of her.

"Your Highness," Mrs. Braun greeted her crisply. "How was your evening?"

"Fine, thank you. And I'd prefer you call me Abelia."

Mrs. Braun didn't miss a beat. "As you wish, Abelia. Shall we begin?" Abbie blinked, stunned, and sat down hard on the suede loveseat. Mrs. Braun signaled the models to enter as she explained, "We weren't sure of your tastes, so we tried to provide a wide variety of options, one of which we hope will please you." She couldn't help but wonder if Braun was being less difficult because she'd just lost her father or because she was trying to ensure her future in the palace. *As if.*

The first dress was strapless and too low-cut for Abbie's taste. She hated feeling like she was spilling out of things, and her ample chest made that style difficult to pull off. The second had spaghetti straps, which she felt was too informal for a funeral; *why had they even offered it?* The third had a high empire waist, which always made her look pregnant. They were all black, which wasn't a problem, but it made them look boring. She didn't want to look boring. This was the last time she was going to see Parker for a long time—she wanted to look amazing. A pang of guilt stung her. This should be about her father, not about her ex-fiancé.

"Which one would you choose?" The words tumbled out of her mouth before she could stop them. Asking Mrs. Braun's opinion was the last thing she wanted to do, but grief and anxiety were clouding her thoughts. She didn't understand how it could only be eight in the morning; she could've gone back to bed and slept until tomorrow.

Mrs. Braun's face wavered slightly, and Abbie knew she must look as lost as she felt. The older woman's voice was pitched softer than her usual tightly efficient tone when she spoke again.

"The dress should be conservative to show respect, but that doesn't mean it can't be skewed a bit young to highlight your beauty. How do you want to feel, in a word?"

"Classy."

Mrs. Braun nodded once approvingly and whispered to her assistant, who quietly withdrew. "If I may, I'd like to see you in a knee-length velvet dress with a lace bateau neckline and three-fourths-length sleeves to keep you warm. Churches are often cold." The model walked in a moment later wearing the dress and Abbie found herself nodding. "A print would be too playful, in my opinion, but that doesn't mean we can't give it a bit more interest than plain black fabric. The velvet would give it texture and interest, especially if you don't plan to wear a crown or much jewelry. The fabric also has a bit of stretch and give, so you won't feel squeezed into anything. Of course, we'll tailor whatever you choose to your body precisely. But the velvet should photograph nicely for the press next to Kurt's dark blue uniform."

Abbie's eyes filled with traitorous tears yet again, and she looked out the window. She heard her mother's chief-of-staff murmur to the others in the room, and they all left without a word.

"Abelia, is it the dresses? You don't like them?"

Abbie shook her head. "How can he be gone? He seemed okay when I saw him...he seemed...I don't know. Not like he was dying."

Mrs. Braun seemed to hesitate, something Abbie hadn't known was possible in her robotic programming, then she sat down next to her on the sofa. Then, without ever looking at her, she reached over and held her hand. Abbie stared at it.

She'd never been touched by the upper-level palace staff before. Sure, maids had dressed them, nannies had wiped their mouths. But tenderly? Never. The touch of a person who's grieving with you is not utilitarian. On the outside, it accomplishes nothing. But on the inside, it grounds you, gets you out of the water and into the lifeboat. It reminds you that your blood is still inching through your veins. It reminds you that even the coldest heart can be warmed again.

The two women sat, their eyes staunchly fixed on the windows, holding hands, tears they both hated glistening on their cheeks.

After a few minutes, Abbie wiped her face and said, "I'm ready to try on the velvet now, Mrs. Braun. Thank you."

"Whatever you wish, Abelia." The older woman rose and walked to the door, then paused. "It is so very good to have you back under this roof. I know you do not intend to stay. But if you desired it, your unique needs could be accommodated here." She straightened. "I would see to it personally, as a matter of pride. We are here to serve you, always." She left quietly.

If this was Mrs. Braun's bid to keep her job, it was a poor one. Her brother was more likely to keep Mrs. Braun on for simplicity's sake than Abelia ever would be. No, this was something else. Deep loyalty to her mother, maybe. What did Mrs. Braun even know about her illness? Maybe she hadn't agreed with how her mother handled it. Abbie filed it away to chew on later as the woman re-entered with her dress.

This was the dress she was wearing now, fingering its soft folds as she waited to be seated at the back of the church. It was literally the last place she wanted to be. It felt too soon to say goodbye; he'd just come back into her life. Selfishly, she realized she'd thought she had more time to make things right. He wasn't old, for Woz's sake. Or was he? The older Abbie got, the harder it was to tell where "young" ended and "old" started.

The hardest part was the service itself. Her father had hated emotional scene-making, just like her, and they relished privately poking fun at people who gushed over things like babies and weddings. Not funerals, though. They had to draw the line somewhere. The royal family was routinely required to attend funerals for heads of state, so Abbie had a lot of basis for comparison, and she had to admit, he'd nailed it. This funeral was so...him. He'd been overshadowed a lot, she realized now. He'd kept himself in a box up on the top shelf of his closet, playing a part for her mother's sake. They'd loved each other; she knew that was true. But now, in this church, listening to his favorite poems (too sentimental, Mother would've said), the bluesy clarinet piece he'd chosen ("Four/four time is standard for a reason," her mother would've commented), even the flower arrangements ("Lilies are too pungent for an enclosed space.")...Abbie realized for the first time that he'd moved on. Not romantically, of course, but personally, he'd moved out from her shadow. He'd moved back into himself.

Tears flowed down her face. She was so ready. So ready to put her mother's voice to rest. So ready to not hear it in her head anymore, doubting her, correcting her. Maybe if she'd grieved her mother earlier, her ghost wouldn't have had to follow her across the continent. But she hadn't. So, sitting in church, listening to the choir singing, when she was supposed to be saying goodbye to her father, Abelia said goodbye to her mother instead. She left Mother's opinions in the trash with her tissues. She left her critiques in the pews with her former staff members. She left lighter.

Exiting the sanctuary, a well-dressed man stepped in front of her and she stopped, surprised.

"I told you we would meet again soon." It was the Warlord-in-Chief, she realized with a start, wearing a tailored navy suit. This time, inside the Veil and away from his magic, he looked closer to middle age, snow-white stubble on his face. He appeared to carry no weapons, but Abbie was taking no chances and did not attempt to advance past him until her security had cleared the way.

As she passed him, Abbie murmured, "Thank you again for your help, and for listening to the pleas of my young tongue."

"Oh, the pleasure was mine. Pardon me, ex-princess." He gave her a sharp-edged smile as he walked away, holding out a hand to another dignitary, and Abbie hoped silently that he would leave soon.

She stood in the foyer, listening to people's soft Sunday voices, thanking people for coming, doing a slow, sad nod. She saw Parker lingering in the back of the church, his white uniform standing out amidst the glut of black. He was waiting to speak to her, she knew. He was waiting until anyone who was interested in their conversation was safely tucked back into their carriages and wagons and walking down Alphonsine Avenue on high heels and shiny oxfords, still drying their tears.

"Hello, Abelia."

"Hello, Edward." Parker's uniform emphasized his strong, lanky physique, but his eyes were rimmed red and his fatigue showed on his face. His gaze sharpened as he took in her cheek fully for the first time.

"What happened to your face?" *Damn, the makeup isn't hiding it.* She'd been afraid of that.

"Hmm?" She feigned ignorance, but his anger was apparent.

"Your cheek, Abelia. What happened to it?"

"I got into an argument."

"With whom?"

"Not important." He looked like he had more to say—a lot more—but instead, he changed the subject.

"These are for you." Parker handed her a small bouquet that didn't look like professional work. "I'm so sorry for your loss." She took the pink-and-white flowers and a sweet fragrance wafted over her.

"Thank you. They smell good. What are they?"

The prince broke his gaze away from her face for a rare moment as he shifted his weight, straightening a gold button on his uniform. "Oh...um..."

Abbie was surprised by his bashfulness as she waved to the last couple leaving. "What's wrong?" He shook his head, still not looking at her.

"Nothing, nothing. I just thought you'd know." He sighed deeply. "It's abelia," he said quietly. "The flowers, they're abelia. I picked them at home, in the National Botanical Gardens. The head gardener had to pretend he wasn't really angry with me, as I left a gaping hole in one of his bushes. Also, I had to stand in a special line to take horticultural products through immigration and customs. Kings don't wait in lines unless they have a very good reason, and now I know why."

Her mouth opened, then closed. Then opened. Then closed. She knew she probably looked like a fish, but she couldn't help but be deeply touched by the gesture. Worn out from fighting a war, still looking for his brother, dealing with his fractured family, his mentor having just died without him getting to say goodbye, his idiotic fiancé dumping him, and here he was, bringing her flowers.

*Idiotic,* she thought fondly. *That describes it perfectly.*

"I've never seen them before. They're beautiful."

"You're aptly named, then."

Abbie stared at him without embarrassment. His face was so earnest, his hurt so raw.

"I was wrong," Abbie blurted. "I'm sorry for how we left things. I'm so sorry, Parker."

"I'm sorry, too, I should've spoken to you before I just—"

"No," she said firmly, stepping toward him and his security people perked up. He waved them away. "No," she said again, "you didn't do anything wrong. It was all on me. Woz, I've screwed this up since day one."

"I'd like to disagree with you."

"Oh?"

"Yes," he said, mustering a microscopic smile. "I'd like to, but I can't."

"Clever," she smiled.

"Couldn't you have come to this conclusion before I went to war?"

"That would've been nice."

"Wouldn't it, though?"

"Mmm." Abbie was edging closer to him. "Congratulations on winning your war."

"I owe thanks to you and Blair in large part. But I did win, didn't I?" Parker rubbed his face. "I apologize, I'm very tired."

"Where are you staying?"

"They've rented a villa right on the banks of the Bunke. Great view, they tell me. Not that I'll see much of it."

"I'd like to see the view with you."

"Would you?"

She couldn't read him; there was a careful distance in his eyes, and she began to sweat.

"It'd give us a chance to talk a little, if you want to."

He folded his arms. "Talk about what?"

"About us." She lowered her voice. "But if you don't want to..."

Parker paused, looking over her shoulder out the window, and she held her breath.

"No, that'd be fine. Eight o'clock?"

"Sure. Maybe you can get some rest."

"Perhaps, though more likely they'll have things for me to do."

Abbie crossed her arms, irritated. "I thought you were running that country. Tell them you need the afternoon off. They work for you, not the other way around, you know." It was strange; she felt a resentment toward his advisors that took her by surprise. They knew he'd never draw boundaries himself, not unless he had a good reason...*like maybe spending time with his future wife. He needs this as much as I do,* she thought. *Maybe more. They're running him into the ground, and it's only just begun.* An idea occurred to her as he mimicked her perturbed stance.

"I am running the country, and believe it or not, it comes with a lot of non-optional activities."

"Your Highness, you look like you're about to fall over. Surely you're not making important decisions in this state. That would be foolish, and you know it."

He breathed out a laugh. "I'm glad to see our journey hasn't impacted your fighting spirit, Your Highness. I'll see you at eight." As he walked away, flanked heavily by aides and security, Abbie signaled Mrs. Braun with a nod and the woman moved smoothly to her side.

"I'll need another dress, Mrs. Braun. Red if possible, and somewhat less...conservative than this one."

"Right away, Abelia."

*He never called me Abs,* she realized. *Or darling.* She stuck her face in the flowers and inhaled.

"Oh, and Mrs. Braun? Please get me a copy of my marriage contract."

# CHAPTER FORTY-FOUR

PARKER THOUGHT HE'D feel better once the funeral was behind him. Riding in his carriage, he watched the mourners leaving and the houses sliding by. He could've fallen asleep right there. He'd done well; he'd kept himself from kissing her, stroking her soft auburn hair, holding her so tight she couldn't breathe, touching her cheek where some bastard had marked her. That was good. But he couldn't help feeling skeptical...what had changed her mind? It sounded like she'd been doing some hard thinking since they'd been apart, which could be good. But why now? What about her health—had something changed there? Did she really think they could just pick up where they'd left off after what'd happened in the desert?

No, he'd be careful. He'd approach this cautiously, leading with his head, not his heart. Duty to his country had meant that he as good as lost his brother, but perhaps it didn't have to mean losing his fiancé as well. The rest of the afternoon was crammed full of meetings; Parker ate dinner through his finance meeting and a cabinet brainstorming session for the agricultural post. He checked his watch. It was 7:45. Damn. He'd really wanted a nap before she came by, but he'd have to settle for a shower and some strong tea instead. He wanted a glass of wine, but he was afraid he'd pass out...he'd always been a bit of a lightweight.

"Gentlemen," he interrupted, "I apologize, but I have an engagement this evening for which I must prepare."

Colonel Brown paged through the stack of papers in front of him. "Sir, we still have five items on the agenda: the diplomatic response to the Grathan mercenaries who responded to Lincoln's call, living arrangements for your siblings and your parents now that you'll be reigning at Bluffton Castle—"

"Colonel, I'm done for today. I have an engagement."

His advisors exchanged glances, and Colonel Brown cleared his throat. "There's nothing on your official schedule after this meeting ends."

"That's correct. It's a personal matter." Parker stood up, and the other attendees scrambled to follow suit. "Good evening, gentlemen."

"Good evening, Your Highness."

Abbie was right; that felt good. They'd adjust to his style of leadership eventually. The decisions and precedents he set now would probably serve him well in the future. He stripped out of the stuffy uniform he hadn't managed to change out of after the funeral—damn, he'd managed to spill steak sauce on it. At least no one could yell at him about it now. As he stepped out of the bathroom, still toweling off, he found that someone had come and laid out clothes for him, khaki pants with a white polo shirt. He chuckled: they didn't know who he was meeting, so how in the world did they think they could pick out what he should wear?

He opened the closet and pulled on a white undershirt with a black dress shirt over it and a pair of jeans. His head hurt. He went back into the bathroom and dug around for some ibuprofen. He caught his reflection in the mirror...he looked like a nerd. An exhausted nerd. He sighed and rolled up his sleeves to his elbows. 7:58. No time for any more improvements now. He wove his way through the unfamiliar house until he got back to the living area.

"Your Highness..." one of the female staffers whose name he hadn't learned yet was hurrying toward him, out of breath. "Your Highness, your guests have arrived."

"Guests? There's more than one?"

"Yes. Her Highness Abelia Olivia Jayne Venenza Ribaldi Porchenzii and Mr. Johann Rohnhart, a lawyer."

"A lawyer, you say? Any idea why he's come?"

"She didn't say, Your Highness."

"Very well. Thank you, Miss...?"

"Scrope."

"Thank you, Miss Scrope. Also, could you please bring me some strong Duke of Darlington tea?"

"Decaf?"

"No, regular, please." The young woman curtsied and pivoted toward the kitchens. *I swear by all that's good and holy, if Abbie's suing me for something I will throw myself in the river.*

Parker stalked out of the open glass doors that led to the balcony, and he heard the soldier by the entrance begin to announce his presence with the long litany of his names...and then suddenly, he couldn't hear anything, because he could see Abbie.

In the lantern light of the balcony, the bare skin of her back glowed. She wore a rose-red gown, which she knew was his favorite color on her, and her auburn hair had been tamed into loose, flowing curls. When she turned, he could see that her lipstick matched the dress. The dress...its silk hugged her hips and her breasts in all the right places, coming together behind her neck in a thin-strapped halter. The dress had a high slit up the side, making her long legs look even longer with those matching pumps on. If he'd thought the purple pajamas she'd worn when she'd yelled at him in the desert were hot, this was much worse, because he knew this was for him. She'd done this *for him*. He hadn't gotten his voice back yet when she spotted him.

"Darling," she said, "there you are." She pressed a lingering kiss against his cheek, then turned to make introductions, wrapping her arm around his waist and drawing him toward the table. "This is Mr. Rohnhart, one of my father's lawyers and a professor at the University of Gelt."

"Pleased to meet you," Parker said, still dazed. *I really need that tea.*

The man offered a deep bow, and Parker acknowledged it with a nod. He was so disoriented; who was this man? For that matter, who was this woman? His Abbie hated squeezing into uncomfortable shoes, yet her head rose well above his shoulder in these. *No*, he reminded himself with a pang, *not* my *Abbie, not anymore.*

"Mr. Rohnhart was one of the men who wrote our marriage contract, and he has something interesting to share with us."

"Won't you sit down?"

"Thank you."

Miss Scrope brought the tea, and Parker took a grateful, scalding sip. *Has she found a loophole? She's being friendly with me; she was touching me. Should I touch her back? Can I touch her back without losing my fragile mind...not to mention the torture for my not-yet-unbroken heart?* He took another gulp of tea. He should've asked them not to give him these dainty cups anymore. He needed a mug. He must've made a face, because Abbie glanced at him.

"What's wrong?"

He waited for Miss Scrope to walk away, then muttered, "I hate tiny tea cups, and this isn't strong enough. I asked for it strong."

Abbie put a hand on his knee.

"Miss Scrope?" she called, and the woman came hurrying back. *How is she learning my staff's names faster than I am?* "His Highness would like this same blend again, this time in a large mug, and he'd like it steeped for one minute longer this time. You can leave the cream and sugar in the kitchen, he always takes it black. Thank you so much."

Parker suppressed a smile at how the woman quickly obeyed despite the fact that Abbie had absolutely no authority over his staff. That never seemed to slow her down.

"Go ahead, Mr. Rohnhart," she prompted as she shifted his tea in front of her and took a sip. Those red, red lips against the white bone china cup sent his mind in another direction entirely, and he neglected to tell her it was caffeinated.

The man cleared his throat. "Yes, Your Highness. In writing the contract, it was emphasized to us that you must both have total flexibility regarding your future ability to reign in either nation. If, by chance, something happened to their planned successors, your parents wanted you to be able to step up and lead, since either of you could be called upon to be the political potentate in your respective countries. And as we see, sadly, that's just what's happened in both of your cases. In most of these contracts, the language is very specific regarding what each spouse's role will be. However, because they wanted the flexibility previously mentioned, these details are not explicitly stated in your contract, since it might be that Her Highness needed to reign in our queendom, or it might be that you were needed to reign in your kingdom."

Parker shook his head, trying to understand where he was going with this. He looked at Abbie, who wore a mask of polite interest and was keeping her eyes focused on Rohnhart. He looked back at the lawyer.

"I'm sorry, I don't understand."

"Just as there's no requirement that Abelia have a royal status in order to enforce the contract, there's no requirement that she gain a royal status in Orangiers upon your marriage."

"So you would be..."

"Mrs. Broward." She reached for his hand, and he couldn't believe his eyes: she was wearing his ring. The one he'd bought for her to maintain the ruse in the Unveiled, the one she'd chucked into the bushes at Blair's. He took her cold hand, tucking it into the crook of his arm, and she leaned into him, resting her head against his shoulder. *I don't believe this. I don't believe this.*

"Your Highness, I would advise you to speak to your barristers before making any decisions...though I see it may be too late for that." A sly smile crept across his face. "In my understanding, if you wanted to make Abelia your wife but not your queen, you are within your legal right to do so as the contract is written. However, forgive my language, Your

Highnesses, but you both have to realize that you are bringing an utter shitstorm down on your heads, and the political cost will be very high."

"Oh, Rohnhart, you're such a pessimist. Everyone loves a fairytale romance," Abbie teased.

The older man chuckled lightly and stood as Miss Scrope brought Parker's mug of tea. The couple stood as well, and this time, Parker extended his hand and the lawyer shook it.

"Thank you for coming, Mr. Rohnhart, on what I can only assume was very short notice. I realize that this may be tricky for you, so we'll do our best to leave you out of it, whatever we decide. But from the bottom of our hearts, we thank you. You have done us a great service today that will not be forgotten."

Rohnhart seemed moved. "It was my pleasure, sir, ma'am. My pleasure. Have a lovely evening together. May it be the first of many."

"Thank you," they said together, but their attention had already turned from the lawyer as he left. Parker crossed his arms in order to keep himself from gathering her into them.

"Leave it to you to find a loophole."

Abbie smiled but said nothing, twisting her ring. She opened her mouth but no words came out. Parker noticed the tears in her eyes, and his defenses took a direct hit.

"What's this? Tears?"

Abbie nodded, swiping quickly at her cheeks.

"It's stupid. I'm stupid."

Parker held out his right hand and bent down to look into her eyes.

"I'm sorry, I don't believe we've met. I'm Edward, and you are...?"

"I'm Abbie," she whispered, taking his hand, smiling, still choking on something between a sob and a laugh.

"No, no, you can't be Abbie. You're almost as pretty as she is, but Abbie's smart and self-possessed and tough. She'd never call herself stupid."

"She might if she just proposed to a prince in the most backwards way possible."

Parker pulled her to his chest and held her then, and she cried harder. He stroked her hair, and she began to quiet.

Without removing herself from his embrace, she said, "I know I can't ask you for an answer now; you need time to think this through. I'm asking a lot, I know that. It's crazy, I know it's crazy, but it might work, and I think it's the only way, and I'm so afraid you're going to say no, and I'm going to be...to be..."

"Alone again."

She nodded. "But more than that, you'll be alone, and I love you, and I don't want you to be alone, and I *really* don't want you marrying stupid Crescena, but if that's what you need to do, if you really need a queen and not just a wife, then you should do it and forget about me and burn my picture and all that." She pulled away from him just far enough to look into his eyes. "Let's face it. She's easy on the eyes and probably a lot less work."

He laughed as he wiped her tears away. "So I'm confused; are you still making a case for us? Or am I to marry Crescena now? You make it sound appealing."

"Us, us," she laughed.

"Glad we clarified that, then." He paused. "You love me?"

Abbie nodded. "I do. And because of that, I'd like to punch your advisors in the crotch at the moment."

"Some of them are women, you know."

"It still works."

"You'd know better than I."

She swallowed hard. "And I'm sorry about the crying. I hate it, too, but it just seems to be happening a lot lately in spite of that."

"I'm so sorry about your dad."

"Even before Dad. Ever since...since you left without me."

"I'm not ashamed to say that I shed a few tears of my own over that decision."

"I know. I'm so sorry, Parker. I know I hurt you. I'm sorry for saying I'd never marry you, I'm sorry I stormed off in the garden that night instead of talking it through. But I'm trying to talk now. I'm being so rational."

He lifted an eyebrow. "Well, we're heading in that direction, anyway...how long did it take you to find the ring?"

"Oh, hours, babe. It took hours. It really set us back in catching up with you. You should've seen Rubald, down on his hands and knees, muttering about finding a cheap piece of costume jewelry when the royal coffers are full of rings ten times better."

They both laughed then, and Parker brought his hand to the side of her face, his thumb caressing her wet cheek.

"I love you, Abelia."

"I love you, too." She stared into his eyes. "When we signed our contract the first time, I didn't know it would feel like this...I didn't know how much...how deeply I'd—" She was tearing up again, and Parker kissed her until she was breathless.

"I'm not saying yes," he said when they came up for air. "I want to, but I have to think this through from all the angles, look into the law regarding our potential children, talk to some lawyers on my side..." He found her left hand and brought it to his lips. "You keep that ring on, all right? Don't take it off just yet."

She nodded. "I won't take it off."

"Promise me?"

"I promise."

"Okay. I'll call you soon."

She lifted an eyebrow. "As soon as you unblock my number, right?"

He nodded sheepishly. "That was childish, I know. But my heart was...broken. I couldn't stomach the idea of losing you like that. Not like that."

He intended to kiss her on the forehead but somehow found her lips again instead.

"Wipe your face before you go inside, there's a bit of a lipstick issue..." she whispered over her shoulder as she walked back toward the house, grinning and biting her lower lip.

Parker wiped his sleeve against his mouth. At least he'd sent her off smiling instead of in tears; the tabloid photographers would love that. He pulled out his phone and began to type.

*Mates, you're not going to believe this...*

# CHAPTER FORTY-FIVE

NEEDING SOMETHING TO occupy her mind, Abbie checked her email in the carriage on the way back to the palace. Work wanted to know when she'd be returning from her bereavement leave, which they reminded her was five days, two of which she'd already used. A terse text message from Kurt informed her that they'd be reading the will tomorrow morning at nine. She saw no reason to attend; Kurt would yell at her about it later if there was anything relevant, and she already knew she wasn't mentioned. Brevsporan law prevented missing persons from being listed as beneficiaries, and her father hadn't been able to get her legally declared found before he'd passed.

Lauren demanded a phone call to update her on everything; they hadn't talked since before she went into Gratha. It took Abbie an hour to fill her in on everything, and Lauren did an appropriate amount of squealing and crying.

But at bedtime, there was nothing else left to think about. *I did what I could do,* she told herself, staring at the ceiling. *I made my case, I left the choice with him. He knows that I love him, that I want him. That's the important thing.* She wrapped her arms around her torso and squeezed. Sleep was clearly not happening tonight. She was too tired to walk the grounds. She tried to read, but couldn't focus on the words, re-reading the same page over and over. She got up, used the bathroom, and had started back to bed when her eyes fell on the letter Kurt had given her, her mother's letter.

She picked it up, feeling the weight of it. It was long. The mere sight of her name in her mother's handwriting felt prickly, painful. *Do I even want to know? What could she say that's helpful? Even if she apologizes, it's too late. She's gone.* She slid her finger under the flap, then stopped. *It doesn't matter*, she told herself firmly and tossed the letter into the fire.

Abbie flopped back into bed, the sheets uncomfortably damp and mussed from her tossing and turning. Her phone plinked with a message, and she figured Lauren had a follow-up question or ten.

*Parker: Are you asleep?*

*Abbie: No...*

*Parker: You drank that tea; it wasn't decaf.*

*Abbie: That's not it.*

*Parker: I apologize for failing to warn you. I was apprehensive, thoughtless.*

*Abbie: No, it's okay. I was nervous, too.*

*Abbie: Still nervous.*

The phone rang, startling her, and she quickly answered. "When I saw you in that dress..." He sighed. "I thought I was dreaming."

"The good kind or a nightmare?"

He chuckled. "The best kind, darling. The kind that ends with both of us wearing nothing."

"That might've made Rohnhart uncomfortable."

He laughed again. "Woz, I missed you. I've missed you so much."

"I missed you, too. I wish you were here." He went quiet, and Abbie knew his wheels were turning, trying to think of something to say. "That's not an invitation, don't worry. I know you need time."

"Do I?" He sighed, and her heart skipped a beat. "I should take time to think and talk to my advisors. But I don't want to."

"Then don't." She said the words on a rush of air, then held her breath.

"Abs," he groaned, and she grinned. *That's what I needed to hear.*

"If you were here right now, I'd kiss you silly."

"Miss Scrope! Bring the carriage around."

ABBIE ALREADY HAD A stress headache, and the camera flashes weren't helping. She stood beside Parker behind the podium, not touching because it wasn't allowed. Whoever made that rule didn't anticipate Abbie, because the rule just made him more irresistible. But sadly, he was out of reach.

"Good morning," he spoke into the microphone, and the packed press room chorused a response, then quieted respectfully. "With my coronation just a few weeks away, Her Highness Abelia Olivia Jayne Venenza Ribaldi Porchenzii and I have a joint announcement to make. As you will remember, we have been engaged for some time, having signed a marriage contract at the ripe old age of twelve." The reporters chuckled. "But since that time, many things have changed for both of our families." He paused. "For reasons she does not wish to disclose, Abelia does not feel she can fulfill the role of queen at this time." A unison cry went up from the reporters, and he held up his hands for silence. "She does, however, wish to fulfill her contractual obligation. We will, therefore, be marrying in six months' time." He had to pause again to regain their attention. "Not as royals, but as private citizens. Abelia will have no official role in the political side of our lives. She will, of course, be supportive as any spouse would be for her husband's work." He turned to check on her and gave her a rakish wink. Abbie managed to keep a straight face—barely. "We will reside at Bluffton Castle, and she will make limited public appearances. Her official title will be Mrs. Abelia Broward, and we will refer to her as Mrs. Abelia Broward." The group chuckled again. "I'll take questions now."

Every hand went up.

"Yes, Johnson."

"Thank you, sir. Will your children be titled, and where will the future Mrs. Broward fall in the line of succession?"

"Abelia will not be in line for succession, but our children will. They will be titled prince or princess as appropriate. Next? Yes, Peckham."

"Thank you, sir. Will Mrs. Broward have diplomatic immunity when she travels?"

"Yes, as a family member of the royal household, she will have immunity, but she won't be traveling with me often. Yes, Holland."

"Thank you, sir. This question is for Her Highness, if I may?"

Parker nodded and stepped aside, gesturing for her to take the podium.

Abbie swallowed hard and smiled at the reporters. *Difficult, troublesome, vital, necessary creatures,* she thought.

"Thank you, ma'am. Have you discussed this decision with your own government, and if so, what was their reaction?"

"Yes, we have discussed it at length with my brother, the Prince Steward of Brevspor, and the rest of the government. They are disappointed, of course, but my brother has been very supportive and understanding." *He didn't start throwing things until we hung up, Mrs. Braun reported.* "And as for my fellow Brevsporans, I hope that they too will extend me courtesy and understanding regarding this very difficult decision. They stand at a crossroads. We have been a matriarchy for sixteen generations, and I know that change does not come easy. But I believe that this is an opportunity for greater equality between the sexes in Brevspor, and my brother is more than equal to the task of stewarding these changes.

"Kurt has innovative ideas, sound economic policies, and the benefit of being heavily involved with both my mother's and father's governments before they passed. He has my deepest love and gratitude, as well as my full support for his government. If the people choose to call up one of the other high-born families to rule, they will be doing themselves a great disservice." More hands went up, and Abbie didn't know their names, so she just pointed.

"Thank you, ma'am. Judson Boote, *The Orangie Online.*" The others snickered. *Oops,* she thought. "It appeared at one time that you might not fulfill your contract, given the amount of time it took you to arrive in Orangiers. May I ask what changed your mind?"

All eyes were on her. She felt Parker move forward and place a hand on her lower back, as if to let her know she didn't have to answer. Abbie threw back her shoulders and looked the journalist in the eye.

"Mr. Boote, I'm a strong, capable woman, and through my own blood, sweat, and tears, I had crafted a life I loved in Gardenia. I wasn't interested in giving up all that freedom for just anyone." She paused. "But your very-soon-to-be king isn't just anyone, and I adore him. As we traveled across the Unveiled, he was my shoulder to cry on, my voice of reason, and my protector—often from myself—and I realized that there's no freedom in all the world great enough to justify giving up all that. Does that answer your question?"

"Yes, ma'am. Thank you."

She leaned forward into the podium. "Wow, you guys actually raise your hands. Orangie reporters are so much more polite than Brevsporan ones." That got a big laugh, and they took that opportunity to flee the briefing room, smiling and waving, of course. Security hurried them down the hall, and Parker squeezed her to him.

"You were wonderful, darling."

"Yeah, I think it went okay. They seemed pretty easygoing about it."

"Uh oh."

"What?" She peeked over to see his phone and read the social media post: "*Good enough for him, but not for us: Edward to wed his Un-queen.*"

"Un-queen? I don't think I care for that nickname." Abbie scowled down at the screen, and Parker tipped her face up toward him.

"As you may recall, we've been called worse." He grinned, and they both laughed, "WHEAT EATERS!"

# EPILOGUE

ABBIE SHOVED THE PHONE at Parker. "You talk to them, I can't..."

Parker put her phone to his ear. "They're in position." He paused. "They don't think Marie and Marc are home, just the girls. They're just doing a little more recon."

Abbie chewed her thumbnail, her other arm tight across her stomach and her body swaying from one foot to another.

"Okay, they're going in. It's just the advance team, two men, no weapons." He paused. "The front door was unlocked." Abbie could hear the screaming in the background and she winced.

"Okay, they're okay. Marie and Marc are out. The girls have agreed to leave with the officials. Here, listen." He passed it back, and she took it with trembling hands.

"Miss Porchenzii, are you there?"

"Yes, I'm here." She just managed to keep the shake out of her voice.

"You were correct in your assessment of the situation. Thank you for bringing it to our attention. Fadline and Theresas have agreed to go to the orphanage tonight until a foster situation can be worked out. It may take some time, because we try to keep them together. But they'll be better cared for than here. Both show signs of domestic abuse, which would be enough to remove them from the home even without your first-hand account. We'll keep you updated on their progress."

Abbie closed her eyes, and her head fell back. "Thank you, officer." She hung up and launched herself into Parker's arms. "We did it."

"You did it, darling. Human traffickers, beware: Abelia's coming for you."

"And yet, they're just two of thousands."

"I know. We have to do more."

Abbie's features hardened. "It's not going to be easy. Gardenia is tough on slavery, but other countries may not be amenable to our meddling."

"Oh, but haven't you heard the proverb? A king's wrath is a messenger of death, and a wise man will appease it."

Abbie smirked. "What about an un-queen's wrath?"

"Oh, that too, darling. Especially that."

# Liked it? Hated it? Leave a review!

Whether the plot moved too fast or too slow,
Leave a review and let us all know!
Was Abbie obnoxious? Was Parker a bore?
Leave a review now; it's hardly a chore!
Goodreads and Amazon, wherever you bought,
Take a quick minute and share what you thought.
Glowing reviews keep my business afloat,
And at parties, they give me a reason to gloat.
*Thanks in advance!*

# Acknowledgments

TO MY FAMILY: THANK you for being my cheerleaders, my encouragers! You always knew I could write a book. Now I know it, too.

To my writing group: for a bunch of poets, you ladies sure give great advice.

To my editor, Sylvia Cottrell: you took this project beyond what I could've hoped for.

To my cover artist, Patrick Knowles: you rock. I'm glad I found someone as talented and patient as you!

To my map artist: Roll for Fantasy website, I was delighted with how it came out!

# If you've made it this far, you deserve a treat...here's a taste of The Un-Queen, coming out June 2019!

ABBIE WAS JUST WASHING up the dishes when there was a knock at the door. That is to say, she was sitting on the couch, snacking, her e-reader propped up on her knees, her hair in a bun, yoga pants and a sweatshirt, thinking that she should be doing the dishes when there was a knock at the door. Abbie checked her watch; 3:02 PM. That couldn't be Parker. His security had come by around 9 AM to sweep her apartment for bugs, bombs and terrorists, much to her amusement. She made them coffee. They said he'd pick her up at 7:00 for dinner. Therefore, when someone knocked at 3:02, she ignored them. The knock came again.

"Go away!" she yelled through a mouthful of popcorn.

"Are you certain? I've come all this way, and I really thought we were past this stage in our relationship," came a muffled, accented voice from the other side of the door.

She was off the couch and throwing the door open in record time. Parker stood there, scowling.

"Abs, you didn't check the peephole. You've got to make sure before you just let anyone in. I could've been a murderer. A very well-dressed murderer." The ex-princess dragged him into her apartment by his tie, wagging her eyebrows at his security to make them snicker before she slammed the door.

**334**

"Oh, hush. I'd know your pomposity anywhere; I could smell it wafting in from the hallway."

Parker mockingly sniffed an armpit, then grimaced. "You're right. How long has this been going on?"

"Since the day we met. You asked me if I would care to 'take a turn around the grounds' with you. You were seven. Why haven't you kissed me yet?"

Grinning, Parker moved into her space, their noses touching, backing her into the wall. "I was politely waiting for you to finish speaking."

"You shouldn't wait for that, it could take forever."

"Well, good news, then; we've got forever."

Abbie slid her arms up over his shoulders. "Say that again."

"We've got forev—" She cut him off, pulling him closer with both arms, kissing him hard.

He pulled back playfully. "Did you miss me?"

Abbie shook her head, leaning in for another hard kiss.

"Not even the tiniest bit?"

She shook her head again, grinning.

Parker sighed. "You're such a liar."

"I know. I have to keep you from getting a swollen head with everyone kissing your royal backside all the time. Did you miss me?"

"I gladly admit that I did. But only every minute of every hour of every day we've been apart, which is 20 days, 480 hours, or 23,800 minutes."

"Pathetic."

"Ouch."

"Buck up, Your Majesty." Using his title reminded Abbie who exactly was pressed up against her, and she suddenly paled. Her apartment wasn't ready to be seen...this was not the first impression she'd intended at all. He was turned away from the worst of it, but he could see into the kitchen if he turned his head...

He brought his mouth closer to her ear and lowered his voice. "You went tense. Are you concerned that I'm looking at the mess?"

She raised an eyebrow even though he couldn't see it. "Stop reading my brain."

"Stop making it so obvious. Also, anyone who shows up four hours early has to realize the place may not be ready for company. Also, I couldn't care less. I'm here to see you, not your apartment." True to his word, Parker did not look around, but Abbie didn't feel better. She still knew it was there.

"Just go out for ten minutes, fifteen tops, and I'll take care of the worst of it." She shoved him toward the door, but Parker dug in his heels.

"Oh, I'm not leaving. I just got here!"

"You gonna fight me?" She pushed him again, and he laughed and adopted a lower stance so she couldn't tip him over.

"Oh no, I'm not as foolish as I look, I'd never fight you."

"Good."

"Additionally, I don't have to."

Abbie crossed her arms. "Why is that?"

"Because of that." He pointed over her shoulder, and when she turned to look, he slipped past her and into the living room, flopping down on the couch, its denim slipcover shifting at the corners.

"Hey!"

"I'm disappointed, darling, that's the oldest trick in the book. Your siblings clearly didn't prepare you adequately for a life in politics."

She came around the couch cautiously as he surveyed the place.

"Where's this mess, then?"

"Ha ha."

"I'm not joking, actually. Does this embarrass you? I didn't realize you were a neat freak."

Abbie's face reddened. "You can't be serious. Look: dishes in the sink, clean laundry still in the basket unfolded, shoes under the couch, my bed unmade..." The flicker of interest in his eyes at the mention of her bed wasn't lost on Abbie, but she decided not to mention it. "Popcorn on the floor."

Parker helped himself to a handful out of the bowl. "Abs, this is nothing. The dishes are clearly from your lunch; you did the ones from breakfast. Fold while we catch up, and I can survey this bed situation later." He winked, and she allowed her lips to hook into a half smile. "This popcorn is very good; what's on it?"

Abbie sat down next to him, one leg curled under her. It felt odd to be so alone with him; they'd always had Rubald and Rutha as a buffer. He didn't seem uncomfortable in the least, and she wondered how he managed it. More practice managing his royal emotions, maybe.

"Avocado oil and sea salt."

"I must mention it to my cooking staff."

"Dude, you can make your own popcorn."

"On second thought, perhaps I will." His attention shifted to her e-reader. "You were reading?"

She nodded. "Not a romance, sorry."

"More's the pity. Though it would explain why you attacked me in the entryway...so unladylike." Abbie grinned. "So what *are* you reading?"

"Work stuff. Government standards for reclaiming food waste for livestock." Abbie pulled the laundry basket toward her and subtly pushed the clean underwear to the bottom as she pulled out a Brevspor Bengals t-shirt to fold.

Parker made a face. "That's what you're reading on a Saturday? Shouldn't you be doing something fun?"

"I was saving my fun for when *you* got here."

"Why didn't you say so?" Parker tossed his popcorn over his shoulder and launched himself at her, Abbie shrieking with laughter as he mauled her, covering her neck with loud kisses. There was a knock at the door, and they paused.

"Everything okay in there?" It was Dean, Parker's lead security.

"Yes, thank you," Abbie called, her laughter returning. "Everything's fine!"

"You're supposed to be protecting me, not her!" Parker called over the sofa.

"We like her better!"

"And who can blame them?" he murmured, his eyes still teasing as his lips went back to her neck, and Abbie let out a happy sigh as he lay her back on the couch. "I missed you, darling."

"I missed you, too, hon," Abbie said, the blood quickly leaving her brain in favor of parts further south, parts that were apparently very pleased to be in Parker's presence again.

"I knew it."

"Shut up." She brought his face up to hers and slipped her tongue into his mouth. His deep groan made her sternum vibrate, and she giggled, cringing a little inwardly at how silly she sounded. Is this what love did to people? He'd been here less than ten minutes, and they were already horizontal...not that she minded. When they'd been kissing for a while, he stopped caring whether he was crushing her, releasing his full weight, pressing her into the cushions. She wouldn't have minded if she could breathe. Maybe if they moved to her bed, they could lie side by side...good Woz, where did that thought come from?

He noticed her wonky breathing and sat up, pulling her with him, pushing the loose bits of her hair away from her face.

"Sorry, I forgot you need oxygen."

"Quite all right," Abbie said, imitating his accent. "Where are you taking me tonight?"

"This is your town; what's your favorite place?"

Abbie had no hesitation. "Martissant's, hands down." She salivated at the thought of their six-mushroom risotto.

"Then I guess it's good that I called Lauren three weeks ago and asked her what your favorite was so I could get us a reservation."

"And when you say reservation, you mean that you bought the place out for the night for security reasons?"

"That's correct, yes." He pulled out his phone, looked at the screen briefly, then put it away. She reached for a pair of capris, glancing up at him.

"You can take a call if you need to."

He glared at her reproachfully. "I'm not wasting our precious time together on work."

"But king work isn't regular work. I realize that," she said as she smoothed out the creases. "I don't want nations to perish because we were making out."

He cleared his throat. "Abs, look at me, and hear this as I intend it." She put down her folding and Parker reached for her hand. "The rest of the world can take care of itself for a little while. Right now, it's you and me. This weekend, I am available to no one else."

"Not a full weekend," she countered, and he nodded.

"No, not a full weekend, but it's the best I could do. You're on my calendar now, every month, and the next person who 'adjusts' your time gets fired."

Abbie smiled; she didn't mind him defending them to his staff one bit. "I got you something."

Parker looked confused as she pulled her laptop out of from under the couch and powered it up. "Are you showing me a picture of it?"

"No, impatient pants, just hold on." Abbie scowled at the screen. She could feel Parker still gazing at her and she tried not to squirm under his open regard. "Ah! Here we go." She turned the screen and plunked it onto the coffee table in front of him.

"What's this? Football?"

She nodded. "To distract you while I shower. I got a paid subscription."

He scowled. "You didn't have to do that."

"Why wouldn't I? You're going to be here more often, so now we can watch those dudes run up and down the field together."

He seemed to be holding back a smile. "It's a pitch, not a field."

"See?" she gestured as she stood. "I have so much to learn."

He looked at her with skepticism. "Can you afford this?"

"Normal people just say 'thank you.'"

"Don't do that. I mean it, can you afford this? I can pay you back for it."

Her hands went to her hips as if drawn by magnetic forces, and she narrowed her gaze. "I'm not allowed to get you presents?"

Parker looked like he could sense the noose dangling in front of him. "No," he shook his head slowly, "no, I didn't say that."

"Damn straight you didn't. I know I'm yours, but you're mine, too. I can skip a few meals if needed."

"Abbie, you are *not*—"

"I'm kidding! I'm kidding," she said, hands up, as she crossed to her bedroom door. She wouldn't mention that she'd been eating less in order to lose some weight before the wedding anyway. She pulled off her sweatshirt, revealing the cotton camisole she wore underneath.

"Where are you going?" There was an edge to his voice.

"I said I'm going to shower. I'll just be a minute; watch the football."

Parker muttered something under his breath, and Abbie crossed her arms.

"Sorry, I didn't catch that."

"I said it'll have to be the best match ever played to effectively distract me from the fact that you're naked in the next room."

Abbie grinned and blew him a kiss as she closed her bedroom door.